Phoenix Rayne

Published by:

G Street Chronicles
P.O. Box 1822
Jonesboro, GA 30237-1822

www.gstreetchronicles.com
fans@gstreetchronicles.com

This work is a work of fiction. The events and characters described herein are imaginary and are not intended to refer to specific places or living persons.

Cover design:
Hot Book Covers, www.hotbookcovers.com

ISBN13: 978-1-9405740-2-8
ISBN10: 1940574021
LCCN: 2013950595

Join us on our social networks

Like us on Facebook: G Street Chronicles
Follow us on Twitter: @GStreetChronicl
Follow us on Instagram: gstreetchronicles

Heels of Love

I dedicate this book to my fans!

G STREET CHRONICLES
A LITERARY POWERHOUSE
WWW.GSTREETCHRONICLES.COM

Chapter One

The Meet and Greet

I was in another one of my "trying to find myself" states, and I had just broken off my third and absolutely final engagement. I am so sick and tired of living my life for someone else, and I am so very glad I woke up from this one before I was in too deep. I wasn't sure where I was heading to this time, but I knew I wanted to be as far away from the south as possible.

I was driving downtown absentmindedly when I called Chelle and she, as usual, invited me out to the Pacific Northwest to stay with her. She lived forty-two hours away from my old life, and it just didn't seem far enough. I arrived on Wednesday, and I was starting the new job that Chelle set up for me on Monday. Chelle had to work the rest of the week, and I wanted to do some major sightseeing. I had never been this far west before, and I wanted to see all I could see. Plus, one of my favorite writers had a series about Vampires in the Pacific Northwest. I had to see the areas she wrote about, and check out a couple of the reservations in this area.

So I woke up bright and early my first day in the Pacific Northwest the next morning, bought a map at the 7-11, and started my journey. There was so much water here, and I had never set foot on a beach before. So I went searching for all the beaches I could find in a three hundred-mile radius. I came across the town the author wrote about in the vampire series. It looked just like my hometown, nothing too spectacular but still nice to see, and I saw the reservation from the books as well. It was nice to see the places she wrote about and all the signs the town and reservation had up promoting the author and the series.

However, I went to four different beaches, and I was not impressed. I was all set to take lots and lots of pictures, but it never happened. Everything was so depressing and cold here. My vision of beaches was hot sunny days with people jogging across the shoreline, but no one jogged across any shorelines here. It was a little past 3:00 p.m. and I thought that since I was about three hours away I had better start heading back. I filled up at a little gas station, and the elderly attendant behind the counter asked me if I was a tourist.

"Well, yes and no."

He laughed, and I explained that I was sight-seeing but was now also a resident of the Pacific Northwest.

"What sites have you seen?"

"Beautiful beaches."

He asked what beaches I had visited, and I told him.

"Well, there's about three more thirty minutes from here that are pretty nice. They are up by reservation country, and you cannot miss them. You can do some major thinking over there. It's worth the drive, and the scenery on the way is breathtaking." He showed me exactly where the beaches were on the map and it was pretty much a straight shot to get there. I had about four more hours of light left, according to my new friend, and I thought that would be just fine. I thanked him, bought a few more snacks, and headed up the highway.

The old man was right: the scenery was breathtaking, and the drive was completely soothing to me. I made it to the beach about forty-five minutes later. It was nice, not crowded at all. There were a few couples there, but other than that, all I could hear was the ocean. I stayed for twenty minutes or so; I took some pictures and collected a few colorful stones.

Suddenly, all hell broke loose; rain started pouring down. The few couples on the beach were now running to their cars, and so did I. Just a few seconds ago, the sun had been beaming, and now it was completely gone and the sky was grey. This was scary because everything was dark here now. There was not a pole light in sight, and the other cars were racing away down the highway. Since I am on the fluffier size of life, I couldn't run as fast as the others could. I made it to the car drenched and heaving for air. I slammed down into the car seat and tried to catch my breath. I pushed several buttons trying to find the windshield wipers in the rental but then pushed the wrong button and the convertible top came down soaking everything in the car and me…again. I tried to stop the top, but I didn't know which button I pushed to make it come down. I jabbed at everything I could find. The car alarm was going off, and the radio was blasting making this scene even worse. Finally, I pushed the right button and the top started coming back up. I will have to remember the button behind the wipers will be forbidden from here on out.

I looked out the windshield, and the rain was pouring down so hard I couldn't even see the beach anymore. I backed up and high beamed it off the beach. I made it a few miles up the highway before I saw a car's headlights coming once they got almost right up on me. They were over in my lane heading straight for me. I slammed down on my horn, and then the car started swerving all over the two-lane highway. Trying to get out of the way, I ran off the side of the road, hit a mailbox, and drove into somebody's yard. The other car kept going.

I looked over and saw a tiny house with a missing screen door and no light on. I grabbed my jacket, put it over my head, and ran to the door. I knocked, but no one came. I ran back to the car and thought I could leave my name and number so I could replace the mailbox. However, there was nowhere to leave a note. I thought about getting the mailbox, but it was in the small ditch next to me floating in water. I pulled out my cell phone and had no signal. I wrote the house number down and figured I could find another house or a store or something where I could call for help.

I drove and drove but never saw another house. I saw a sign pointing up the road that said "Station 1 mile," so I followed the side road. I went up a hill and saw a guard station but no guard. The rail was up to pass on through, so I did. I saw identical houses on both sides of the street. All the houses were in a straight line like the military. It felt like I was on an Army base.

I made it a few more feet up the block and saw a giant boulder. Then I saw the dead end sign. I put the car in reverse and looked behind for oncoming traffic. The street was clear. I looked back up towards the dead end sign, and there sat a man on the boulder. I jumped and gasped; no one had been there a few seconds ago. I turned around to reverse again and backed up as far as I could go. When I faced forward towards the man, he was not on the boulder anymore. I looked out the passenger window, and nothing was there. I turned around to the driver's side window, and there he stood right in front of my driver's side window. I screeched this time and slammed on the gas. The car was screeching too, but it wouldn't move; it was deep in mud. I tried it again, and the car still wouldn't budge.

The man stood and didn't say a word. He came over towards the car with a ready-for-war stance. His walk was hard and rough, his shoulders never moved. It looked as though they were trained to be still. Both of his arms were hanging straight down on both sides of his body. His hands were bald up into a tight fist and his veins looked as though they wanted to burst through his skin. He had long, jet-black hair that draped over his eyes, a strong jaw, and a clenched fist. He wore a white Henley shirt that stuck to his chiseled chest and dark denim jeans that were dripping. He just stood there, and I couldn't look at him; I imagined him with a hatchet and a long black raincoat. Damn, Ms. Meyers and her stupid vampire books, and curse me for going sightseeing.

I texted Chelle, "I went sight-seeing like I told you I would this morning, and now my car is stuck in the stupid mud. I am on this reservation, and there is someone outside the car staring at me through my driver's side window. I just wanted you to know where I was."

I ended the fierce text and laid the phone down on the passenger's side car seat. The man at the window started tapping, but I wouldn't look at him. I couldn't help but picture him with a hatchet. Making it this many years alone, I've learned if you don't stare at people in their eyes, don't remember their features, and definitely don't remember their emotions, they will more than likely let you live.

The man tapped on the window again, but I still didn't look at him. The rain had completely stopped now, and there was a hint of the sun coming back out. I tried to get a side view glance at him, but at the angle he was standing, it was impossible. I imagined him with a dozen tribal tattoos and piercings everywhere. I unhooked my seat belt, pulled my purse open and yanked out my mace. I was not going out without a fight. If he tried to rape me, I would spray him in the face with mace and try to break off his dick. I grabbed my cell phone again, still no signal.

The man tapped one last time at the window. "Get the hell away from me, psycho," I screamed at him.

"Your phone isn't going to work up here," he said in a deep voice.

"Please just leave me alone; I'm just passing through and I got lost," I told him.

"I'm not going to hurt you; I'm trying to help you," he said. "You cannot be here; you are on private property. Visitors, who have not been cleared, are not allowed."

Oh dear God, I am going to have to fight this whole damn neighborhood.

"I live right up the street. I'm going to get help. Don't move. And don't try to pull out anymore; you're only making it worse," he said in his psycho voice.

I nodded, still not making eye contact with him. I still hadn't seen his face, so maybe he wouldn't hurt me.

As the psycho walked away, I noticed he didn't have his hatchet anymore or his malice. I must have imagined them both, but they seemed so real. My eyes followed him, and I saw exactly what house he went into. As soon as he walked in, I slammed on the gas again and heard nothing but grinding noises. I tried it repeatedly and still nothing.

A thought came to me then, maybe I wasn't that stuck, he could have been lying. Maybe he was going to get other people to help him kill me or maybe he was going to get a garbage bag to put my body parts in after he was done with me. I gave up; I swallowed my fears and just opened the car door to take a look for myself. I could barely see the wheels now; they were really stuck in some deep mud. I looked around and there was nothing I could do, there was nothing around to try to wedge the wheels out of the mud. I heard voices coming from across the street, I yanked my head back up, and there stood the psycho and three more psychos with him. I slammed the door back shut, locking it. They would have to bust the windows open and yank me from the steering wheel. I started saying the Bible verses of the 23rd Psalm; I cursed myself for not remembering all the verses.

The psycho and the other three psychos made it back to the car. Still not making eye contact with any of them, I looked straight ahead. I noticed one of the psychos had a bright red Mohawk and several tattoos. They mumbled something to each other, and then I heard one of them say, "I told her," and I thought they were probably talking about me. Psycho #1 told me not to move, and I am sure he could tell I tried getting out the mud again.

Just then, Psycho #1 shouted at me to gun it; I didn't see any of the psychos anymore. I froze for a minute. "Go!!!" someone yelled out. I gunned it and nothing. "Stop!" I heard someone yell now. So I froze again not saying or doing anything. "Go!" someone yelled again. I gunned it again, and then I could feel some moving under the car. "Stop!" someone yelled again, and I stopped, and then all of sudden I felt a burst of relief. The psychos were not psychos at all; they were really trying to help me get out of the mud. I felt terrible; I had called the man on the boulder a psycho to his face. Well, from the side of my face that is.

"Okay, again! This tone was more pleasant. I did as he commanded, and then the car eased up onto the street. I threw my head back onto the seat, trying to catch my breath. I had done absolutely nothing, but I felt the warm relief from not being a victim of a vicious attack.

The three men walked away from the car. Mud covered them from head to toe. When I woke from my shock of relief, I pushed two of the window buttons accidentally pushing the one behind the wipers, the forbidden one. Both windows rolled down plus the top again. I yelled, "THANK YOU!!!" One of them threw their hand up and the others just kept walking towards the house.

"Do you think you can find your way out now?" he asked. I turned slowly and there stood a bare-chested mud god. Now that his shirt was off, I noticed just how ripped his body was. His jeans were covered in grit and grime, but he was a sexy being.

"Now you need to leave, you people act as though you can't read the sign that says, 'Private Property.' You do not belong here and you're not welcome." My mud god spoke again, but these words were harsh; he talked down to me as if I was a peasant. I frowned at him, and then the anger welled up in me. He said "Your kind."

"My kind!" Now I knew from my college classes on American History that a lot of Native Americans didn't care for Christopher Columbus; I mean, he did take their land; but God, I didn't take it and why was he being all rude to me now. Doesn't he understand how "You people" sounds to an African-American person? It's like a slap in the face; he might as well have called me a colored girl. I was slowly realizing now he only helped me so I could get out of here because "My kind" didn't belong. How racist was this? He treated me like an old whore on the streets, and that pissed me the fuck off.

"Wait, that came out wrong," he begged, and that was all it took for the hurricane in my body to start. I screamed at him from the top of my lungs. I told him about the stupid vampire books and then about the beach and then the mailbox. I told him I just moved to the PNW and that I hated it and I hated him. I called him a racist, and then I told him I needed to let the people know I would pay for their mailbox. He was grinning at me now and that just pissed me off even more. I screamed at him, asking if he knew the people in the little house, and then he laughed and said yes.

I watched his face and then the fury in me rose. He looked like he was about to bolt away from the car. "Well, if you're done laughing at me, Jackass, why don't you tell me who the family is so I can contact them about the mailbox so that "My kind!" can leave this warped world.

"Hey, there is no need to--"

I interrupted him. "No need? Did you really just say, 'No need?' You racist son of a bitch…kiss my fat ass. I'm a minority just like you. Our skin is the same color almost and…you know what? Screw this and screw you! Where is the closest police station?"

"Ma'am, I'm real sorry if I offended you, but I really didn't mean it like that. I was only-"

I interrupted again, "POLICE STATION!" I demanded him, looking straight ahead now. There was nothing but silence for a long moment.

He bent down, and then he rested his arms on the window seal. "There is a ranger station three miles up to the left."

I slammed on the gas and bolted out of there. I made it down the hill and saw the guard station was well secured with two guards now. They tried to flag me down, and I just flipped them the bird and gunned it some more. I dove about two miles up the road and saw the sign for the ranger station. I turned into the well-lit parking lot. As soon as I parked in the parking lot, my phone started buzzing and chiming like crazy. I guess I was back in signal range now.

I yanked my purse and phone out of the passenger's seat. I walked up to the door of the ranger station and pulled it open. There was a woman sitting behind the desk painting her nails and two guys in brown matching uniforms, playing chess. When they heard the bell ring, they all shifted as a kid would in school when the principal was coming. They all watched me.

I walked straight to the woman and said, "Excuse me, Ms.," trying to hold back my anger as much as possible and fighting back tears with every word.

"It's alright now. Don't make a fuss," she said while getting up and coming around the counter. She pulled two tissues out the box on the counter and wrapped her arms around me. "Lil Samson up from the reservation already called and filled us in. He's a really nice boy, and he was just all torn up about what had happened." Her words really made me break down now. She pulled me over to a chair and patted me on my shoulder. "There now, it's okay. J.P., go and get her some water," she told one of the men at the little table.

I told her my full name, but then I said, "Everybody calls me Cricket."

"We will, too, Cricket. I am Charlotte, and this is Kenny and J.P."

The guy named J.P. handed me a cup of water, and I drank it all. Charlotte had me write my information down. She asked me where I was from, and I told her and they all opened their mouths wide.

"Well, how in the world did you get way up here?"

I told her I had just moved.

"You are far from home. Welcome to our state."

My cell phone started ringing at that very moment, and it was Chelle. I asked Charlotte to excuse me for a moment.

"Hello" I answered. "What the hell, Cricket? I thought something had happened to you. I called the police station and everything."

"I'm sorry it's a super long story. I'm at a ranger station now, and I will call you back when I get back on the road," I pleaded.

"You better Missy," she snapped back. Then the line disconnected.

The office phone started ringing then; Charlotte jogged over and answered it at once. "Ranger station," she sang. "Oh, Lil Samson, yes, she's here. Would you like to speak with her? Okay, then," she said into the receiver. "Honey, he would like to speak with you."

"I gotta go now. Thank you again so much for all your help." I turned around and walked toward the front door. I didn't have anything to say to that racist asshole.

"Oh, she's still a little upset." I heard Charlotte whisper into the phone as I walked out. When I got back in the car, I called Chelle immediately. I gave her the two-hour version of the story, going into full dramatization mode.

"You went all the way up there by yourself? Cricket that was too far," she yelled through the phone.

I told her I was coming straight home and that I needed a serious hot shower. When I pulled into the garage, Chelle hung up the phone, and the garage door opened wide. She ran over to me and hugged me as tight as I could stand it. She had a hot bath waiting for me, and she said she would make us some hot chocolate. When I got out of the tub, she had a pair of my softest pajamas on the sink.

I walked into the living room, and she brought in a tray with two huge mugs, one filled with about a thousand mini marshmallows and the other plain.

"Awhhhh, thanks, Chelle," I crooned. She smiled at me, and we both sat down on her big oversized couch. I sipped on my hot chocolate, and a marshmallow stuck to my nose. We both fell out laughing.

Chelle made me tell her the story again, and then she gave out a big sigh.

"What?" I asked. "Nothing. Keep going." she grinned.

I started back up, and then she rolled her eyes at me.

"What the hell is wrong with you?" I asked with a laugh.

"Okay, so you've called him uncouth, rude, prejudice, and a

hunky ass," she answered.

"Yea, so what?" I snapped back.

"Soooo…just how cute was he?" She asked with a grin.

"Wait a minute. I NEVER said he was cute!" I shouted out.

"You didn't have to…Okay, so you are safe, clean, and dry now. I am going to bed." she answered.

I sat there stumped for a long moment, and then went upstairs to bed. I woke up with extremely puffy eyes and a silent house. I knew Chelle was gone to work now, and her two boys were at school. I got ready for the day. I wanted to go to the job and check out how long it took to get there.

I got there in forty-five minutes with no traffic, so I would need to give myself an hour and a half drive time on Monday. I stopped at a gas station and grabbed an apartment guide for the city. I searched and searched, never going further than a twenty miles radius from the job. After looking at fifteen apartments and getting almost thirty applications, I was completely exhausted. I got back to Chelle's house a little after eight, and she told me my plate was in the oven. We talked and laughed for almost an hour. We reminisced about the old days and how things used to be. Chelle made me listen to her read back my encrypted text that I had sent her, and then she wanted to analyze it. She then told me I watched way too much CSI.

While I was getting ready for bed, my cell phone rang. I knew it was my mother, but then I thought about it. I was three hours behind her; she wouldn't be calling me at this hour. None of my friends from back home are speaking to me right now, so I knew it was not any of them. Everybody was mad at me for moving across country and canceling the wedding. I didn't want to hear any of their sighs right now anyway. I picked up the phone and realized I didn't recognize the number. I had only had this number for three days, and I didn't have a lot of Washington State numbers in it. I answered it and waited for the caller to ask for the person who previously owned this number.

"Hello?" I answered.

"Cricket?" he asked.

"Yes, this is she; may I ask whom I'm speaking with?"

"This is Jyme." The unfamiliar voice said.

"Uhh, okay"...I waited for more information besides his name.

He laughed and said, "I'm the guy who helped you get out of the mud last night."

I sat straight up now, giving him all of my attention.

"Hello," he called out.

I hung the phone up immediately. It rang again, and I pushed ignore and lay down quickly.

The next morning I woke early. And the house was silent. I stumbled around for a few minutes, and then my cell phone rang again. I recognized the unknown number at once. He was calling me again, "Hello," I answered.

"Look, I talked to Sal. That's the man's mailbox you knocked down. I told him I would come down and fix it, and he was cool with that. So the mailbox is back in the land of the living."

I didn't respond.

"Are you still there?" he asked.

"Yes, I'm here," I said. "You really didn't have to do that, and I will pay you for your services," I said in a rude voice.

"Listen, I wanted to do this, and I feel horrible about what I said. Charlotte told me you were from the South and that you took total offense to what I said."

"Wait a sec. Did she give you my number?" I snapped.

"Yea," he said it like, "What's it to you?"

"Unfuckingbelievable! the rangers are now giving out people's private numbers. I mean, that's my own private information," I trailed.

"It's not like that around here," he said.

"Okay, I'm done with this conversation. Thank you, and have a pleasant day." I hung up the phone and threw it to the foot of the bed.

The rest of the weekend went by fast. Chelle took me to the Space Needle, and then we took a tour on a big duck tour bus. One minute we were riding in the street, and then the duck turned into a boat, and we were floating in the water.

Today was my first day at my brand-new, swanky job at the world's famous coffee company. Their corporate office just happened to be in the PNW. My job was low-key; I am now a full-time mystery shopper, aka THE SNITCH. I feel like a traitor; I have to visit coffee stores and buy stuff, and then rate my service. I knew one day someone would find me out; then I would get it. I know the saying, *snitches get stitches is true*. Chelle knows the marketing director, and she hooked me up big time. I get a company car, credit card, and an unlimited supply of the world's best coffee.

I walked into the office wearing my best black suit and spiked heels. The receptionist's eyes got wide, and then she smiled at me. She greeted me and asked how she could help me. I gave her my name, and then I told her it was my first day.

"Oh, Mrs. or Ms." she asked.

"Ms. But….please call me Cricket," I insisted.

"Sure thing," she said. "I'm Ophelia, but everyone calls me O."

I followed her as she showed me the bathroom, conference rooms, and the kitchen. We finally made it around to my office; well a box with no windows is more like it. Well, it was not a box, but it didn't have any windows. I would have to liven this up a bit, because it was a little depressing.

"Well, if you need anything, just pick up your phone and dial zero. D'Artagnan, will stop by in just a moment," she stated.

"Uhmmmm, D'Artagnan? I asked.

"Oh yes…just you wait and see," she smiled.

I placed my small, cardboard box on my desk and started unpacking. Three picture frames, a high heel tape dispenser, a purse post it holder, and a sterling silver letter opener set…I was done.

There was a knock at the door, and I focused on the doorway. I sucked in a quick breath because there was a six-foot six Adonis standing at my door. He stood with his hands crossed over his chest and he leaned into the doorframe. He gave me a cocky smile and his eyes looked as though they could see right down to my thong.

I had to catch myself because my eyes were wandering too far down south. I jerked myself right and made eye contact with him.

He gave me a crooked smile. "Hi Eugenia. I'm D'Artagnan, your partner in crime." He strolled over to my desk with his hand out.

"Hi, it's very nice to meet you. Please call me Cricket," I said, gripping his hands and shaking.

"Well, you are not what I was expecting at all," he said.

"Yea, they ordered a medium but got a 2X instead," I laughed, losing eye contact now.

"No, they normally don't hire pretty girls," he said with a smile.

"Oh, that was a good one. Now does that normally work on the girls?" I asked pulling my hand from his. He got a tighter grip and led me over to my desk. He had just crossed the personal space bubble I had up.

"Now I wouldn't know that because I don't fool with girls," he growled.

"Oh, so do you like little boys?" I breathed out. He looked me over as if he could see straight through my clothes, and I suddenly felt exposed.

"No princess, I like grown women who know exactly what they want." he growled again. "Oh, so you're into Sugar Mamas." I grinned.

At that, very awkward moment my phone buzzed, and I heard O's trilling voice bursting through the speakers, "Cricket, you have a package at the front desk."

D'Artagnan didn't ease up on the grip; I glared at him and then glanced down at my prisoner hand. "Well, first day, and you're already getting little trinkets," D'Artagnan said.

"Uhhh, Cricket?" O asked.

"She'll be right there, O," he answered.

"Oh, okay, D'Artagnan," she said in a dazed voice.

The speaker died out, and then D'Artagnan smiled at me. "We have a meeting in ten minutes in the Caramel Mocha Conference Room." He finally let my hand go, and I quickly raced out of the room.

I prayed all the way down the hall that I didn't stubble over an invisible line on the floor. Walking this fast, with this weight, and in these heels was dangerous. I made it to reception, and O was on the phone. She pointed to a clipboard on her counter and motioned for me to sign it. I saw a line with my name printed on it and an X beside it. I signed at the X, and then O pointed around the corner to a room with the door wide open. Boxes and boxes and then more boxes. I saw a large flower arrangement with the most amazing flowers I had ever seen. I picked up the large arrangement with both hands and wobbled back to receptionist. I sat the arrangement on O's desk and waited for her to get off the phone. She was writing a message down and I decided to hunt for a card in the arrangement. I had no luck finding one.

The flowers were in a frosted vase. I looked and looked for a card, and nothing. I heard people talking in the hallway and looked up at the clock. I had four minutes before the meeting. There were twenty-eight flowers in the vase, and they were beautiful. All of them different colors and styles. I looked again; no card. I would have to research this later; I left my office and the sweet smell of the flowers.

D'Artagnan stood at the end of the hall, holding a thin folder. I walked past him, not saying a word; then, he appeared next to me. Neither one of us said a word as we walked into the conference room. He pulled my chair out for me at the long table before the meeting and after.

At the end of the day, D'Artagnan stood by my rental car. I unlocked the door with my wireless entry, sliding my briefcase in the passenger seat. Reaching to shut the driver's door, D'Artagnan cleared his voice. I looked up at him.

"Cricket, I just wanted to apologize for my behavior earlier. Please let me make it up to you?" he asked.

I just sat there, looking at him.

"I was the new guy here for nine months. And my parents taught me better than that," he stated. I watched him, and he had transformed into a different person. He seemed genuine now; the cocky asshole had finally left the building.

"I accept your apology."

"Please let me make it up to you. Dinner at Palisade, or maybe Maximilian; and my treat?"

"Rain check?" I asked.

"Sure, but we will sit down together real soon, and I will wine and dine you, Ms. Hooper." he smiled.

"I'm positive you will, Mr.—uhhhhh?"

"Crain. D'Artagnan Crain," he chimed.

"Where does the name D'Artagnan come from?"

"Let my mother tell it, and she says it's Romanian; but my father says she was obsessed with *The Three Musketeers*. My baby sister's name is Echo," he said.

"Echo?"

"Greek Mythology. She was a famous nymph."

"Oh, well that is interesting," I mumbled.

We sat in an awkward moment. "Well, I'll see you in the morning," I stammered. D'Artagnan gave me crooked smile and then a hundred watt show with those sparkling whites. I swallowed hard as he walked away from the rental.

All the way back to Chelle's, I thought of the flowers. I knew deep down exactly where they came from, but I couldn't admit it to myself. They were tall, strong, mysterious, and wild things. I knew he had to be the one who sent them. They were him all the way down to the last steam. I had no idea how my mud god somehow had found me

Later that night when I got ready for bed, I looked at a number I had never called before. I finally tapped the screen, and my phone started dialing. It rang three times, and then a stern voice answered.

"May I speak to Lil Samson Jyme," I asked.

"Speaking," he laughed.

"I owe you an apology, and I assume a 'Thank You' is in order as well," I said.

"What exactly are you thanking me for," he asked.

Oh, so he wanted to have one of *those* conversations…I didn't take him for the gloating type, but I guess I was wrong. "Well first off, for helping me get out the mud, second for repairing the mailbox, and third for that amazing floral arrangement. They're beautiful, and I'm so grateful."

"You forgot one," he said.

"Uhmmmmm." I answered.

"And for not killing you." he answered.

I sat there not saying a word. I knew my breath was getting heavy, but I didn't know what to say. "I'm really sorry about all that," I whispered.

"We're even," he answered, disconnecting the line. I sat there looking at my cell phone until the backlight went black. I sat and thought for a moment, this man could have killed me and chopped me up into tiny pieces and no one would have found me. But I was intrigued and almost addicted to the mud god; not the possible murder on the reservation.

G STREET CHRONICLES
A LITERARY POWERHOUSE
WWW.GSTREETCHRONICLES.COM

Chapter 2

The First Date

On my way to work the next morning, I needed a little musical courage to help me through the day. Beyoncé was blasting about her video phone when the song was interrupted, it was a number I recognized, but had decided not to save in my contacts. The touch screen car stereo was blinking bright, and the speakers were chiming in my ears. I touched the screen and answered the phone.

"Lunch at twelve," His voice was not asking, and I didn't know how I felt about that. All I could think about was, *what would Beyoncé do?*

"Alright," I said. For one brief second, there was silence, and then Beyoncé was back in my ear on the second chorus. I smiled and then I frowned. I didn't even get a chance to ask him how he knew where I worked. I had never told him that before, and we didn't know the same people, so how did he know? He just hung up the phone; no farewell, no goodbye, nothing.

At eleven thirty, I grabbed my makeup bag and headed towards the ladies' room. As soon as I stepped out into the hall, I ran smack dead into Mr. Crain. (In order to keep our relationship professional, I decided to call him 'Mr. Crain.') I dropped my halfway-zipped makeup bag, and he lost his folder full of papers. I went for his papers; he went straight for my makeup bag and grabbed at the rolling lipsticks and liners.

He took a deep breath. "Cricket, that fragrance you're wearing is remarkable."

"Thank you."

"May I ask what it is?"

"I'm not sure. I swiped a couple of sprays from my roommate's vanity this morning," I answered.

"Oh, I didn't know you knew anyone here. That makes me feel better," he said.

I gave him a strange look. I frowned at him then I felt the heat rising on my face. I tried to hold it back, but I felt my eyebrows narrowing. I knew now I was scowling hard at him. I tried to pull myself together because in all honesty, no matter how much he was stepping into my private boundaries, the man was still my boss.

He explained. "No, I meant, I worry about you being all alone in the big city," he sputtered.

"I used to live in New York and Atlanta. I think I'm safe here," I snapped.

"I didn't mean-"

I interrupted, "Don't worry about it," I said, pulling my makeup back out of his hands and handing him his folders. I turned and headed towards the bathroom again. I refreshed my face and stepped back into my office.

O buzzed my phone. "Cricket, your twelve o'clock is here," she chimed.

"Thank you, O. I'll be right there." I grabbed my purse and smoothed out my black, ruched dress. I walked down the hall and turned towards the reception area, but stopped as soon as I saw the back of his head. Lil Samson Jyme had his hair pulled up in this funky, but very sexy ponytail bob thing. He wore a white button down shirt with denim jeans and a pair of brown boots. He was on his cell phone and didn't notice when walked into the room.

I looked over at O, but she was not looking at me at all. She was in this misty trance; her eyes never left him.

"O, I'll be out the office for the next two hours at a lunch meeting."

"Yea, okay, Crick-" is all O said.

As we left the building, two women walked up to the entrance, and Lil Samson pulled the door open for them. Still on his cell phone, he didn't notice the two women stumbling over each other as they tried to get a better look at him. I walked up behind him and just stood there. He smiled into the glass and I walked through the opened door. When I passed through the door, he held a hand out for me and I placed my hand into his. We walked down the hall to the elevators. I hadn't held someone's hand since junior high. It was kind of nice.

The elevator dinged, and he told his caller he would get back with them after his lunch meeting. He hung up the phone, placing it into his back pocket. He didn't look at me or speak. I watched him in the steel elevators doors, and he was smiling.

Just then, the doors opened, and out spilled three women and two men. The women did double takes, and the men stared. One of the men in particular, stared us both down with an open mouth. D'Artagnan Crain stood there with two big brown bags from the deli across the street.

"Cricket, I didn't know you were leaving the office for lunch. I brought you something back from the deli."

"Yes, I am," was all I said. The elevator door started closing, and Lil Samson placed his hand in the door to stop it. D'Artagnan finally shuffled out of the way, and with my hand still in Lil Samson's, we stepped into the elevator. As the door shut, D'Artagnan was still staring at us. On the lobby level, we walked out the front doors. As soon as we stepped outside, the big clock at the top of the building chimed signaling that it was noon.

"Do you like sushi?" he asked.

"Yes."

"Banzai has the best sushi, and it's not far from here."

"Okay."

We walked over to a sleek, black Ford pick-up. The chrome wheels were shining and massive. Although the truck looked luxurious, I could tell that if this truck needed to climb a mountain, it could do it without a sweat. While still holding my hand, he opened the door. I stepped up on the running board, and he finally let my hand go.

I pulled my seat belt on at once and took a quick peek at the back seats. They were leather and the color of red brick. The truck looked brand spanking new. The carpet had obviously been freshly vacuumed, and the whole thing smelled great.

He climbed in and ohhhh…watching him climb into that truck with those jeans and those boots made my toes tingle. He put his seat belt on, and we pulled out of the parking lot. The radio station was playing Beyoncé's, *Video Phone*, and I busted out laughing. He whipped his head over at me with a strange expression on his face. I waved it off and explained that it had been a long day.

When we arrived at the restaurant, we sat down, and he ordered a sampler platter. I ordered sake while he had coke. We both had the soup.

He watched me, not saying a word, and the silence was killing me. "So, what do you do for a living?" I asked.

He smiled and then he took a gulp of his soda. "I'm a fisherman," he answered. I couldn't help but think of the killer from *I Know What You Did Last Summer*. Then, I shook that image off and thought of the Gordon's fisherman picture on the frozen dinners.

"What?" he asked.

"Excuse me?"

"You got this look on your face," he answered.

"I'm trying to picture you fishing, and I can't see it," I explained.

He wiped his mouth with the cloth napkin. "I go out into the deep waters on a boat. I normally wear a tank top, shorts, and fishing boots," he explained.

I got a very steamy image in my head of him. His tank top was stuck to his skin and he wore khaki cargos with black work boots. "Oh yes, I can picture that."

He gave me a smile. Then, his phone rang. He looked down at the screen, then he told me what he wanted to eat, and then he excused himself from the table.

I sat there feeling a little uneasy. I didn't take him to be the type that stayed on his phone all day. I waiter came to take our order and I told him what we both wanted.

When he returned, the waiter was coming over for our refills. He sat down and apologized to me for being rude. He explained that the call was urgent and he had to take it. I asked him about life growing up on the reservation. I told him if it was private, I understood, but he brushed that away. He told me I could ask him anything I wanted to and that gave me chills. He seemed so open like a book and that made me a little nervous. The waiter came with our food and we dug in. Jyme explained how fishing in the ocean was and how they call him the "Fish Whisperer." He told me his mother use to tease him by saying whenever he came into the kitchen when she was cooking fish that they would try to jump out of the frying pan to get near him. His eyes were soft when he spoke of his mother. I listened to his smooth, velvety voice. I think I could listen to this man if he read the phone book to me. The waiter came back over when we were just sitting there talking and gazing into each other's eyes to give him the check.

"Do you want dessert?" he asked.

"No, I didn't see anything I wanted," I said.

"What's your all-time favorite dessert?" he asked.

"Um, I guess cheesecake."

"Cheesecake? Okay, I know a place." He held his hand out for mine, and then we were off.

When the radio came on and One Republic was crooning in our ears, Lil Samson Jyme looked over at me cautiously, and I had to control myself from busting out laughing again. He thought I was crazy; I had to stare out the window and bite my lip.

"What is your name Lil Samson or Jyme?" I asked.

He grinned. "My name is Jamison, but my friends call me Jyme."

"What do you want me to call you?" I asked.

"You can call me whatever."

We pulled up at a place called The Confectional. He turned the truck off and told me to stay put, so I did. He walked over to my side and opened the door for me. He held my hand as I got out and he didn't let go. We walked hand in hand on the small sidewalk. I could smell the yummy goodness from the around the corner. He let my hand go when he opened the door for me. Then he captured it again when we got on the inside. He made these small circle movements inside the palm of my hand and I felt tinkles in those tingling spots. He ordered for me and I was pleased. As soon as my fork touched my tongue, I felt little tingles in my mouth.

Jyme laughed and asked, "You're feeling that one, aren't you?"

"Mmmm. Yes, I am. This tastes so good that it should be illegal. This cheesecake would mend any broken heart," I answered.

"Huh, I beg to differ," he whispered. I looked over at him and he was looking down at his cheesecake. He seemed like he was far away now. I didn't want to say anything to him, but this mud god sitting across from me is absolutely scrumptious. What woman in her right mind would let him go? I really hope he doesn't own a machete.

I had a bite of my caramel slice, and Jyme took a bite of his Mochaccino.

"So, have you had many broken hearts?" I asked with a smile.

"No, just one."

"Well, I've had a few, but you know what they say. What doesn't kill you makes you stronger."

"How many boyfriends have you had?" he asked.

I gave him a wide-eyed look and then said, "Do you mind if I finish my dessert before we discuss our sex partners," a little fire in my tone. How dare he ask me a question like that on our first date?

"What?! I just asked you how many boyfriends you had. I never mentioned anything about sex."

"Boyfriends, sex, what's the difference? I was annoyed now.

"What?"

"Look can we go? I need to get back," I said.

"You told the girl at the desk you were taking two hours; you still have forty-five minutes." he frowned at me.

"I need to prepare for a meeting," I answered. He looked me over once and then sucked in a breath before getting up and holding out his hand for mine.

I ignored it and walked towards the door. We both put our seat belts on again, and then Jyme placed his hand over mine. "I'm sorry if I offended you in some way, but I've only had one sex partner. I've only had one girlfriend. All this is new to me, and I'm trying not mess this up," he stated.

I looked at him closely. He didn't seem to be lying; he seemed ashamed of something. I couldn't put my finger on it, but something was there. I nodded my head.

He removed his hand from mine and started up the truck. When we got back to the office, he left the truck running and walked over to hold the truck door open for me.

"Have dinner with me tonight?" he asked this time.

"May I ask you something?"

"Yes."

"How old are you?"

"Twenty-seven."

"I'm older than you," I explained.

"So? I'm sure it's not by much."

"Well, let's just say, I was in kindergarten when you were born."

"So what?" he asked.

I smiled at him. "See you tonight then."

When I made it back to the office, O was grinning like the cat that caught the canary. "What?" I asked with a laugh.

"Oh my, he looked scrumptious."

"I wouldn't know. He was not on the menu," I answered. I passed her desk and started down the hall.

"I got a feeling he was," she called out.

I sat down at my desk and pressed the message button. I had two messages from Mr. Crain. The first: "Ms. Hooper, please contact me at your earliest convenience," and the second: "Cricket, please see O about your company phone." I picked up the desk phone to call Mr. Crain, but before I could finish dialing, he walked into my office.

"I asked you to call me back," he snapped.

"You do see the phone in my hand? Actually you asked me to call you back at MY earliest convenience," I answered.

He sat down across from me, and I could see him transforming from Mr. Crain to D'Artagnan. He stiffened and I could see the veins in his neck bulging. His jaws were locked, he held his lips tight, and his body was mimicking a statue.

"Did you have a good lunch with your friend?" he asked.

"Who said he was my friend?"

"Well, you two were holding hands like you were teenagers."

"Did you have something you needed to speak with me about? You called me twice," I asked.

"We need your mobile number in the system, and you need to activate your company phone."

"Alright."

He sat there watching me, and I stared right back at him. "D'Artagnan, is there anything else?"

"Well, you'll start in the field tomorrow. I'll let you start with five locations in town." he explained. He sat there in a long awkward silence again.

"Alright then, is there anything else?"

"Just make sure you check with me after each shop, and I will need your company number as soon as you get it from O," he explained.

"Alright, I will get right on that," he still sat there, saying nothing.

I got out of my chair and went straight to the receptionist, leaving D'Artagnan sitting in my office.

I explained D'Artagnan's request. She opened a drawer at her desk and handed me a brand-new Blackberry.

"I thought you were going to use your personal cell?"

I thought about that for second, in my acceptance letter, it said for me to change my personal voicemail on my cell and that the company would split the bill. I had already changed my voicemail on my phone to include the company address, my office phone, and my work email.

That was it. That's how Jyme knew my work address. He had called my phone and gotten my voicemail.

O gave me the instructions for setting up my company voicemail and gave me the number to call for setting up my teleconference user name.

I went back to my office, and there was no D'Artagnan in sight. My phone chimed, and I recognized the number that I still had not saved.

"Hello."

"Italian?"

"Sure." We both sat there not saying anything. I didn't like it. "Where?"

"A restaurant called Mondello. What time do you get off?" he asked.

"I start out in the field tomorrow, so I will need to prepare for that. I will just meet you there, let's say, seven."

"I will pick you up," he demanded.

I swallowed hard and then stammered, "Let me get back with you on the time and the pickup place." I sounded like he was making an order for fresh meat.

"Okay," he answered, sounding confused.

I hung up without a goodbye. He made me so nervous.

I rushed up to reception area, "O, is it okay if I stay in corporate housing tonight?" I whispered.

"Oh yeah, I forgot to give you the keys. I'm sorry things have been crazy around here. We have you down for ninety-one days and those days will start today," she advised.

"WOW!"

"I know, right? SWEET," she crooned. She handed me the keys and gave me the printed out instructions. She told me the condo was fully furnished and that they already had fresh sheets and towels stocked. The condo was three blocks from the office.

I texted Jyme my address and got right to work preparing for tomorrow. My desk phone rang, and I pressed the speaker button since my door was shut. "This is Cricket."

"And this is Michelle."

"Hey roomy."

"How does Pizza and beer sound for dinner tonight?" she asked.

"Oh, Honey. I'm sorry. I already have plans, and I won't be coming home tonight either."

"What, Bitch?" she asked.

"I'm starting my territory tomorrow, so I will stay in the corporate housing tonight. And I actually have a date."

"WHAT?" she yelled.

I yanked the phone from its cradle and pressed it to my ear. "I was going to call you and give you with all the details, I swear."

"Rewind and start over!" she yelled into the phone. I brought Chelle up to speed on everything. She "uh-huhed", gasped, and OMG-ed in all the right places. Chelle was such a great friend.

"Hey! What reservation did you say he was from?"

"The one over by Amanda Park," I answered.

"That's what I thought. One of my besties is from there."

I knew Chelle would want the scoop on him so she could do what she did best: unofficial research. I gave her all the information I knew. She seemed satisfied and made me promise to text her back tonight while I was at dinner with him and to call her as soon as I got back to the condo.

After I finished my prep for the next day, I made it to the condo at a quarter after five. The parking attendant gave me a sticker to place in my car for the garage. I grabbed my suitcase out of the truck. I always kept a suitcase full of clothes and shoes just in case. My mother embedded this preparedness into my brain. She said, "You never know when you'll be stuck somewhere and can't get home."

I placed the keycard in the door of 808. As soon as it opened, I was surprised to see a basket full of my company's logo mugs, travel cups, coffee samplers, chocolates, nuts, fruit, and a bottle of wine. I took the basket to the kitchen, and there was a kickass coffee maker all chromed out on the counter. I opened the cabinets: nothing but our signature coffees and dishes. The fridge was stocked with creamers, syrups, and sauces. And in the freezer was every flavor of ice cream we carried. I slammed the freezer door, cursing them for trying to keep me in my size sixteen. Even now, I was rudely knocking on eighteen's door.

I walked back into the foyer and entered the living room. The color scheme was silver, grays, and greens. All the walls were brick except for the bathroom. The bathroom walls looked wet, but it was just the high gloss shine giving it that wet look. I showered and put on a pair of black stiletto jeans, a black paillette tank top, a leather jacket, and a pair of Pink Bottoms platforms. I only wore two silver rings on my fingers and a pair of silver hoops. I had too much boob action going on for a necklace. I went light on the makeup, only wearing mascara and lip gloss. I wrapped an infinity scarf around me three times, grabbed my clutch, and then headed down.

The desk attendant stared at me; I walked over and introduced myself. I explained that I had come in through the garage earlier. The door attendant held the door open for me, and I saw the black Expedition. Jyme got out the truck and walked towards me. He was wearing a cream cable knit sweater, denim jeans, and boots. I didn't know how I was going to keep my hands off him this evening. We both wore our hair down for our second date. His was longer than mine was, but I'm sure I probably had some of his cousins or aunts in my extensions blend. I wanted to run my fingers through his coal black hair, but I knew I had to control myself.

He held the passenger door open for me and helped me into the front seat. He shut the door and I pulled my seat belt around me. As I leaned over to secure the lock, I noticed a shadow in the back seat. I jerked, and then there were two different laughs coming from the back of the car. When Jyme opened his door, the dome light came on, and I saw two men sitting in the back seat. I unlocked my seat belt and jumped out the truck in the blink of an eye. I left the door open and headed back towards the attendant. "What did you say to her?" was all I heard coming from the truck.

I heard footsteps coming after me, and I yanked my head around. "I'm not sure what sick games you had in mind, but I don't get down like that."

"Whoa, whoa, whoa...Wait!" he begged, stepping in front of me. "I told you that two of my friends popped up, and now we would have two joining us for dinner. You didn't get my text?"

"WHAT?" I yelled back at him.

"I texted you, forty minutes ago," he explained.

I pulled out my phone and touched the screen; nothing happened. I tried to power it up, and the battery symbol popped up on the screen. My phone was dead; I had forgotten to charge it. "Ohhh." I said.

He stood there, staring at me.

The door attendant opened the door and looked at us. "Is everything alright, Ms.?" he asked.

"Yes, I'll be right there," I answered.

"Why?" Jyme asked.

"I need to go and get my other phone . . ."

He interrupted me, "I have a micro USB charger in the truck. You can charge it there."

"Look, you are seriously shadowing my comfort zone right now. I will meet you at the restaurant," I snapped back at him.

"I can ditch them if you want me to," he said.

"It's not a problem. I would just rather drive myself that's all."

"You will be there?" he asked, staring me straight in the eye.

"Yes, I've already told you that."

He ran his fingers through his hair and walked back towards the truck.

I stepped into the building and went straight towards the elevator. "Is everything alright Ms. Hooper?" Randy, the clerk, asked.

"Yes, everything is fine. I just decided to drive myself," I said.

"Ms. Hooper if you give the valet your valet key, he will bring your car around every time you need it," Randy stated.

"Oh well, I will have to do that. Thank you, Randy."

I rushed back to the condo and grabbed the Blackberry off the counter. I clicked on Chelle's number and listened to the ringing.

"What up, Trick?" she answered.

I explained what I needed, and she was more than happy to oblige.

A few minutes later, I walked into Mondello, and there was a beautiful, plus-size Native American woman waiting at the entrance.

"Ayashe?" I asked.

"Cricket?" We both nodded and smiled.

Chelle couldn't make it to me in time, so she sent the next best thing: her friend Ayashe, who just so happened to have been from the same reservation Jyme was from. I felt at ease when she put her arm through mine. We both walked back over to the hostess, and I gave her Jyme's name. She looked a little confused then waived over a waiter. He brought another chair to the table set for four.

Jyme stood, and then his two counterparts did as well. They all greeted Ayashe, well, everyone but Jyme. He didn't say a word, just stared at me. I asked one of the men next to the empty chair to scoot down. He did so, and then we all sat down.

I was glad for the warmth of the restaurant. It was time for the twins to make a grand appearance. I pulled off my leather jacket, and Ayashe removed hers as well. The waiter was back taking our drink orders. I made sure I would really act this show out. "What types of white wines do you have?" I asked. I unwrapped my infinity scarf slowly, pretending as if I was seriously listening to what the waiter was saying. Once I was done unwrapping, I answered him: "A glass of the Mandrarossa."

The waiter's eyes widened and he gave me a cheerful look. The three men at the table were in awe at the showing of the twins. The girls had never let me down before, and I needed them to put on a superb performance tonight. The twins were the only way I knew to take my nerves away.

Ayashe ordered a glass of the Pinot Grigio Delle Venezie.

I held one hand around my neck and the other up, trying to catch the waiter's attention. "Excuse me. Can we just get a bottle of the Delle Venezie instead? I asked.

The waiter agreed and said we had made an excellent choice.

I turned back around and focused on the menu in front of me. My phone chimed in my clutch; I opened it and pulled out the phone.

"Cricket, this is Kanoke and Loon. You guys, this is Cricket" Ayashe introduced. They both nodded at me, and I smiled at both of them. I touched the screen of my phone; I had a text from Jyme.

"Are you mad at me?"

I hit reply and typed, "No. Why?"

I turned to the man next to me, worked to remember his name, and said, "Kanoke, did you guys already order?"

"No, we just got drinks."

I finally noticed that the two guys were dressed in almost identical gear. Both wore jeans, t-shirts, and boots. Their leather jackets hung around the backs of their chairs.

My phone chimed again, and I looked up at Jyme. He was staring at me with no expression whatsoever on his face.

I looked down at my phone, and the screen read, "How do you

know Ayashe? And why did you bring her?"

I hit reply: "She's a friend of a friend, and she was bored."

The waiter was back with our bottle and two wine glasses. He took our orders. I ordered the Pollo Al Cartoccio, and Ayashe got the Braciole. The guys ordered, and once Kanoke was done, I asked him if he'd been here before.

He told me Jyme was the one who went out to these fancy, pansy, restaurants.

"Why?"

"Ever since the breakup, he has been on this 'learning all types of other cultures' kick." My phone chimed, and I turned from Kanoke. The screen read, "You're making me jealous."

I felt the warmth all the way down to my toes.

"You're the one who wanted to have a party tonight," I texted back.

I turned to Ayashe, "Have you ever been here before?"

"No, but I've heard excellent things about it."

"Jyme, what made you pick this place?" I asked from across the table.

"You don't like it?"

"No. I think the ambiance is amazing."

"I came here a few months ago, and I liked the food," he said.

"Well, after that fabulous lunch today and then that amazing cheesecake, I'm starting to believe you are the food whisperer."

Kanoke and Loon both stared at Jyme.

Ayashe stood and excused herself for the ladies' room.

Jyme stood as I was about to join her and walked over to take Ayashe's seat. He put his hand on my forearm.

Kanoke and Loon both stood and walked away from the table.

The whole scene happened in less than ten seconds, but it was the most intense ten seconds I had ever experienced.

"Leave with me now," he pleaded. He turned so I could see nothing but him.

"Where do you want to go?" I croaked out. He placed a hand

on the side of my face, and then his fore fingers gripped the back of my neck. He pulled me closer to him and dug his face into my hair. I could feel his hot breath on my ear, and then my skin was covered in chill bumps.

"I…" is all that came out of his mouth, and I closed my eyes. "I don't care where, I want you alone, now," he whispered.

Everything inside of me melted. I let out a whispered "Oh," and he chuckled in my ear.

"Shall we?"

"I can't," is all I could get out.

"Why not?" he growled in my ear.

"Ayashe," I answered coherently. Someone behind us cleared their throat, and his hypnotism session on me was released.

I let out the breath I sucked in when he first touched me.

Two waiters stood there with our plates.

Jyme continued sitting in Ayashe's seat. She came back to the table, went straight to Jyme's seat, and poured herself another glass of wine. I liked Ayashe. She had this easy air about her. Chelle had been certain of Ayashe's presence before even speaking with her. She seemed like a ride or die friend.

Jyme had ordered the Fettuccine Di Mare. His platter was full of mussels, calamari, prawns, and claims. Everyone started digging in immediately. After a minute or so, we were all gushing over our dishes. Soon after that, the massive sharing session began with everyone eating off of everyone else's plate. The portions they gave us were so hefty that everyone could share several times.

After we were all stuffed, Jyme ordered everyone coffee and requested a piece of each dessert they offered. We all turned to look at him; he started laughing.

"They only have six; we can all share," he explained.

I had to excuse myself. My three glasses of wine were running right through me. I placed my napkin on the table and looked at Jyme. "Excuse me I need to get by; I have to go to the ladies room." I turned in my seat, and he gave me a wicked smile.

He leaned over and brushed my long extensions over my shoulder. He put his lips right up against my ear again. "Can I see you later tonight?" he asked.

"Um, I need to think about that"

"Okay." He stood and held his hand out for me.

I gave him a smile and grabbed my clutch. I placed my hand into his, and he pulled me up.

We both walked to restrooms, hand in hand, and got a few stares. He walked me to the ladies' restroom.

Once the door shut, I almost ran to the stall; I had to use it emergency style now. My bladder was at ease, I felt like a new woman. I blotted my face and reapplied my lip gloss.

As I stepped out the ladies restroom, there he stood. He reached out for my hand, and I slid mine into his. The desserts were arriving when we returned to our seats. Once again we all shared, everyone getting a little of everything.

"So Jyme, when was the last time you saw Elle?" Ayashe asked.

CHAPTER 3

All Hell Broke Loose

Everyone stared at Ayashe, and then their attention went to Jyme. I swallowed a spoonful of the lemon sorbetti, and noticed no one else was enjoying his or her dessert. I put my spoon down with a clank and swallowed slowly, trying not to make a sound. All three guys at the table looked uneasy, and Ayashe looked chilled. She was up to something; it was obvious. She had saved this performance for the ending, and I wondered why.

Jyme sipped on his coffee then turned to her. "I guess seven or eight months now," he answered. Kanoke and Loon both were looking as if breathing was hard to do now.

"I hear she's engaged to that guy," Ayashe told him.

"Cricket, what kind of…what do you do?" Loon asked.

I hadn't really heard his voice all-night, and he definitely hadn't addressed my presence before now. "I'm an Auditor." My boss told me in my interview that I was never to tell anyone outside my department what I did. He told me to find a lie and stick with it.

"How long have you been doing that?" Loon asked.

Everyone's attention was on me now, and the twins were not even ready for their encore performance. I had my accessible bra on, once I unhook these straps and the twins have full range. It's all over for anyone who likes breast. I didn't like this unannounced spotlight. "About two days now," I answered.

I looked over at Jyme, and he was looking for the waiter. It was obvious Ayashe had hit a nerve, as was obviously her purpose. She would have to dish once we got outside.

The waiter came with the check, and Jyme handed him a credit card. I was going to pay for Ayashe's dinner since she did me a solid on such short notice. I whispered to Jyme, "I was going to pay for Ayashe's dinner; I didn't bring her for-"

His glare silenced me. "I don't want you to see me like this," he growled.

"Like what, what's wrong?" I asked.

"I have to go, right now. I will call you later," he answered. He stood up, and Kanoke and Loon mimicked him. All three of them left the table, and I saw Jyme meet the waiter halfway. He signed the bill and grabbed his card. He didn't look back as he left the restaurant.

I felt my eyes burning, and then I pulled myself together. Ayashe was silently finishing her Tiramisu. I moved one seat over and leaned into her.

"Sooo…who's Elle?" I asked.

"I'm going to let him tell you that one," she answered.

"How well do you know him?"

"I know of him, but I know his friend Sheen better," she answered with a giggle.

"Oh, do tell?"

"I met Sheen one summer, when I was visiting my Grandmother on the reservation. He was friends with my cousin, and they hung out together the whole summer. He was my summer of firsts, and I fell head over heels for him. He had a girlfriend, but they were taking the summer off, so to speak. We met up in this small cave and it was nice. I soon found out though, that it was both of our first time. That made it even sweeter, he was gentle."

I watched her while she talked about him; she had this sparkle in her eye. She smiled and then took another sip from her glass. "And then what happened?"

"Oh, you know...we grow up and moved on."

"When did you see him last?"

"About three months ago. He works for Jyme now."

"Oh."

"That was ages ago, and I happen to know for a fact he's in a serious relationship now."

I gave her a small smile, and then my phone chimed. I reached into my clutch and pulled it out. That number I knew well now appeared on the screen and the text read, "Can I please see you tonight?" I couldn't help but feel all warm fuzzies inside now, after hearing her story.

"When and where?" I hit reply.

I was intrigued by the Elle subject; I had to know more. My phone chimed, and I read the screen. "Where do you feel safe?" I thought about it for a minute and thought of the perfect place. I saw it yesterday on my drive into the city.

I responded, and soon after, Ayashe and I left the restaurant. I thanked her again and made her promise to let me take her out to a real dinner this weekend.

It took me twenty minutes to get to my destination. I unplugged my dying phone, and I had two strong battery bars holding on. I put the phone on vibrate and sat in the back in the shadows. There were a few people up front, and no one gave me a second glance. I should have gone upfront, lit three candles, and said a prayer for all three of them. But my feet wouldn't let me move. I sat there waiting for him instead. I thought about my old life and then I started feeling sorry for myself. I don't get like this too often, but Catholic churches are my weakness. I sat there another five minutes or so and then he sat down right beside me; I almost didn't recognize him. He wore a sweat-suit and sneakers. He left his hood on his head, and he was taking deep breaths.

"Did you run here?" I whispered.

He nodded.

"Where do you live?"

"On the reservation," he whispered back.

"But why are you in Seattle?" I asked.

"I work here," he answered.

"You fish here?" I asked.

"I own my own fishing company." My eyes widened, and I blew out a frustrated breath.

"I wanted to tell you this tonight, but things got a little carried away, and then you showed up with Ayashe," he said.

"You told me you were a fisherman," I hissed. A couple of people a few benches up turned around and stared at us. I did the sign of the cross, and then I bent my head.

"Are you Catholic?" he whispered.

"No, I'm Methodist."

"Why are we here?" he asked.

"Methodists don't leave their churches open twenty four hours a day."

"This isn't right." He shook his head in disgust.

"God is God, and He doesn't care what church I'm in." I whispered.

"I'm sorry about tonight. I've never been on a date with someone I don't know," he explained. "Kanoke and Loon both work for me, and they wanted to meet you. They didn't believe me when I told them I was going on a date. I normally go by myself to nice restaurants and watch other people on dates," he explained.

"Who is Elle?" I whispered.

He swallowed and then looked at me. "My ex," he whispered.

"Oh," I answered, I kind of figured that, but I needed him to say it.

"She really messed me over, and it took me a long time to get over her," he stated. He put his head back down, and two people left the sanctuary. I could hear the door creek open and shut.

"Are you over her?" I asked.

"Yes."

"Are you sure?"

"I'm positive."

I pulled his face toward mine; I needed him to make eye contact with me. "Well, why did you get so upset when Ayashe asked you about her?"

"I wanted to tell you about her myself, and she caught me off guard. She pissed me off," he explained.

I watched him, and he didn't blink. His big full lips were moist, and I just wanted to lick them with my tongue. I had to suck both of my lips under my teeth; I bit down hard trying to compose myself. I was in a church for goodness sake.

"Let's get out of here."

"Good," he sighed.

I did the cross thing again and an awkward curtsey thing. He pulled my hand into his and held the squeaky door for me. We walked out into the light mist and headed towards the rental.

"Do you need a ride?" I asked.

"I can walk."

"Get in," I demanded. We both slid into the car and buckled up. He pushed the seat back as far as it could go and leaned back.

"How tall are you?"

"6'4."

"Which way do I go?" I asked him as I approached a stop light.

"Take a right at the light," he answered.

We rode in silence for a while before he pulled my hand into his. He touched each one of my acrylic nails and he played around with my owl ring.

"You like bold pieces of jewelry," he said.

"Yes, I do. I get bored quick with regular pieces," I explained.

"How about people? Do you get bored of them quick?"

"I don't know," I lied. I knew the answer to that question far too well. That is why I keep running from people. A house in the suburbs with a white picket fence and the two point five children terrified me. I hate the same old, same daily routine, day in and day out.

"Make a right at the next light," he said.

"So what do you normally do for fun?" I asked.

"I like all sports, and I like all kinds of toys," he smiled.

Just hearing him say he likes all kinds of toys made my toes tingle. I had to grit my teeth to hold back my feelings. Lust, pure lust that is all it was. I didn't know him well, but I did know him enough to have a bond with him.

Cricket get a grip, I scolded myself silently.

"Why are you grinding your teeth like that?"

"Uhh," I said. He'd caught me, and I didn't have a lie to give him.

"Make a left at the next street," Jyme said. He was watching me carefully now.

Dammit, he probably thought I was about to have a fit or something. Shit, I didn't want him to think I was a nut.

"What are you doing tomorrow evening?" he asked.

"Nothing that I can think of; why? What's up?"

"Pull in there."

We drove into an apartment complex. He told me to pull up to the silver box. He had me punch a number in to open the gate. I parked right next to his truck and put the car in park.

"My cousin plays in a string quartet, and they're pretty good. They have a show tomorrow night at one of the amphitheaters across town. I thought we could grab a bite to eat then go."

"Sure that sounds fun," I said. This tension between us was about to get out of hand. He had released my hand when we pulled into the parking lot, and I longed for his touch again. He had traced the lines in my palm, and it felt so good. His fingers had traced repeatedly, and then all of sudden he stopped. It was hard to concentrate when I was driving, but I am strong and I could handle this.

He unhooked his seat belt, and my heart fell. I didn't want him to leave, but I couldn't ask him to stay either. He leaned over to me, and I leaned into him. He went straight to my ear again, and the chill bumps resurfaced. It took everything in me not to press my lips against his and then force my tongue into his mouth. He kissed me softly on my cheek and left it wet. Then, he opened the door and walked away from the car.

I sat there, still not awakened from his hypnotic trance. I let the window down a little, and then I started the car up. Fresh air would help me right now. I collected myself and pulled out of the parking lot. Once I made it up the street, I took out my phone. It only had one battery bar now, so I plugged it up immediately. I touched the screen on the car radio and activated the navigation system. Once I had the condo address in, I called Chelle.

"Trick, where have you been?" she yelled.

"Church," I answered.

"Ohhh, okay," she answered. I filled her in on dinner.

Then, she told me Ayashe's version. Ayashe had told Chelle how cute Kanoke had gotten and Chelle seemed very interested. Ayashe also said, she thought Jyme and I made a really cute couple. And if we ever had any children how good looking they would be. Then she went on to say, how much of a sin it was for us to be together. She said we were both model worthy and that it wasn't fair. She also told Chelle that if Jyme could ever get over Elle, I would be perfect for him. That did sting me a little, I had to admit, and it does sit in the back of my head as well. But other than that *almost melt down* this evening, he seems okay.

Chelle then went in on how she felt about the date that she didn't attend. She went on and on about how everyone has seen him but her. I reminded her Ayashe was the only person that she knew that had seen him. Then she went on about Elle and wondered how she looked. She said Ayashe told her, "She's no Cricket." That did make me feel a lot better about the whole thing.

I told her about the Catholic Church, and what he had said.

"I don't know about him, Cricket. Ayashe is being extremely secretive about him for some reason. I asked her if he was a good person, and she said he's no worse than the others from the reservation. Then, I asked her how he was financially, and she said,

"Cricket should ask him that."

"What does that mean?" I could tell she knew something she wasn't telling me.

"All I know is that he owns a fishing company or something," I answered.

"I thought you said he was a fisherman?" she asked.

"That's what he told me. Then, he said he owned his own company,"

"Where does he live?"

"On the reservation, but he had me drop him off at some apartments," I said.

"Well, what does your Spidey sense tell you?" she asked.

"I think he's been extremely hurt; I think the woman before me must have been really hard on him."

"From what Ayashe said, I think so too."

"What did she say?" I asked.

"She said they sent him to another reservation for like three months and that he came back like a zombie. She said he hardly talks now, and he never smiles. She said it's like the fun in him is gone," she explained.

"Oh, so he's like damaged goods or something?" I asked.

"Sounds like it."

I pulled into the garage at the condo and lost all signal. I sent Chelle a text immediately and told her that I was at the condo and that I was headed to bed. I got out of the car and handed the attendant my valet key with my tag number. He advised me to give them ten minutes' notice when I needed my car pulled up front.

The elevator doors opened and there stood Mr. Crain. He had some little PYT hanging on his arm. I moved out of their way so they could exit the elevator and stepped in as soon as they got out; I pressed my floor and kept my head down.

As soon as I walked in the door, I climbed into the shower. Just as I got out, I heard my phone chiming on the charger. I ran over, and I had two missed calls from that number that made my toes tickle. As I stared at the phone, the doorbell rang. My heart started racing; I put my bathrobe on and sprinted towards the door. I looked out the peephole with a smile and then I eased away from the door slowly. D'Artagnan Crain was standing in front of my door. He rang the doorbell again, and then he started knocking.

My phone chimed, and I tiptoed back to the bedroom. "Hello," I whispered into the phone.

"Why are you whispering?"

The doorbell rang again, and then D'Artagnan pounded on the door.

"Who the hell is that?" he growled.

"It's my drunk boss. I think he's harmless," I answered.

I heard a car alarm chirp and then the slamming of doors. "What are you doing?" I asked frantically. He didn't answer me. I heard the car starting and then the blasting of the stereo.

"Hey now, you don't have to come over here. I'm not that kind of girl."

He said nothing.

The doorbell rang again three times in a row, and I rushed to the closet. I pulled on some sweats and yanked on some socks.

"Look, you really don't have to come over here. He's drunk, and he'll stop eventually," I said.

"Let the front desk know you're having an overnight visitor and give them my name," he demanded. The line went dead; I ran to the kitchen for the emergency number. D'Artagnan banged on my door again, calling out my name. I wondered why the other guests hadn't called the front desk yet. I found the front desk number and ran back to the bedroom. I couldn't use the speaker pad on the door because D'Artagnan would hear me. I dialed the front desk and Randy was still on duty; he agreed to let Jyme up. About two minutes and four doorbell rings later, I could hear muffles and then a thump. My phone chimed, and I answered.

"Open the door," he growled. I opened the door wide, and the sight I saw was unbelievable. Jyme stood there in a leather jacket with no shirt underneath. A pair of grey sweat shorts and sneakers and that was it for his ensemble. D'Artagnan was now passed out on the floor, and he had apparently wet himself because his khakis were damp in the seat. Jyme walked in and then closed and locked the door behind him.

He pressed me up against the foyer wall and lay against me. His lips pressed up against mine, and then he licked my lips with his tongue. It was as if his tongue was knocking to get in; I opened my mouth, and he slid it in with mine. We played tongue wars for only a couple of seconds.

His phone rang in his pocket, and he growled loudly. He pulled his tongue out and removed his lips from mine. I wrapped my arms around his bare back, and I stood on my tiptoes so I could kiss his neck. I got two kisses in when he yanked my ponytail and my head cocked up to meet his eyes.

"I'll call you in the morning," he spit into the phone. He dropped it on the floor, yanked his coat off, and started kissing me again. He slung both sneakers off and then wrapped both of my arms around his neck. He placed both of his hands under my butt and then told me "Come on." I jumped up, but with all this ass and hips, I didn't jump far. He had to do all of the work. I wrapped my legs around him, and we headed to the bedroom as I held on for dear life. I've never had a man in my adult life pick me up like that. He didn't break a sweat nor did he seem out of breath.

He kicked the French doors open, and I slid down. He placed both hands on either side of my face, and then he kissed me softly. He removed his hands from my face and shifted around a little. I put my arms around him and immediately noticed he was butt-naked. He had shrugged out of his shorts, and now he pressed against me. I was fully dressed and then I remembered I had pulled on a sports bra but no panties. How embarrassing was this? I was supposed to have on some sexy little number, and that was not the case. Shit, when was the last time I shaved. Oh no! This was going to be a complete nightmare. He was about to see the wild kingdom, and he would probably need a weed whacker to find his way in. Well, it was somewhat dark with only the light from the bathroom around the corner.

I sat down on the bed, and I was about to take my sweatshirt off. I looked up, and I was eye level with his dick. Let's just say it freaked me the hell out. "What the hell is that?" I screamed.

He kneeled down, and we were almost eye-to-eye. "Wait, wait. I'll go real slow. I swear I won't hurt you," he pleaded. I sat there in utter shock; I had never seen anything like that before in my life.

"It won't fit. I am not a virgin by no means, but I assure you that will not fit in me. And if it does, I will have to go to the emergency room."

He dropped his head, and his floppy ponytail split into two pieces. I stood up, and that anaconda was back in my face. I shut my eyes and moved away from it. I heard the French door doors open and shut. I opened my eyes, and he was gone.

I sat in the bedroom for at least twenty minutes. I opened the French doors, and Jyme was sitting on the couch in his boxers. His shorts lay across the back of the couch. He had gone and picked up his coat and his shoes. He sat slumped with his head in his hands. I knew his last break up was bad, and I didn't want to set him back. I felt awful, and I was almost positive that I had overreacted.

I walked over to the couch and kneeled down in front of him. He dropped his hands down to the couch cushions, and then dropped his head to the back of the couch. He was staring up at the ceiling, so I couldn't make out his facial expression. But, according to his body language he was pissed. He was stiff and his breathing was quick. I placed both of my hands on his knees, and he didn't move. I slowly slid my hands over to his and then slid my fingers through his; he still didn't move. I thought it was safe to really touch him now; but I had to test the waters first.

I waited for a minute, and then I stood up and straddled him. He wrapped his arms around me. He kept his head leaned towards the back of the couch. I leaned over and kissed his lips. I had to kiss him twice before I could get a reaction out of him. He finally sat up and stared at me.

"Don't be afraid of me, Cricket," he pleaded. And my poor heart just stopped. I felt horrible and he was feeling even worse. He squinted his eyes and held me tight.

"I'm not." I laid my head on his chest, and he rubbed my back until I fell asleep.

I was out maybe fifteen minutes when the doorbell rang. I jerked my head up, and Jyme held me in his arms tight. "Get up," he said.

I stumbled to my feet, holding on to him for balance. We both walked over to the door, hand in hand. He looked out the peephole, and then he stiffened. "What's up with this asshole?" he asked. I looked out the peephole, and then I shut off all the lights. I grabbed my phone from the counter and tugged for Jyme to follow me. I dialed the last number I had called. I pulled the covers down, and then I pushed Jyme down to the bed. I told the attendant that I was in 808 and that a drunken man was ringing my doorbell. I advised the attendant that I was in the bed and needed to get back to sleep. The doorbell rang again, and then he started knocking again. The attendant assured me someone would be right up to handle it. I told him I didn't care who it was and that no one needed to speak with me. I just wanted to get back to sleep. He assured me the safety of the building and then told me someone would be right up. I ended the call, got up, and shut the bathroom lights off. I walked back into the bedroom and slid into Jyme's arms. He kissed my forehead, and I snuggled deeper into his chest.

I woke up to Jyme gently rubbing my face and a faint alarm going off. I turned, and the phone was not on the nightstand where I left it.

"You grabbed it and chucked it on the floor about fifteen minutes ago," he explained.

I giggled and shook my head. My sweatshirt was all twisted and one of my arms was hanging out of the sleeve.

"You sleep like a wild animal," he laughed.

"I know, I'm not sure why I do that," I answered.

"I like it. You're so free when you sleep."

I righted myself and slid out of bed. I found my cell phone at the foot of the bed. I went to the closet and pulled out my outfit for today. A white button down, black wide leg trousers, and a red knee length trench coat. Jyme was on the phone in the bedroom, and I saw the extra toothbrush and mouthwash on the sink counter. I scooped them up and handed them to him while he was on the phone.

I stepped into my stilettos and walked into the front room. Jyme went into the bathroom and started brushing his teeth. I picked up his shorts that were hanging over the couch. Something fell out of pocket; I bent down to pick it up. I gripped it, and there was a swooshing sound. I looked down and it was a blade with ridges. He had a black rubber knife in his pocket. I looked down at my hand, and blood was dripping from it.

I screeched and dropped the knife back on the floor. I heard the water in the bathroom cut off and ran to the kitchen sink. I turned the water on and held my hand under it. I stomped my foot twice trying to cut back some of the pain. Jyme stood there beside me then grabbed a dishtowel.

"NO," I yelled at him. I looked around and saw paper towels on the small table. "Can you hand me some paper towels?" I asked. He went to the table and yanked off some paper towels. I wrapped my hand up and looked in all the cabinets. I looked under the sink and yanked out the little white box. I cleaned the wound and Jyme helped me bandage it up. I found some disinfectant under the sink. I yanked some more paper towels off the roll. I went back to the living room to clean the blood off the floor. Jyme pulled the disinfectant and the paper towels from my hands not saying a word. I went straight to the bedroom and called the front desk for my car. I looked down at myself, and there was not a spot of blood on me. I was relieved because I really didn't want to change clothes. I turned the bathroom light off and ran smack into Jyme. He placed both hands on each side of my face. We made some serious eye contact, neither one of us saying a word. His cell phone rang from the other room. We both shifted, and then I pulled away from him.

I slid my coat on and grabbed my purse. He had put his shoes and coat on, this time zipping the jacket. We road down on the elevator in silence, and he held the elevator door for me while I stepped out. I thanked the attendant, and then we both exited the building. I stepped out and walked straight to the rental not saying a word to him.

I got to my first assignment for the day, and this location was extremely busy. I decided to go inside since the drive thru was wrapped around the building. The parking lot had cigarette butts, and there were a few napkins with the company logo scattered over it. I walked in, and someone immediately greeted me. There were four people ahead of me, but the barista took my order instantly. I ordered a breakfast sandwich and a hot tea. There were three free tables, so I decided to stay for a while.

I pulled out my laptop and connected to the free Wi-Fi. I went to get my order and asked for some raw sugar. She handed me two packs and a stirrer. I made sure my computer screen was not facing anyone who could see. I sent my evaluation over to D'Artagnan.

My phone chimed, and I pulled it out. It was *that* number, but I didn't answer it. I was working, and I didn't want to talk to him right now. My phone beeped this time, and I knew I had a voicemail. I touched the screen to listen to my voicemail. The first three messages were from Chelle, and then the last one was him.

"We need to talk about this morning; I don't want us to pretend like it never happened. I don't want to do this over the phone. Can we meet for a quick lunch?"

I looked over my schedule, and I texted him back, "I have a gap from one to three today. I will be in the Pike Place area."

He answered my text immediately. "I will meet you at Maximilian in the Market at 1:15."

I quickly knocked out two more of my assignments. I had sent

D'Artagnan all three of my evaluations, and he hadn't responded to any of them. I called the office, and O answered. I asked her if D'Artagnan was in, and she told me he was out sick. I asked her how many company condos we had in the building I was in. She told me we had six, and then she mentioned that several employees, including D'Artagnan, actually lived on the premises. She also told me that we all get a hell of a discount there because the owner of company owns that building. I asked O if there were any other condos on another floor I could stay in. She said there was an empty one on the tenth floor, a corner condo with two bedrooms. She said that D'Artagnan would have to sign off on it. I assured her he would do so. She said I could swing back by, get the key and move right up there. O said the cleaning crew comes daily and that they would move my stuff for me. I thanked her and promised when I was back in the office we would have to do lunch, my treat, anywhere she wanted.

I walked into the Pike Place store and the service was on point. Immediately, the man behind the counter greeted me with a wide smile. The service was speedy fast. I ordered some black and white cookies and Naked Juice. I made it to the restaurant five minutes after I was done with the evaluation, and he was already waiting on me. He had showered and changed. He now wore a long sleeve pullover with a pair of khakis, brown loafers, and a brown jacket. His hair was still a little wet and pulled up in this funky ponytail. He looked amazing, and I honestly think he had no idea.

We both had lemon water and a cup of soup. I ordered the PNW Salad, and he had the Salmon Grille Sauce Homard. We started the talk before our entrees arrived.

"I don't want you to be afraid of me. I'm not *that* guy," he pleaded. I watched him, and he was seriously concerned.

"Look, I'm from the South and you having a knife or a switch-blade isn't an issue. The problem I have with you is that you didn't tell me. You left it in your stupid shorts pocket. I could have lost my fucking hand," I snapped at him.

He gave me a wide smile and then he pulled my bandaged hand into his. "I'm sorry," he smiled.

"I accept your apology." We finished our lunch, and I had an hour and fifteen minutes to spare. I desperately needed to get an hour of shopping in. I started to say goodbye to Jyme, but he stopped me.

"You said you had a two hour gap; we still have plenty of time.

"I do, but since I'm staying in Seattle this week, I desperately need to buy a few things to hold me over."

"From where?" he asked.

"Over on Northeast Northgate Way."

"Okay, I'm heading that way. Follow me there," he said.

"You're going to Northgate Way?"

"I'm going to Northeast Northgate Way," he corrected.

"You are such a bad liar."

"And something's telling me you are way too good at it," he said.

I smiled at him. "But you will never know the truth." I teased.

"I'll learn you soon enough." We left in separate cars for Northeast Northgate Way.

CHAPTER 4

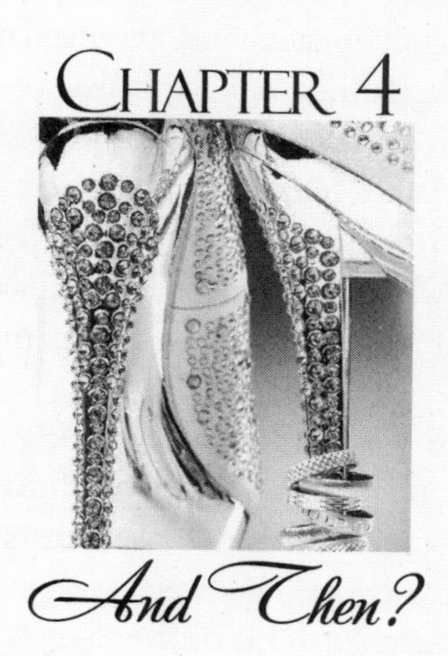

And Then?

I picked up a sequin tee, a tuxedo-front long sleeve in white and black, a shimmering drape neck shell, a palette sequin cami, three non-iron, button-down shirts, a sequin poncho, an ikat sequin embellished blouse, a sequin trim knit cardigan, and a dolman wedge sweater. I then added three pairs of jeans, two pair of trousers, and one pencil skirt. I had to turn and go back to the intimates. I got five matched sets and two nightgowns.

After all my coupons and credits, my total added up to be $1,360.41. Jyme handed his credit card to the sales associate. I looked over at him, and he wouldn't make eye contact with me.

"I've money to spend here," I snapped.

"So do I," he said. The sales associate handed him his card back, and he signed the pen pad in front of him. She gave him the receipt, and then he looked at the bottom of it. "Look, you saved $386 dollars," he teased.

I rolled my eyes at him and grabbed four of the bags while he grabbed the other six. I slammed my bags into the trunk of the rental and waited for Jyme to put his bags in so I could go. I held the trunk door open with my arm and my purse and keys in the other hand. He slowly placed each bag in one at a time. He was really pissing me off now. He put the last bag in the trunk, and I was all prepared to slam it, but he caught it and yanked me in front of him. We were both staring at the trunk full of bags.

He wrapped his arms around me and unhooked my coat. He placed both of his hands under my shirt. Then, he told me to close the coat back up. I obeyed like a good little girl. He pulled both cups of my bra down, and then he started seducing the flat quarter. He dug his face in my hair until he reached my ear. "Is anybody watching us?"

I looked around. "No," I whined out, "No."

"Look at each and every car facing us," he demanded. I looked at every single car slowly, and then, those quarters were turning into erasers fast. Jyme made me check every single car. He made me whisper to him what color I was watching each time.

"Oh God, what about the people behind us," I moaned.

"They don't matter; they can't see you," he assured. He licked my ear and got even closer to me. "Do you feel that on your back?" he asked.

"Yes." I answered. "It wants you, badly. Do you want it?" Each word he spoke made me tingle deep down inside.

"Yes." I answered.

"Are you scared of it?"

Those erasers were now about to break off. I couldn't take much more of this. "Jyme."

"Shhhhh. Answer me," he demanded.

"Yes." I answered.

"Why?"

"Oh God…Because it's too big." I answered.

"I told you I would take my time with you. I wouldn't go fast, and I would go nice and slow. And you would be just as wet, if not more, than you are right now." he assured.

I made some serious gargling noises. I was at the edge and about to jump off.

"Now do you want it?" he asked.

"Yes," I shifted and leaned closer up against him.

"I've wanted to do this to you ever since you brought those luscious things out at the restaurant," he explained.

I shifted myself again, and I was about to blow my top.

"Are you scared of it?" he asked.

"NO," I growled.

He chuckled and then he removed one of his hands, and then he pulled my head around until his lips met mine. He gave me lots of tongue, and the next thing I knew, both of his hands were out of my shirt and he was walking away from me, heading towards his truck.

I watched him with my mouth wide open. I was sizzling all over, and he just left me standing here like this. I was ten times madder at him than before. I melted into the driver's seat. I looked in the glove compartment and blessed the baby wipes I had in there. When I made it to my next assignment, I went straight to bathroom with the baby wipes in my purse. I needed a serious shower after that lust session in the parking lot, but the wipes would have to do for now.

The bathroom on this assignment was actually disgusting. The trash looked as if it hadn't been emptied in a good long while; the floor was grimy, and the soap dispenser was empty. I snapped a few quick pictures and forwarded them to D'Artagnan.

When I stepped out into the shop, it didn't get any better. The floor needed mopping, trash needed pulling, and the sugars were empty. The employees all looked bored, and no one was smiling. I remembered that when I walked in I was not greeted at all. I snapped a few quick pictures since no one was paying me any attention. I pretended I was texting all the while I was recording and snapping pictures.

I got another Naked Juice and tried to get a muffin, but they were out. I then tried a slice of the cake of the day, and then I moved on down to the cookies. I bit into one of the three cookies I ordered, and there were hard as bricks. This location was out of everything, and it was only three thirty; they still had another five and a half hours in the day to go. D'Artagnan had told me when something like this happens; he needed to get emergency assistance in the shop. I would call this location a warzone, and it needed a cleanup crew badly. I had to hurry up and get out of the shop before someone remembered what I looked like. Although I don't think anyone here would remember anything.

I got into the rental and called D'Artagnan's cell phone. O said he was out sick, but he hadn't given me any information on how to contact him when he was out. The phone rang two times, and then he answered.

"Cricket?" I knew this conversation would be awkward, but I would have to grit through it.

"D'Artagnan, I know you're sick, and I apologize for calling you like this

but-"

"Cricket, you can call me anytime, no matter what," he stated.

"Well, I'm at my last assignment for today, and this shop needs an emergency clean-up crew" I rushed. I told D'Artagnan that I had forwarded pictures and two videos of the shop. He told me he had received them, and then he told me to get out of the parking lot so he could make a call to the district. I pulled out of the parking lot, letting him know that no one in that shop would remember anything. He told me I had done a superb job with all of my evaluations and that he was extremely proud of me.

We had an awkward silence, and then I bolted into the elephant on the phone. "O is going to contact you about me moving up to the tenth floor. I told her that the eighth floor was extremely noisy, and I hardly got any sleep. So I would greatly appreciate your approval on this issue," I stated.

There was silence on the phone, and then he cleared his voice.

"Cricket…I'm-"

I interrupted him, "That's all I have for you today."

"Okay, that's good. I will contact O immediately. And I will talk to you tomorrow," he said.

I disconnected the line and sucked in a deep breath. My top lip was sweating, and I felt hot. I cracked the window, so I could get some fresh air as I drove to the office.

I got the new key from O and handed her my old one. O was a professional; she knew something was up, but she didn't pry. I stepped into my office, and my phone chimed. I recognized the unsaved number and gave the phone a huge grin. "Hello," I tried to sound annoyed.

"Hi," he teased. I felt the heat rising in the back of my neck. I walked over to my office door, shutting it.

"Did I catch you at a bad time?" he still taunted.

"Is there something I can help you with Mr. Samson?" I asked.

"How do you feel about Creole food?" he asked.

"It's fine." I answered.

"But do you like it?" he asked.

"I've been to Louisiana several times, and I enjoyed the food."

"Pick you up at six?"

"Alright."

"Are you still upset with me?"

"NO." I growled.

"Well, if that's no, I don't want to hear your yes," he chuckled.

I couldn't help it; I grinned from ear to ear.

"Ah, there it is. Did I hear a smile approach your face?"

I cleared my throat, and then I was back to serious. "Is there anything else I can help you with?" At that very moment O buzzed me and told me I had another delivery. "I have to go," I grinned into the phone.

"Can you do me a favor?" he asked.

"What?" I snapped. "Can you wear that sparkly off the shoulder piece tonight?"

I sucked in a deep breath, my heart was racing now. Just the thought of his hands on me made my mouth water. I blew out a slow breath, and then I calmed myself. "I will see what I can do. See you at six." I hung up and went right to reception area.

The sight of this delivery was…the vase was massive, and it had that cracked look, and it held the most peculiar flowers I had ever seen. All of them were amazing, but there was one that stood out from them all. You could tell the florist had arranged all the other flowers around this one. There were twenty-eight flowers, and there was a syllabus to explain what each one was. The one flower that caught everyone's passing eye was something called a Rafflesia Arnoldii Corpse. It had no stems, leaves or visible roots. It had five buds that were each the size of cabbages. It was blood red with beige spots all over it. The arrangement now had groupies surrounding it. Everyone was mesmerized with the arrangement. O looked as if she would cry if I removed it from her desk. I plucked the card out and gave it one last sniff. "Enjoy them O," I called out to her.

"Ohh, Cricket!" she crooned. I walked back towards my office. I could hear more people walking up admiring the flowers. I heard O tell each one of them, "Oh, they're not mine, but one of bosses insisted that they stay here for everyone to admire," she chanted.

I closed my office door and opened the card. "I hope you enjoy these bold and very non-boring flowers." I pulled my phone out immediately and went straight to the contacts. I stored Jyme's name and gave him a very special ringtone: Beyoncé's, *Video Phone*. That song meant a lot to me even though the lyrics hadn't a thing to do with him.

Randy buzzed me at five fifty advising me that Mr. Samson was on his way up. I unlocked the door and stood there for his arrival. I had managed to wear the little sparkly off the shoulder number he had requested. I decided to wear my hair up in a rhinestone banana clip. He wanted my neck exposed for some reason; he wouldn't have asked me to wear this shirt otherwise. I wore dark denim stiletto jeans with sparkly platforms. I had diamond hoops in my ears, and I wore a gaudy ring. My make-up was flawless, all except for my lip gloss, which resided in my clutch. He opened the door, and I walked towards him. He froze as I sauntered over. He wore a black fitting V-neck t-shirt with a grey opened vest, denim pants, and a pair of black boots. His ponytail was underneath a black fedora. He shut the door, and I wrapped my arms around him.

"Thank you for the flowers." I pressed my lips against his, and he pressed me against the sidewall. His fingers intertwined with my silver chain belt. We kissed very nosily, and our breathing belonged in a porn video. His hand rubbed every inch of me, and I tried to mimic him. My cell phone chimed, and we stopped, both of us breathing as if we ran a marathon.

I pulled away from him and walked over to my clutch. I had a missed call from the front desk. I called the number back, and Randy told me that I had a delivery. He said he would send it right up. I went into the new and massive bedroom and applied my lip gloss.

This new condo was even more amazing than the other. This one had two bedrooms and three walk-in closets. I also had two and half baths and two balconies. This color scheme was silver, grays, and royal blue, and I loved it.

There was knocking at the door, and I asked Jyme to get it. After I applied my lip liner and lip gloss, I walked back into the living room. There was an arrangement of a dozen white roses sitting on the coffee table. I looked at Jyme puzzled. And he gave me the same look right back. I walked over to the arrangement and plunked out the card. It read, "Please consider this arrangement as my white flag" and it was signed D'Artagnan.

"These are from my boss," I explained.

"The drunk guy from last night?" he looked annoyed.

"Yes." I answered.

Jyme held the elevator door for me as I stepped out.

"Why is he sending you flowers?"

"I guess he felt bad about last night."

"Are you going to keep them?"

"Jyme, there just flowers."

"Whatever," he said with an attitude. I reached for his hand

and he ignored me. I put my hand into his and he finally closed his hand around mine. We walked hand in hand towards the front desk; Randy stood and straightened his jacket. "Ms. Hooper."

"CRICKET!" I growled.

"Cricket." He smiled at me, and I ginned back.

"If you don't mind me saying Mr. Samson, Cricket, you're a vision," he explained. I felt my cheeks heat up, and I thanked Randy for his compliment. Jyme nodded back at him.

The door attendant held the door for us, and Jyme helped me into the truck. I immediately looked over the back seat to make sure we were alone; we were.

We walked into The New Orleans Creole Restaurant. There was jazz music playing, and everyone looked cheerful and upbeat. We sat immediately and ordered lemon water. I had the Eggplant Lafitte with a side salad, and Jyme ordered the Oyster Bayou with a side of red beans and rice. We both oohed and ahhed through the entire meal. The food was good, and I told him this was my new favorite spot. We ordered a bag of beignets to go. Jyme swore we could eat them at the amphitheater. We made it twenty minutes early; I grabbed the beignet bag, and he went to the back of the truck. He pulled out a cooler, a large piece of plastic, and two blankets. Once we made it down the stairs, he told me to take off my shoes. He pulled his off, and I did the same; we walked onto the grass barefoot. Once we had made it down the small hill, I could see why he packed what he did. Everyone was stretched out on the ground. We passed a few people that spoke to him by name.

Once we got up towards the front, everyone started calling him Lil Samson and nodding at me. He found the spot he wanted and laid the plastic down putting both blankets on top. He helped me down to the ground and then joined me. He opened the cooler, and it was filled with Perrier water, and canned Cokes. A few people walked by, spoke to Jyme, and then stared at me. It made me feel a little uncomfortable and out of place. Jyme told me that they were not used to seeing him with anyone. He said he was a loner, so this was new for them. I felt better after he explained the situation.

The lights came up on the stage, and the strings started. They first played a little whimsical number, then a bolder piece, and then a soothing light piece. A few of the couples stood up and started slow dancing to the music. It was very sweet, and I turned around and around watching them all. Some were seated, as couples were up dancing, snuggling, kissing, or dancing to the music. Jyme kissed the side of my exposed neck, and then he shifted around me. I was now sitting in between his legs and I felt my neck get hot. He wrapped his arms around me, and I laid both of my arms on top of his. The strings played slow pieces for the rest of the concert. Jyme kissed my exposed neck repeatedly. He took his time, and he didn't rush. He did the tracing of the palm thing again, and I felt like a stupid naive teenager. This man gave me chills, and I couldn't imagine any other place I would rather be. It had only been three days, but in these short days, I had such strong feeling for him. I turned to kiss him, and it was soft, gentle and sweet.

We gathered our things after the concert, and several people came up to him. I noticed almost everyone in the audience was Native American. I could count the few people that were not on my hand. Then, I remembered all of the string players were Native American as well. The grass was covered with people now, many more than I saw when we first got here. Most of the Native Americans had tattoos and exposed piercings of some sort. It made me a little nervous, and I moved closer to Jyme, wrapping my arms around him. He was talking to a group of people, and he turned to kiss me on my forehead. He pulled me closer to him, and after a few more long minutes, they said their farewells and we departed. I looped my finger into his belt loops on his jeans. The crowd was so thick, and I didn't want to get separated from him.

When we made it back to the truck, I wrapped up into him and kissed him slowly. Someone cleared their voice behind us, interrupting our passionate moment. There was a beautiful Native American woman with dark hair flowing down her back. She was holding up an obviously drunken, grey-headed Native American man. Beside them, a younger version of the woman and a buzzed cut Caucasian man stood next to her. Jyme sucked in a deep breath, and then he said something to them in a language I didn't recognize. I watched his mouth, but my ears didn't understand a word of it. He said a few more words, and then they all looked at me. He turned to me and introduced everyone to me. Brad was the Caucasian man's name, Patty was the younger woman's name, Jenimine Julin was the beautiful woman's name, and Big Samson was the drunken man's name. I shook everyone's hand except for the drunken man. I froze after Jyme spoke his name to me.

"This is your family?" I asked.

"Yes." Then he introduced me to them by my name and nothing more. Jenimine Julin looked me over and then she spoke that language again. She apologized immediately, and then she called me a good luck charm. She kissed Jyme on his check and said, "So you finally found one."

She turned to me and said, "Call me JJ." The drunken man mumbled something, and then they all laughed, well everyone except for Jyme and me. They said goodbye and walked away from us. JJ called out to Jyme from a distance. "Bring her to me this weekend." He nodded and helped me into the truck.

Once we made it out the parking lot, I started. "Your mother and sister are so beautiful," I stated. He said nothing in response to me. We rode in complete silence back to the condo. He pulled up-front and my heart dropped. I was hoping he would stay the night tonight. I needed him to stay with me tonight. He opened my truck door for me, and I slid out into him. I pressed all of myself onto him, melting into skin. He wrapped his arms around me and kissed me on my cheek.

"You're not coming up?" I breathed out.

"No, not tonight."

I pulled back from him so I could get a better look at his face. "Did I do something wrong?" I asked.

"No, not at all, my workweek starts tomorrow. We fish all day Thursday and go to the markets on the weekend," he explained.

My feelings were now officially hurt. I pulled away from him, and headed towards the door. He caught my arm before I reached the door. "Come here," he breathed.

"Look, don't start something you're not going to finish," I explained.

I left him with a double meaning and walked into the awaiting opened doors of the building. I crossed my arms and kept my head down as I passed the front desk. When I stepped into the elevator and the doors shut, the tears starting falling. He was supposed to have followed me into the elevator, and he was supposed to be rubbing and tugging at everything while I unlocked the condo door. Then, we should be peeling each other's clothes off. Then, we should be making some hot passionate love. Instead, I was stepping out the shower pulling my bathrobe on and collapsing on the bed.

The next two days were monstrous. D'Artagnan was acting like a wounded puppy, and I hated it. O was out sick at the office, and the temp kept calling me instead of sending all of my calls to my voicemail. Plus, I hadn't heard from Jyme in over forty-eight hours.

I drove to Chelle's on Friday night so I could pack some more of my things. Ayashe was there, and we opened a bottle of wine. Chelle lit a fire since it was a little chilly outside. She served bruschetta and a chocolate cake. We sat on the floor surrounding the coffee table with dinner forks. That cake didn't have a chance in hell.

Chelle and her current Boo were on the outs. He lied to her about his whereabouts a few days ago. She said a friend of hers snapped pictures of him at the bar with some slut. Ayashe's ex was tripping with the child support. She said he was determined to give her exactly what the State demanded him. He told her someone had told him that she goes out every night to the clubs on his dime. So he stopped giving her the extra money he used to. Her ex was slick though; he had four different businesses, but he was only claiming one of them to the authorities. She promised him a long time ago that she would never tell and he agreed to always take care of her. He was now going back on his word and she barely had a leg to stand on. Ayashe said she knew if she told on him now, he would just quit his jobs and then she wouldn't get a dime from him.

Then, I had to fill them in on my drama. They looked me over a couple of times, and then they both asked me if I had called him. I thought about it, and then I realized I hadn't contacted him at all, not one time in the now fifty-two hours we hadn't spoken to each other. I excused myself and went into the restroom. I dialed the now-saved number in my phone, and it rang once.

"Cricket?"

"Hi."

"I'm really sorry about the other night. I should have followed, and we should have…" he drifted off.

"It's okay."

"No, it's not. It's my family; they make me crazy. Can I come see you?" he asked.

"I'm not in Seattle," I said.

"Where are you? I can come to you."

"I'm in Olympia for the night."

"I can come there. I don't mind the drive," he pleaded.

"No, it's kind of late."

"Meet me somewhere, anywhere."

"No, not tonight." I said.

"Are you getting back at me for the other night?" he asked.

"No, not at all," I assured him.

"Will you come and see me tomorrow at work?"

"Where is work?"

"I'm working in the University District tomorrow, right next to that department store you shopped in," he explained.

I thought for a minute. He had said that he had business to take care of over there, and he was telling the truth. I thought he was just being facetious. "What time?"

"Come at twelve."

"Alright, I'll see tomorrow," I said.

"I can't wait to kiss you," he whispered, and there they were, the tingles.

Ayashe and Chelle tagged along with me the next day. I insisted on them bringing a change of clothes. Being in Jyme's presence, there was no telling where we would end up. When we got to the market, we grabbed a map from the information booth. The market was extremely crowded, and we barely made it through. We went down one row, then two rows, and then three rows. We went back to the information booth, and the two women inside asked what we were looking for. I told them Jyme's name because he had never told me the name of his fishing company. Both of women looked at me and started laughing, asking if we had ever been there before.

"Keep walking down this street, and trust me you can't miss them," the older woman said.

We walked and walked and then walked some more until we could see a crowd of people at the end of the street. We pushed our way through, and then we could hear music and some sort of chanting. All of a sudden, there was flying fish. Fish were tossed and thrown into the air, and the crowd went berserk. We finally made it to an opening, and then I got the full effect of the show. There were nine men standing before us. Two were out front, and the other seven were behind tables under a big tent. One guy had a wireless microphone across his head, and his voice belted through the large speakers. He threw a fish at the man standing directly across from him and that man threw the fish at the first guy standing next to him behind the tables. All the while, the microphone man chanted, "If we drop it we buy it."

The first man threw the now clean fish to the second man. The second man then threw the now skin free fish to the third man. The third man sliced the fish right down the middle and threw that fish to the fourth man. The fourth man had a huge hatchet-like knife.

Just then, I got a good look at him, and my heart stopped. Jyme was the fourth man with the big hatchet. He wore a white tank top with khaki carpenter shorts and sneakers. You could see his biceps and all of his arm muscles perfectly. He looked scrumptious. All the men wore the exact same get up, but Jyme looked hella hot.

There was a man standing right next to him, and I saw that I knew him, too. Jyme handed Kanoke the fish, and then Kanoke did something to the fish and threw it to the next man. I knew this man, too. Loon did something else to the fish as he tossed it to the last guy. All of this happened in less than thirty seconds. There was a huge digital clock hanging over the tent above them that said so. The sign over the tent read, Samson and Son. This went on for the next four or five minutes or so. I was in awe at the performance, and I couldn't keep my eye off Jyme.

He finally looked up when it slowed down. He searched the crowd, and then his eyes landed on mine. He gave me a big grin and started chanting something that sounded like Poke. They sung the name repeatedly throughout the crowd. All of a sudden, a man who looked identical to all of them ran from behind the tent and took Jyme's spot. The crowd whined and shouted, NO!!!! Jyme smiled and placed both hands over his heart. The women fucking lost it then. I hate to admit it, but I was a little disappointed for his departure as well. That was until he nodded for me to follow.

I pushed through the crowd with Chelle and Ayashe on my heels. The guy with the mic looked us over, and then Kanoke chanted something at him. He opened the small gate for us to pass through. We went around the back and a saw a mobile home stretched out, the door wide open. As we stepped up into the mobile home, the wood grain almost blinded us. The mobile home was kickass, and it had all the trimmings. Two guys dressed in the same identical gear as everyone else sat in front of a big flat screen, playing some gaming system. Ayashe called out to one of them, and he stood and walked towards her. He hugged her and nuzzled his nose into her hair. Chelle walked over to the dining area with Ayashe. I stood in the kitchen and heard, "pissst." I turned completely around and saw a cracked door. Then, a finger beckoned me. I went to the door and was yanked in. I was pressed against a wall, and then I felt his wet skin all over me.

Jyme had showered and was not wearing anything but a towel. His hair was wet and wild. His hands and fingers searched for any gathering of my skin.

"I missed you, Cricket," he growled.

"I missed you, too."

Jyme licked and sucked on both of my ears, and it drove me crazy. He squeezed both cheeks of my butt. I reached under his towel. He froze and pulled back from me. He saw that look in my eyes, and I didn't say a word. He reached over and locked the door then led me over to the bed with him. He sat down and pulled me on top of him. I could feel him straight through the thick fluffy towel.

I bent down to kiss him, but he drew back. "I'm not going to hurt you," he whispered. I nodded at him, still trying to meet my lips with his. He pulled back again, and I closed my eyes, I tried to push down the heat coming from that juicy place.

"Open your eyes and look at me," he whispered. I obeyed, and his face was calm and soothing. He wrapped both arms around me. "I'm not going to hurt you," he explained.

"K," I breathed.

"We're not going to do *that* here."

My mouth fell open, and I sucked in a breath.

"We can do *some* things here, but not that," he stated.

I was still shocked; I couldn't believe he was setting me up for failure.

"Don't worry," he said. He pressed my worry line flat on my forehead. "I'm gonna hook you up," he assured.

"Now?"

"Right now."

I wore a white, V-neck t-shirt with a pair of khakis shorts. I still had my dark denim jacket and Ugg boots on. Now, I could never ever get away with an outfit like this back home, but this was the norm here. I pulled my jacket off and let it drop to the floor. I stood up and pulled my shorts off and repositioned myself right back over him. He pulled both of my cups down from my black lacy bra. He started sucking and biting, and I bit back my moans. His hands cupped both cheeks of black lacy panties. He slipped a finger in and then another. He pushed his fingers in and out and in and out. I was going crazy straddled on top of him. He was still calm and cool, and I was loving having that shit.

I opened his towel, and I literally had to use both hands to massage him. He closed his eyes and parted his lips a little. The more aggressive I got, the more he liked it. I licked both of my hands thoroughly, and he watched me with wide eyes. "Cricket," he called out.

I went right back to work on him, and he started squinting. His fingers slowed, and I started rubbing up against them myself. This was making me so hot, and I knew I only had maybe about a minute left. "Oh…Oh God," I whispered.

"Wait for me," he breathed. My head was spinning, and I was feeling so light headed. I knew it was about to happen and oh my, it was going to be a good one. "I…I can't, I can't," I whined.

"Wait a minute, wait a minute, wait." his mouth and eyes opened wide. He moved his fingers as if they were on a mission now. "Okay, come on," he whispered.

I dropped my forehead down onto his. We were both panting and sweating. Jyme turned my head, and now his lips were against my ear. I didn't know what he was about to say, but his breath up against my ear was going to be the end for me.

"Cricket," he growled.

"Oh God, Jyme. I'm cumming," I whined.

"Will you be my girlfriend?" he strained.

I gripped him so hard and tight now; he raised us both from the bed, turned us around, and then my back pressed against the bed. He was grinding into me so hard. We couldn't get close enough; we both tugged and pulled at each other. Both of us were so crazed and hungry for the other. We were now humping like horny teenagers. He yanked my head to the side and sucked my ear lobe, and that was it for me. He pulled back a little and started murmuring in my ear.

"Will you be my girlfriend?"

"Yes, oh GOD yes!" I shuddered.

Jyme followed right behind me; he buried his head in between my breasts, and I couldn't move. He let me shower first and then got back in. I clung to the big fluffy towel for dear life. He had entered the bathroom buck naked without a courtesy knock. I was not ready for him to see all of this yet. I slid back on my stain-free panties underneath the towel and carefully put on the rest of my attire. I had to use one of Jyme's ponytail holders to pull my hair up. Wearing it down was no longer an option.

I stepped out of the bedroom, and there was not a soul in the mobile home. I pulled my phone out, and I had a message from Chelle. We went to get something to eat in the market. Jyme came out of the bedroom, pulling me against him. He wore a black t-shirt and denim jeans.

"Did you mean it?" he asked. I could taunt and play around with him, but I could tell this was not the time or place. There was something there in his eyes that warned me not to.

"Yes."

Just then, someone burst through the door; one of the guys dressed identically to everyone else entered. "Man that was the easiest three hundred bucks I've ever made," he explained.

One of the two guys behind him said, "You ain't seen nothing yet." They all froze when they saw Jyme and me standing in the kitchen. They started backing up and apologizing saying, "Sorry Lil Samson."

"You cool," he answered.

Two of the guys looked everywhere but at us, they sat down on the couch connected to the wall. The first guy that burst through the door just starred at us. He finally shifted and turned when one of the guys behind him cleared his throat. He walked over towards the fridge and pulled out a soda. There was an awkward silence in the mobile home. I gave Jyme a kiss and told him I was going to go find the girls.

"Let me get some shoes." He left me standing in the kitchen with the two guys watching a documentary. They both looked bored and out of place. I stepped out the mobile home and shut the door.

As soon as I turned the corner to the side of the tent, Jyme called out to me. I spun around and ran smack into him.

"Why did you leave?"

"I just stepped out to get some air."

"You okay?"

"Yeah, I'm fine" I answered. I pulled out my phone and texted Chelle. She told me they were on their way back. After a few silent and very awkward minutes between Jyme and I, staring at everything but each other, I saw Chelle and Ayashe walking back up to us. I started walking towards them, and Jyme pulled me back.

"What is it?" he asked.

"Nothing," I lied.

"Did I do something?"

"No, nothing," I said.

Chelle and Ayashe walked up. "Chelle, this is Jyme: Jyme, this is my bestie, Chelle." They shook hands and then we all stood there in silence. "Well, we better go," I said. Chelle and Ayashe looked weirdly at me, and then they turned away from Jyme and me. "Call me later?"

Jyme shook his head slowly, and I started to walk away from him. I made it maybe two steps, and he stepped in front of me, making me stop in my tracks. The tears were just surfacing, and he knew it.

"What the fuck did I do?" he pleaded.

"Nothing," I rolled my eyes.

"You didn't mean it."

"I'll talk to you later, okay?" I asked. He nodded a slow nod, and I speed walked to catch up with Chelle and Ayashe. No one said a word until we got to the car.

"Cricket, I've never seen you this emotional over a guy. What the hell happened?" Chelle asked.

"I don't know why I'm so emotional about him. He is just so different from anybody I've ever met. The way he makes me feel it scares me so much. I like him too much." I cried.

"What's wrong with that?" Chelle said.

"He just, he's just…" I choked.

"Obsessive and over the top, and you're in love with him." Ayashe said.

I watched her in the rearview mirror, and she was staring out the window.

"What?" Chelle asked.

"She thinks they're moving way too fast," Ayashe said in a dry tone.

"Cricket, do you love him? Wait. Tell me exactly what happened in there," Chelle asked.

I filled her in.

"And then," Chelle asked.

I filled her in some more.

"And then," Chelle asked again.

G STREET CHRONICLES
A LITERARY POWERHOUSE
WWW.GSTREETCHRONICLES.COM

CHAPTER 5

Girlfriend

We made it back to the condo, and I hopped into the shower. I tried to wash away all the pain I was feeling. Everything was happening too fast, and I couldn't breathe. Jyme didn't understand that I had recently broken a one-year engagement. I was nowhere ready for another one. Beyoncé was singing from my cell, and that just made me cry harder. I stayed in the shower until the water turned cold. I stepped out and wrapped my robe around me. I pulled my phone off the counter and opened the bathroom door. Someone had his or her finger pressed down on the doorbell. I went to door and looked out the peephole, and there he stood. I opened the door wide, so he could enter. He walked in, not saying a word to me. He went and sat on my bed with his head in his hands. I shut my eyes and shook my head. *Unfuckingbelievable,* I was going to kill Chelle.

I sat right beside him on the bed. We sat there in silence for a while, and then he finally looked over at me. His eyes were swollen and red; that image right there made my heart melt. I've never had man shed tears over me before.

"I'm sorry" he squinted.

I could tell this man had been hurt to the core and he needed this in his life right now. And I could give this to him; I mean, it's just a little title how much harm could that do? "I'm your girlfriend" I assured him.

He pulled me onto his lap. And we sat there forehead to forehead for a moment. My stomach growled so fucking loud that I couldn't do anything but cover my face.

"WOW," he laughed.

I was so embarrassed, and I had nowhere to hide.

"Let's get something in that belly."

I wore my new dolman wedge sweater and I pulled on a pair of skinny jeans. I slid into some nude platforms and placed two pearl studs in my ear. I wore my rhinestone banana clip again, with a huge rose ring. Jyme wore a rust color sweater with denim jeans. He had light brown boots and a light brown jacket to match his ensemble. Chelle text me and said everyone was downstairs parked on the street. Jyme and I went down to meet up with everyone. We all ended up pilling into the Expedition and still had room to spare. Chelle, Kanoke, Ayashe, Sheen, and Poke all sat in the back. We went to a Moroccan restaurant called Marrakesh. Jyme said he had already ordered our meal. We were getting something called the Mechoui plus water and wine to drink. We had to sit on the floor, and it was the coolest thing ever.

Once our food arrived, the half-naked belly dancers appeared. They wore jeweled bras with bright wrapped skirts. None of them wore shoes and they all seemed to be enjoying themselves. There was so much food on the table, and we laughed for the rest of the night. Every time we emptied a bottle of wine, another would appear. Chelle stood up with the belly dancers, and they taught her how to belly dance but with all the alcohol in her system, it didn't look too good. Jyme took care of the bill and we made him let us take care of the tip.

We loaded back up into the Expedition and Jyme made us all buckle in. I thought for a second; everyone else had wine or beer, but Jyme drank nothing but water and tea.

He leaned over and whispered in my ear, "Can I stay with you tonight?"

"Yes, boyfriend!" I yelled a little too loudly.

Jyme dropped the boys off at the hotel and Chelle and Ayashe got out with them.

"HEY! Where are you Tricks going?" I yelled out the window.

"We're staying here, Ho!"

"Bye then." I yelled back.

Jyme buckled my seatbelt back up, and I leaned back and sung with the radio. When we pulled in front of the building, Jyme's Beyoncé song was playing. I turned it up and shouted with the radio. Jyme opened the truck door and helped me down. I slid down into him and sang all the way to front the doors. I had just made it to the chorus when we got to the front desk. Jyme handed Randy his keys and mumbled something to him. I was still singing and had just started to seduce Jyme at the counter. I slid my body up and down against his very slowly. I felt his bulge growing and I cupped him. He smiled wide then he caught my hand and laughed a nervous laugh at me.

"Stop it Cricket," he strained. Randy shuffled through his papers nervously. I started kissing Jyme on the side of his neck and I tried to unbutton his pants. He stopped me abruptly clearing his throat loudly. He waited for Randy to find the form he needed to fill out so the valet would park his truck in the garage. Jyme turned to look at me face to face; he placed both of his hands on my forearms.

"Stop," he said.

I gave him the military salute and started singing "Sergeant Pepper." I went back over to the door attendant, and he gripped the door so I couldn't get out.

"Dance wee me," I slurred.

He laughed and said, "Anytime, Ms. Hooper." He held his hand out for me and hummed a tune I had never heard before. We waltzed and waltzed, and then Jyme came over and cut in. The door attendant kissed my hand, and I tried to curtsey but almost lost my balance. Jyme straightened me, and then I air-kissed the door attendant and Randy. They both caught my kisses, and I leaned against Jyme. The elevator dinged, and we walked in.

As soon as the doors shut, I slammed Jyme against the wall. "Kiss me," I hissed like a snake. Jyme tried to push the tenth floor button, but I insisted on him kissing me first. The elevator went down all by its self; I had to grip Jyme for balance. Someone got on from the basement, but I was too busy trying to undress Jyme's clothes to care. Jyme was actually letting me semi undress him. He was not stopping me like before. He whispered in my ear, "Not tonight."

I pulled back from him. "Why not!"

He grinned and placed his pointer finger over his mouth.

"It's not too big; it'll fit; we can try," I begged. He just stood there shaking his head. "It's the BIGGEST I've ever seen in my WHOLE life but…pleasssssse," I hissed out. The elevator dinged, and I turned around and straightened myself. There was a man standing there in the elevator with his back towards us. The doors opened, and D'Artagnan turned to face us. He nodded and stepped out of the elevator.

My face fell. I was so ashamed of my behavior. Jyme walked up to the front and pressed the tenth floor, and I started crying. "Shh, Jyme said and pulled me into him. "What's wrong?" The elevator door opened, and we walked out. I was sobbing and shaking uncontrollably. I stayed in Jyme's arms until we got into the condo. I sobbed into his chest once we were behind closed doors.

"Cricket?" We walked to the bedroom, and he sat me down on the bed. He went into the bathroom and turned the faucet on. He came back with a wet towel and a glass of water. I drank the water, and he laid the cool towel on the back of my neck. The towel felt so good, and I calmed down. He handed me two tissues, and I blew my nose. Then, he handed me two more. He shrugged out of his jacket, slid out of both shoes and pulled his sweater off. He kneeled down and pulled both of my platforms from my feet. He shut off the light and slid into the bed pulling me into him. I felt safe and warm in his arms, and I was just about to drift off.

"You love me, don't you?" I asked. There was nothing but silence in the dark, and then I heard a faint, "Yes, I do."

I woke the next morning to Jyme nuzzling into my neck. I snuggled up to him. And then I smelled my body wash. I sniffed hard at him, and then I opened my eyes. "You showered."

"Yes, I did."

Something came to mind just then, something in what he just said. It felt like a déjà vu moment, but I couldn't quite put my finger on it. The buzzer rang from the speaker in the wall in the living room. I got up and walked to the front room. I pressed the button and spoke into the speaker. "Yes," I called out.

"Ms. Hooper, you have two guests at the front desk," the box stated.

"Yes, please let them up."

"Right away." the box answered.

I turned, and Jyme stood right there. He gave me a big grin and pulled me up into a hug. I pulled back from him.

"Okay…can you let them in? I need a shower."

Jyme unlocked the door and followed behind me. He closed the French doors behind us. I turned to look at him, and then I heard the front door open. Chelle and Ayashe were talking a mile a minute.

"I'm going to hop in the shower real quick, you guys," I called out to them. I heard a faint, "ok" between their chatter. I turned from Jyme and headed toward the bathroom.

"Cricket?"

"Yeah?"

"What's your real name?" he asked.

"Eugenia Hooper."

"What's your mother's name?"

"I don't know."

"What's your father's name?"

"Forrest," I answered.

"Do you have any brothers or sisters?"

"No."

"Where were you born?"

"A little town in Tennessee." He watched me and followed me all over the bedroom. I gathered my clothes and underwear together for the day. "I'm going to get in the shower now." I shut the bathroom door and got into the shower.

About a minute later, Jyme knocked at the door.

"Yeah?" I yelled.

"Can I come in?"

"Why?"

"I just want to talk."

"Alright," I sighed. All I wanted was a nice quiet shower and now that was not going to happen. He opened and shut the door. I heard the toilet lid clink.

"What's your favorite color?"

"Anything that sparkles."

"How many times have you been in love?" he asked.

"None." I answered.

There was nothing but silence for a long moment. "Why?"

"I don't let people in."

"Why?"

"Because people can't hurt you if you don't let them in."

"I stared at you all-night, and I wondered what you were dreaming about. I was in a long relationship with Elle, but this seems like the first time somehow."

I turned the water off and cracked the shower door. I pulled my robe down and wrapped it around me. I stepped out of the shower, and it all hit me like a ton of bricks. I looked at him and remembered everything. "You love me," I stated. I watched him very carefully.

He stood and then he walked right in front of me.

"Yes, I do."

"You can't. I will never love you back. I am broken; I am

seriously beyond repair I swear to you. I'm not making this up, I'm not loveable," I warned.

He stood there, not saying a word. He walked right up on me and pulled our bodies together. "I don't want to wake up without you next to me anymore."

"Jyme, I'm not capable of love. I'm not even a hundred percent sure that I love me."

"I can help you make your heart strong enough to love both of us."

"GOD, you're not listening to me. You're going to literally hate me," I told him.

"I'll carry the weight for the both of us for now, but I'm going to need your help later on down the road." he smiled.

"You're impossible." I laid my head on his chest and held him tight.

"Will you go to the reservation with me today?"

"Why?" I asked.

"Because you're my girlfriend and my mom wants to get to know you."

"Um, alright" I breathed. "I need to drop Ayashe and Chelle off first."

"Okay, I'll drive."

Jyme had to stop by the apartment and change clothes on the way. Chelle decided to get the scoop while Jyme was inside.

"So GIRLFRIEND, dish…and I mean now," she demanded. I filled them in, and they accused me of lying when I told them nothing happened. Chelle explained that their sole purpose of staying at the hotel with the guys was to insure I got some. Ayashe begged to differ; she explained that she really wanted to spend some time with Sheen. I asked Ayashe what the story was with them, and she explained that she was still legally married, but that her husband pretty much abandoned her and her kids. She said the reservation frowns upon outside relationships, no matter what. She said she wanted to be with Sheen, but the reservation would never approve.

"Once you're in, you're in for life with them," Ayashe breathed.

"So how much money do you think Kanoke has?" Chelle asked.

"You like Kanoke? YOU SLUT!!!!!!!!!" I screamed. We all burst out laughing, and Jyme got back in the truck with a huge grin.

"I could hear you guys laughing all the way in the apartment."

"So Jyme, what do you think Kanoke's net worth is?" I asked.

Jyme gave me a strange look, and we lost it again. Ayashe had to let down the window because she laughed so hard that she started choking. We were giggle boxes all the way to Olympia.

My phone beeped and I checked the text message. It was from Ayashe, and I started to turn around and ask her what she was doing, but something in my gut told me to leave my mouth shut. The screen read, "You need to eat before you get there, and Elle will be there today. Prepare yourself for the worst; this isn't a friendly visit."

"OK, THX."

"Is everything okay?" Jyme asked.

"Yeah."

We dropped the girls off, and I jumped out the truck, hugging them both extra tight. It was so much easier getting in and out of the truck in flats. Jyme had insisted that I dress down a little. So I wore a gray t-shirt with a sequin pocket, skinny jeans, and a pair of grey sequin Toms. "Can we grab something to eat on the way?" I asked.

"No. We can sit down and enjoy a meal somewhere."

"Alright," I smiled.

"How about brunch?" he asked.

"Sure."

"I know a place."

We pulled into a restaurant called O'Blarney's, an Irish pub. We had a fabulous brunch and were both stuffed. We went a different way than the way I went before to get to reservation. We drove up through the mountains, and everything looked so fresh. We pulled up in front of Jyme's house, and I saw the big boulder sitting at the dead end street. I stared at it for a moment; that day seemed so long ago, and it had only been two weeks. I jumped out the truck and followed behind him.

He held the door open for me, and I entered the little house. I walked into a living area; there was a brown couch and two matching chairs. A flat screen TV hung on the wall, and a couple of dozen picture frames covered the walls. I laid my jacket down and went straight to the pictures. There was so many of Lil Samson and his baby sister. I saw the pictures of him through the years, and then, there she was.

Elle was everywhere in this house and that made me swallow hard. She looked very plain, and I wondered if he liked that in a girl. From the looks of it, we were total opposites. We both were brown skinned, but she was skinny and wore light blues and beiges. I didn't see any pictures of her with her hair down. She seemed to wear it up constantly.

Jyme yawned wide and wrapped his arms around me. He nuzzled into my neck, and I leaned back to kiss him.

"Why don't you take a nap?" I asked.

"Come lay down with me?"

"No, I think I need to get this over with."

"Get what over with?"

"The screening and the test from your mother and sister," I explained.

"They're not like that," he assured me.

"Have you ever dated someone that didn't belong to this reservation?"

"You already know the answer to that."

"Trust me. They are trying to feel me out."

'Women," he yawned.

"Don't try to figure us out; it will make your head hurt." I told him.

We walked out the door, took five steps and walked into another house. Mrs. JJ, Patty, an elderly lady in a wheel chair, and two older women sat at the small kitchen table. They all greeted us both and sat me down at the small table. Patty squeezed my hand, and I squeezed hers back. We all wore our pleasant faces in front of Jyme.

Jyme explained he was going to go take a nap before we had to go back this afternoon.

"Oh, new love, I remember those late nights," Mrs. JJ giggled.

I felt my neck getting hot, and Jyme shook his head at his mother. He kissed my forehead and went out the door. As soon as the door closed, all of the smiles were gone. Well, all except for Patty's; I had a strong feeling hers was genuine.

Mrs. JJ was pulling dishes in and out of the oven.

"Mrs. JJ, can I help you with anything?" I asked.

"No, I want you just to sit your plump ass right there so I can keep an eye on you," she hissed.

I sucked in a deep breath and then released it. I sat there and didn't say another word until they asked. And believe you me, they asked. They asked me my age, my weight, how many sex partners I'd had, where I was from, why I moved to PNW, what I wanted with Jyme, if he'd given me money, if he paid me for my services, if I had any kids, if I'd ever been married, why I had never been married, if I'd had any abortions, what religion I was, where I worked, where I lived, what I drove, and about the quality of Jyme's and my sex life.

When I told them we really didn't have one yet, they all looked surprised except Mrs. JJ. She gave a wicked grin and turned her back on me. She pulled the last dish out and then told me to go and get Lil Samson. On my way out, I heard her say, "He will be here in five seconds going off on us. You watch and see."

I went back over to the little house and quietly walked down the hallway. I looked in the bedroom directly across from the bathroom, and there he lay. I slid in next to him, and he pulled me close. I let the tears roll down silently; I would never tell Jyme about what just happened. I didn't want to give them the satisfaction.

I let Jyme sleep for another twenty minutes or so. I slid over on top of him and kissed him all over his face and chest. He moaned, and then he yanked me back down on the bed and he was on top of me. He mimicked my actions, and I just lost it. His room was dark, and I felt comfortable with the dim light coming from the other room. I lifted my shirt over my head, and then I unhooked my bra and let it drop to the floor.

"Babe?"

"Yes?" I breathed.

"Wait, let me go lock the front door."

He came back into his room, shut and locked that door as well. He pulled his t-shirt over his head and slid back on top of me. He placed one nibble after other in his mouth. The licking and sucking started getting very sloppy. He was enjoying every single second of this. "Thank you for coming with me," he said through kisses.

"You're welcome."

"Cricket, can I try something?"

"Yes." I tried to prepare my mind and body for the anaconda. He unbuttoned my jeans and then he slid them and my panties down.

"I've wanted to do this for a while. If I'm bad at it, just stop me, okay?"

"Alright." He slid my legs apart and went deep-sea fishing. He got three licks in, and I rose from the bed. "Right there. Oh God, lick right there."

His tongue moved faster than a ceiling fan on high speed. My hands twisted all up in his hair. "Jyme, Oh my God that feels so good. Babe, it's so fucking good."

Jyme went in deeper and deeper with his tongue. "You bout to make me cum," I yelled.

"Cum all on my tongue. I want to taste you."

And with that sentence I lost every single thing I was clinging to. I clutched and jerked as if I was having a seizure. The orgasm wouldn't stop because he was still flicking his tongue inside of me.

"Jym-e—sto---op," I finally croaked out. He stopped and wiped his mouth with his hand and licked his hand.

"That is so fucking hot," I breathed.

"Does that happen like that every time?"

"That has never happened like that."

He leaned up on one elbow and traced both of my breasts with his fingertip.

"Why won't you let me see you?" he asked.

"I really need to rinse off before we go back to your mom's." I bent and picked my bra up and re-hooked it. I pulled my t-shirt back overhead. I held my jeans and panties in my hands as I walked across the hall.

A few minutes later, we walked hand and hand over to his mother's house. There was an addition in the kitchen now. Well, let's just say one and a half additions. Elle sat in the chair that had earlier been occupied me. She was holding a baby who couldn't have been more than five or six months old. The baby was obviously mixed with something other than Native blood. I stared that baby down trying to see an inch of resemblance, and I saw nothing.

Jyme had told me that she had done him wrong, and I was guessing she went out and got pregnant with someone else. Jyme looked at Elle, and then he stared at his mother. No one at the table said a word, and Jyme pulled me into the living room with him. Two men sat on one couch; Big Samson was slumped in a chair. Jyme and I sat on the opposite couch, hand in hand. He wrapped his free arm around me and kissed me on the cheek. We all stared at the flat screen. Jyme leaned his back on the couch, and I melted into his side. We had both dozed off when I felt a hand on my knee, and then I opened my sleepy eyes. Elle stood there with the sleeping baby in her arms.

"I'm sorry I didn't get to introduce myself earlier; I'm Elle," she held her hand out for me to shake it. I faked a big yawn, and I thanked the heavens for Jyme's grip on the other hand. I crossed my leg quickly hitting Jyme's kneecap hard. He jerked up and stared at Elle.

"Get the hell away from her, Elle," he snapped.

"I was only introducing myself. She does have a right to meet the whole family," she grinned.

"You're not part of this damn family."

"Well, you know what I mean," she taunted.

Jyme jumped up from the couch like a rocket. Big Samson stirred and then he had a visual on his son. "Lil Samson when did you get here?" he slurred.

"A while ago," Jyme said. He pulled me to my feet, and I followed him.

"Hey, who's your friend?" We walked through the kitchen, and Jyme yanked the door open.

"Lil Samson, Wait. What did she tell you I said?" Mrs. JJ asked.

"What the hell are you talking about?"

She looked at me, and I stared right back at her.

"What did she do to you?" he said at me. I just looked at him, not saying a word. "And you weren't going to tell me?" he snapped. I tried to pull my arm out of his too tight grip.

"Lil Samson, calm down. You're scaring her," she soothed.

"I don't know why in the hell I thought I could bring someone normal around you nut cases," he yelled.

"Jyme," I said. I tried pulling my wrist from his hand, but it was no use.

"Lil Samson, you're hurting her. Let her go." Mrs. JJ put her arm on his shoulder, and Jyme bucked up at her so hard. I squeezed my eyes shut and started screaming.

The next thing I remember I was sitting up against Jyme's chest on the floor. There was a cold towel around the back of my neck and on my forehead. I looked around, and I didn't recognize anyone. I got up off the floor with Jyme's help; I pushed him off me and ran out the kitchen door. I went back to Jyme's house and went straight for my jacket. I pulled my cell phone out the pocket; I had no signal.

Jyme stepped in the door after me; I turned and wailed into him. "Don't you fucking come near me, and don't you dare touch me," I screamed.

"I won't, Babe. I swear. I'm just gone sit right here. I'm not going to come near you," he pleaded. I paced across the floor back and forth. I scratched my arms like crazy and bit the skin around the acrylics until they bled.

"Babe, how long have you been having panic attacks?" he asked.

"Is that what that was? I've never had one before," I choked out.

"Shit, Cricket, I'm sorry, Babe."

I continued pacing the floor back and forth; my heart was still racing.

"I don't think we need to go back tonight; I'll get you home in time for work in the morning," he said.

"Alright."

"Maybe a hot shower will help you calm down."

"Alright."

"Cricket, I know you don't want me to see you naked. I know that. We can turn off all the lights, but babe, I can't let you go into the shower by yourself as shaky as you are."

I noticed he had moved right next to me, but he still didn't touch me, which I was grateful for.

There was a knock at the door; Jyme went to answer it. It was Mrs. JJ and Patty; I turned my back on all of them and walked to the bathroom. I set the toilet lid down and sat on it. Jyme came in with two fluffy towels and two washcloths. He handed me a hair tie, and then he stepped out the bathroom. "I'll knock before I come back in," he said.

I stepped out of my clothes and folded them across the sink. I stepped into the hot shower with my washcloth. Jyme knocked and opened the bathroom door. He shut the lights off immediately, and it was pitch black in there. He slid in behind me and closed the curtain back. He reached around me and pulled something away from the wall. He squeezed a bottle and then gently pressed the soapy towel against my back. I could smell the Irish Spring shower gel. He washed my back, shoulders, legs, and arms. I turned to face him and he did the same for the front. He washed my neck, breast, stomach and front legs. I grabbed the soap and squeezed some onto my towel. I washed his neck first; then his chest. He bent down to my shoulder and kissed my neck, and then he pulled me up on him and kissed my lips.

"Cricket, I'm sorry. I keep scaring you, and I know you're going to—"

"Shhh." I silenced his cry. I turned him around, so I could wash his back. He pressed my front against his back. He pulled my hand around him to his well-swollen Anaconda.

"I want you, Cricket," he whispered.

My toes started tingling, and the feeling was rising up. "Finish washing yourself off." I washed all of my crooks and crannies. He finished before me, of course.

"Let me go find you a t-shirt." he said.

I stood in the shower washing my crannies again, giving them a good rinsing. He came back and told me he was putting the t-shirt on the sink. I asked if he could throw my undies and jeans in the gentlest cycle he had on the washer. He agreed and switched on the light as he shut the door.

I turned the water off and stepped out the shower. I rubbed myself down with the fluffy towel. There was a bottle of baby oil sitting on the bathroom sink. It was not Aveeno, but it would have to do. I rubbed it all over my body, trying to moisturize my skin. I used the fluffy towel again to wipe the extra baby oil from my hand. I pulled the long t-shirt over my head and opened the bathroom door.

There he sat on his side of the bed. He wore nothing but a pair of boxers and his hair loose. I shut the bathroom light off and walked straight into his now pitch black bedroom. I made it to the bed and slid between his legs. Our fingers intertwined with each other's. He wrapped his arms around me and laid his head on my stomach. He squeezed me tight so I placed both of my hands on the back of his head. I stood there for a minute or two and decided to run my fingers through his hair. As soon as my finger reached his scalp, I heard a soft moan coming from his throat. I kept going, both hands over his scalp giving him a light massage. This started driving him wild, he started tugging and pulling and grabbing at everything. He then yanked me on top of him; I loved this rough side of him. Both of my knees dug into the bed on both sides of him. I reached down and yanked my hand back; his anaconda was hanging out of one of the legs of the boxer. I wondered how he kept that thing from falling out. He has to wear whitey tighties or something close to the skin. That thing seriously needed its own zip code.

I am sure Elle had that little bastard baby with no problems whatsoever. If she had to endure this thing over the years, I'm sure he stretched her coochie all the way out. Why am I thinking about her and him now, *so gross. Okay, focus, Cricket, focus.*

He swears he wouldn't hurt me, and I want to believe him, but I can't. I didn't want to just let anyone in, but I was falling fast for this man. I've seen the one-eyed monster from down below, and he looks like he could do some serious plowing. I didn't want my coochie stretched out from his plow. Plus, I'm damaged goods, and I don't see him opening that closed book anytime soon. My heart started pounding, and I tried to suck in deep long breaths, but it was not working. He sucked in a deep breath, and then he nuzzled his face between my breasts.

"Not tonight," he sighed. My heart dropped. I knew he knew I was terrified of that thing, and now we were not going to do it.

"I'll try," I whispered. He nuzzled some more and then wrapped his arms around me tighter.

"You're not ready for it."

"But I want it," I whined.

"I don't think you do, not yet anyway. But I'm a patient man, and we will get there. You have a lot of walls I need to knock down first."

"But you want to," I explained.

"But I'm enough of a man to know you're not ready," he said sternly.

"But we need to do this to connect," I said. He slid a finger in me and started sucking softly on my neck. He slid that one finger in and out of me repeatedly. He then slid another finger into me, and I squirmed. My fingers dug into his scalp, and I cocked my head back.

"Look at me," he growled.

I dropped my head back down towards him. The light in the room was very faint, but I could make out his head and eyes. I reached down and started massaging anaconda through his boxers. It was rock hard, or maybe this was its soft stage; I didn't have a clue. But an idea hit me, and I knew what we could do. I pulled his fingers out of me, and he sucked both of his fingers like he was drinking a Slurpee.

"That is so hot," I whined.

"You taste so good," he breathed. I shifted myself so I could sit down on the Anaconda. I started grinding him so hard. He gasped, and then he started shifting with me.

"Oh God that feels so good," I breathed. I could feel his monster thriving through juicy lips, but the boxers would hold it captive so that it wouldn't slip in.

"Cricket, SHIT," he shouted. I rode him harder and harder, the friction from his boxers and the hardness from his monster were pushing me over the edge.

We both panted and grinded each other so hard; I felt that lightness inside rising. I dug my fingers into his scalp deeper, and he moaned loudly. His grip around my waist tightened, and my lips reached his ear.

"I'm about to cum," I breathed.

"No, Babe. Wait for me," he strained. I was not going to last too much longer, and I knew what to do to bring him over. I put my lips right up against his ear. "I'm your girlfriend," I whispered.

"Cricket," he growled.

"I'm your girlfriend," I whispered.

I felt the lightness taking over my head and then it worked its way down to Juicy. I pulled him tighter to me and then he came, too. We both sat there in a hot sweat, panting and jerking.

"I love you," he crooned. I giggled into his ear, and then he pulled back and kissed me. "And you're going to fall in love with me."

We both got back into the dark hot shower again. Jyme gave me another T-shirt to sleep in, since my last borrowed one was soaked with sweat. I got my jeans and undies out of the washer. I hung my bra and panties in the laundry room to air dry, and I tossed my jeans into the dryer. We both crawled into the bed underneath the cover.

"Your bed is so soft, and it sucks you in."

"I promise you this is not the bed I had with her."

I didn't say a word and wondered what made him say that.

"Where did you come from that day?" I asked.

"The woods."

He knew exactly what day I was talking about. "What were you doing?"

"My grandmother had just done a sort of reading on me that day. And I took a walk into the words to clear my head."

"What did she read from you?"

"She said good fortune and good luck was coming soon. Usually when my Grandmother does a reading, it happens real fast," he explained.

"How did you end up on the boulder?"

"I always sit there. I just stepped out the trees and sat down like I always do." We sat in silence for a moment, and he pulled me tighter. "When I called the ranger station back, Charlotte told me your name was Cricket." He took deep breaths. He was struggling with something, but I didn't know what exactly. "My people believe in the nature of things, something so small to the human eye means so much to us. As you can see we live a little differently here, and materialistic things are not important. We believe that good fortune and good luck are symbols, and one of those major symbols is crickets."

"We didn't meet by accident, did we?" I asked in a whisper.

Jyme kissed my forehead and squeezed me tighter. "I don't think so."

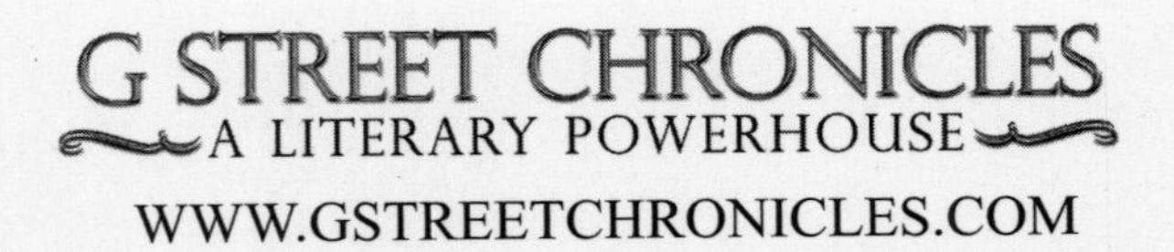
G STREET CHRONICLES
A LITERARY POWERHOUSE
WWW.GSTREETCHRONICLES.COM

CHAPTER 6

We were meant to be

Jyme woke me early the next morning with kisses. He said he had to go and run a few errands before we left. It was five a.m.; I cursed the morning light. He slid out the bed, and I saw the anaconda had gotten bigger, full length in fact. He had major morning wood, and he paid it no attention. He didn't even seem to notice that I was shattering into pieces from the sight of the beast. He kissed me again before he left, and then I heard the truck starting in the driveway. He pulled out and headed down the hill.

I got up to use the restroom; I rinsed my mouth out with mouthwash on the counter. Since I was all alone, I decided to be nosey. There were two other doors shut down the empty hall. I cracked open the first one I came to, and it looked like a workshop. There were wicker baskets everywhere, and all of the utensils to make them. Rolls of fabric lined up against the walls, and there were workbenches and lamps all over the place. I shut that door and moved further down the hall. I cracked open the last door and was hit in the face with a strong smell of cinnamon. This room obviously belonged to a grandmother. There was a floral comforter with matching pillows, drapes, lamps, and even a robe. There was a dresser full of perfumes on top with no labels on them. A walker and two walking canes sat next to the bed. This bedroom's bathroom door was open, and I could see the floral influence had seeped in there, too. I pulled the door back shut and went to retrieve my clothes.

I had just won the fight with my jeans over my hips when I heard a knock at the door and sat up. I tried to breath, but the jeans were still fighting me. I unbuttoned them and prayed that the zipper would be strong enough for the both of us. I opened the front door, and there stood Jyme's mother. Mrs. JJ was holding some dish of some sort. I held the door open for her, and she walked straight to the kitchen. I sat down on one of chairs in the living room and waited. She sat down in the matching chair across from me.

"So you're answering the door like you're the woman of house," she laughed. I didn't say a word to her; I just stared. I sat both of my feet flat on the floor.

"Well, you two are obviously not having sex because you're still walking," she said.

I still said nothing to her. I crossed my arms praying for Jyme to hurry up.

"You should see his father's; no, you should have seen his GRANDFATHER'S," she yelled with a loud laugh.

Something inside me shook, and I closed my eyes and turned my head away from her.

"All I can advise is, get an aloe vera plant and coat after every time."

I stayed silent; I refused to have a sex convo with this woman.

"But poor Elle she suffered the most, she's just so small framed. Nothing we did helped her. Nothing. But you're a *bigger* girl, so you may do fine."

We both sat there in silence, and then she took in a deep breath.

"You know he's already in love with you if you haven't figured that out already," she told me.

"He's been in love before," I said.

"SHE SPEAKS!"

"I'm no different than any other girl."

"Oh, but see, that's where you're wrong. You're independent, you're plump, you're smart, you're gorgeous, you're an Alpha, but you're also broken, and you will never truly love him."

I heard a car door shut outside and pushed out a deep breath of relief. He walked in, and his eyes went straight to mine and then to his mother's.

"If you said something to piss her off I swear, I'll cut you off," he yelled.

I stood, walked over to him, and wrapped my arms around him. "She didn't say anything."

"I don't believe you," he said.

"Nothing happened, Lil Samson," she lied.

"I need to get you out of here and away from them," he said.

"You need to call Loon; he's been looking for you," she said.

"Shut up!" He yelled back at her. I touched the side of his face and our eyes met for a moment. He kissed me on my forehead and then he pulled me with him. He started towards the hall where the phone was.

"Jyme," I whispered. He turned around to face me. He stood there waiting for me to speak.

"I'm okay in there with her; go take care of your business. I mean she hasn't killed me yet." I said to him jokingly.

He gave me a small smile then he nodded at me and I turned and went back into the front room with her. He went into the hall and used the phone mounted up against it.

Mrs. JJ went into the kitchen and came back with a pile of something on a saucer with a biscuit.

I looked at the saucer and shook my head. "I don't want it." After I spoke, I realized I was being rude and was acting like a little kid.

"It's just a sausage casserole," she snapped.

"I'm not hungry," I said.

"Well, at least eat the biscuit."

"I'm not hungry."

"It's just a damn biscuit," she growled.

Now I knew where Jyme got his growling technique. I pulled the biscuit off the saucer, and she grinned at me. This biscuit was not going anywhere near my mouth.

He walked back into the kitchen, and she handed Jyme the saucer with another biscuit on top of it. He held the phone in one hand and started eating.

Well, I guess she had been feeding him all his life, and she probably wouldn't kill him. But I didn't think that rule applied for me. Jyme ate that stuff on that saucer, all the while still on the hallway phone.

Mrs. JJ stepped into the grandma's bedroom and shut the door behind her. I went to the restroom, crumbled that biscuit into a thousand pieces and flushed it down the toilet. I washed my hands once, then twice, then three times.

Jyme hung up the hallway phone and told me he was ready to go. Then, he said he'd be right back; he needed to go next door and tell his grandmother goodbye. I went into his bedroom to get my jacket and now-dead cell phone. Mrs. JJ stood in the hallway staring at me. I knew she was looking at me, but I paid her no mind.

"You said he's been in love before and that you were no different than any other girl. He has never missed a day of work for anyone. Loon thought something had happened to him and that he was dead somewhere. That is how I know he is in love, and that is why you are different. He never loved Elle like that; she was just his entertainment. And you're his life and soul."

Jyme opened the front door, and Mrs. JJ walked towards the front room. We left right after that, and Mrs. JJ's words made my blood turn cold. I looked over at Jyme in the driver's seat, and he smiled. I wondered who would break who first, would I him or would he me. This strong, sexy, trustworthy man was going to make a permanent dent or be a beautiful addition to my heart.

I made it to my first assignment in plenty of time. I really needed to focus on my tasks for the day and push Jyme way to back burner. I had been over absorbed with him, and it was starting to show. I looked drained and my eyes didn't have their normally sparkle like usual. I felt sluggish and I longed to hear his voice and feel his touch. I missed his arms around me and I wanted to taste him on my tongue. I had to snap out of it and get a better grip on my grounds. If this is how addicts feel, I know why they relapse.

I walked into the shop and was greeted immediately by a cheerful face. I ordered a latte and blueberry scone; she offered to up sell me, and I took the bait. The shop was not that busy, but the drive thru was booming. It was so warm and clean, maybe the cleanest I had seen.

I decided to pull my laptop out and sit for a spell. Beyoncé sung from my phone, and I grinned from ear to ear.

"Hi there," I chimed.

"Hi there."

"What are you doing?"

"Stuff."

"What kind of stuff?"

"Stuff I need to do."

"You're impossible," I laughed.

"Can you do lunch?"

"Why do you keep feeding me? I need to lose some weight so I can get out of these double-digit jeans. That will never happen if I keep hanging out with you." I joked.

"Why would you want to lose weight, and I wear double digit jeans."

"Guys jeans don't count; your double digit jeans are really a single digit, according to the women's law."

"Whatever. Are we doing lunch?" he asked.

"Sure," I sighed. I laughed into the phone and grinned at his voice. "So what extravagant restaurant shall we visit today? *And will we be close to the water?*"

"What was that?"

"That was my British accent; it comes out sometimes. And I-AM-NOT-ASHAMED-TO-ADMIT-IT."

"You're weird," he said with a laugh.

"And you're sexy." We both sat there in silence.

"I love you," he said.

I sat there frozen. What was I to say if I didn't feel the same?

"Cricket?"

"I'm sorry. I need to go. Text me the address for lunch." I disconnected the line before he could respond.

The cheerful face appeared in front of me. "Excuse me, we just got these samples in, and I see you enjoyed your scone."

I looked down and realized someone had stolen my scone right off the table. Then, I wiped my mouth and realized I was the thief.

"Would you like to try one of our new cheesecake treats?" she asked.

I nodded.

And she placed one on a napkin in front of me. "Now if you like them, you will have to come here to get some more. We're the only store in the *WORLD* that's serving these. We're kind of like the companies guinea pigs."

"Thank You" I said. She walked away and asked the table next to me if they were interested.

My phone beeped, and I checked the text message. Jyme had texted me the address and nothing else.

I texted him back. "See you at 12:30."

He never responded.

At 12:30, I walked into The Purple Café and Wine Bar, and the hostess approached me. I told her I was meeting someone, and she guided me through the restaurant. I saw Jyme and pointed towards him. She grinned at me with a thumbs up. "Good choice."

He stood and held my chair out. He wore a cream, long-sleeve Henley unbuttoned, denim jeans, and brown boots with a brown jacket hanging over his chair. Jyme was a very well-dressed man, and he had the body to wear damn near anything. He gave me a quick peck on my lips and sat back down. He just sat there and stared at me, not saying a word.

I picked up the menu and tried to use it as a wall against him. I chuckled and coughed, trying to hold back my grin. I ordered the Champagne Battered Alaskan Halibut; Jyme ordered the Seared Hanger Steak.

We sat quietly staring at each other. "You don't drink at all," I asked.

He shook his head no and looked down at his Coke. "Do you cook?" he asked.

"I can, but it's safer to eat out," I laughed. "Tell me about her."

He looked over at me and then looked back down at the table. "Why?"

"Never mind," I sighed. I looked at the tables on both sides of us; the people there looked happy and full of conversation.

Jyme sucked in a deep breath and then blew it out. "I've had over a year preparing for you; I'm not about to mess that up now. What do you want to know?"

"How were you two together?" I asked.

"Nothing like how we are. She is what someone would call a plain Jane. She didn't like to go anywhere, she didn't like to do anything, and she would get pissed every time I left. Sometimes my job would have me traveling all over the state and into Oregon. I would ask her to go with me, but she didn't want to. Then, she would want me to stay at home with her, but I've a family to support. You have seen my dad; he is not capable of doing anything. I started my own fishing company when I was twelve. I've known Elle since I was born," he explained.

Our food arrived, and he paused for second before cutting his steak. "At the very end of our relationship, she started going to visit her sick grandmother up at this reservation a few miles up from ours. There is a store closer to her grandmother's reservation that she used to go to a lot. She met this guy there one day, and all of sudden she was pregnant."

"How did you know it was not yours?" I asked.

He looked up at me and moved in closer. I leaned in, too. "We hadn't had sex for months; every time we did she would be out of commission for a week," he whispered.

I closed my eyes and sucked in a deep breath. "You telling me that does not help our situation, you do know that right?"

Jyme dropped his fork and knife on his plate, and they made a loud clinking sound. A few people at the nearby tables stopped to watch us for a second. He sat back and started pinching the flesh between his eyes.

"She was not a good match for me," he hissed.

"She was not a good match for what? Sex or just for breeding purposes?" I laughed.

"It's not *just* the breeding," he whispered.

I dropped my fork on my plate. Those same few people watched us extra close now.

"What do you mean it is not *just* the breeding?" I asked.

"Cricket, we believe in large families," he said.

"Oh, my God."

I reached for my bag on the floor and dug through it.

"Cricket, CRICKET! Don't leave from this table."

I found my wallet and pulled out two twenties. I laid them on the table, pushed my chair out, and took my jacket from the back of my chair.

Jyme stood quickly and dug into his wallet. He snatched my two twenties off the table, and I turned away from him. I had just made it to the entrance door before I felt the grip on my arm. I froze in the doorway. A man trying to enter the restaurant held the door open for me.

"If you don't let my arm go, so help me God, I'm going to start screaming," I threatened. The man holding the door stared more closely when he heard me and then saw Jyme on my heels.

I walked as fast as my Stilettos would allow me to. I pulled the car keys out the jacket pocket and unlocked the door before I got to the car. I wanted to get in and slam Jyme out. I was maybe four steps from the car when Jyme stepped out in front of me with his palms face up. "Cricket, listen to me. I'm not letting you leave until you hear me out. You are blowing this all out of fucking proportion. You think I am just going to let you up and leave over something so stupid. It's really not what you think!" he shouted at me.

"Move," I yelled at him.

"Cricket!" he yelled again.

"Move out of my WAY," I yelled back.

Jyme moved from in front of me. I yanked the car door open and slammed it. I tried to start the car, but my hands shook so badly that I dropped the keys. I threw my head over the steering wheel and bawled like a newborn baby. I had never been this emotional in my life and over a guy nonetheless. I was not sure what this man had done to me, but I didn't like feeling like this. I had control of my life not anyone else, but I just could not seem to get a handle on it. I had my very first full-blown panic attack less than twenty-four hours ago, and now I was working on my second.

"Cricket, open the door," he soothed.

I really started crying hysterically then. He opened the car door and leaned in. I tried to push him away from me, but the air started getting thick and air was no longer entering my body. "I can't breathe," I wheezed. I heaved and heaved, and nothing was happening. I could hear people asking if I was okay, and then a man asked Jyme if he knew me. Jyme answered that I was his girlfriend and that I was having a panic attack. A woman asked if she should call an ambulance. Jyme yanked me out the car and I tried to fight him off me.

"CRICKET, STOP FIGHTING ME!" he yelled. He held both side of my face, so we could make eye contact. "I'M GOING TO BREATH AIR INTO YOU AND YOU PUSH IT BACK OUT TO ME. UNDERSTAND?" he yelled.

Jyme then put his mouth on mine and pushed hot air into my

mouth. "Give it back," he mumbled. I did, and we did this over and over. I finally felt like I was breathing on my own. I heard a woman say, "Here is a cold cloth, sir, and some water." Jyme put the cold cloth on the back of my neck and opened the water.

"Cricket, drink some water."

I sipped and then sipped some more. I looked down at the glass bottle and thought, *Who in the hell gives away Voss water. What kind of swanky place was this?*

The crowd had died down some and a man who said he was a physician asked if he could check my pulse. I sat back down into the rental, and he checked me over. "What's your name, love?" he asked in a thick accent.

"Cricket," I whispered.

"Cricket how long have you been having panic attacks?"

"I had my very first one last night,"

"What happened during the attack?" he asked.

"I blacked out."

"She passed out," Jyme corrected.

"Did something or someone upset you, last evening?"

We both looked over at Jyme, and he stiffened.

"What about today? Did something or someone upset you again?" he asked.

I didn't dare to look over at Jyme this time. I just nodded my head, too afraid to hear my own voice now.

Someone handed the good doctor a black bag, and he opened it, pulling out a stethoscope. "Your blood pressure is high, and your pulse is still racing," he said. "Who's your family physician?"

"I don't have one yet" I said.

"Yet?" He placed both of his hands on the both sides of my neck. He pressed down hard with both of his hands; he did this a couple of times.

"I just moved to Washington State two weeks ago." I told him nervously.

"Oh, from where?" he asked.

"Tennessee."

"You don't have an accent," he said.

"How would you know?"

The doctor laughed and then handed me a business card. "I believe you will live, but you need to see *someone* about those attacks."

"Are you taking on new clients?"

"No, but I'm willing to make an exception. Call the number on the card and tell Judy I told you to call."

"Thank you." I smiled at him.

"No problem, love." He closed his black bag and walked away. I watched him until he got into a Mercedes SUV. I turned and pulled my legs back into the rental.

Jyme squatted at the door and leaned his forehead on my thigh. It took all I had not to dig my fingers into his ponytail. "I've got to go," I said.

"Don't leave me."

"I've got to go back to work."

"You know what I mean."

"I have to go."

"Can I see you tonight?" he asked.

"Not tonight."

"Why not?"

"I just need some space."

"Cricket, don't do this. I don't think like that anymore, I've told you. I rarely ever go back to the reservation. Babe, please?" he begged.

"I'll call you tomorrow sometime," I said.

"Cricket, I have to see you tonight. I've got to touch you and feel you tonight," he begged.

Jyme leaned into the car and pressed his lips against mine. He kissed me twice and got no response from me. "Cricket, kiss me." He kissed me again and still no response. He kissed the side of my neck, and then he went to my ear. "Cricket, I need you, I want you, and I have to have you."

I shifted and parted my lips. Jyme took full advantage of this moment. His lips found mine in seconds, and he forced his tongue into my mouth. I kissed him back fiercely, and then he started cupping my breasts. I woke from his hypnotism, realizing where we were. I pushed him off me, and he started back at my ear.

"I love you. I love you, Cricket, and I only want you and nobody else. Tell me you don't want me right now. Tell me," he demanded.

"No," I whined.

"I'll see you tonight, okay?"

"I hate you," I cried out.

"No, you don't. You love it when I do this," he teased.

"No, I don't." Hot tears ran down my face now, and Jyme was getting deeper and deeper in the car with me. Thank God, the parking lot was almost empty, and I didn't see a soul walking around.

Jyme stuck his tongue in my ear, and it broke me. I hadn't a thing else to hold on to; I was a complete goner. I prayed I didn't have an earwax buildup in my ear, but if I did Jyme didn't care. I cursed my ears for being so damn sensitive. That tongue of his was my kryptonite, and I wanted to rip it from his throat.

"Tell me you love it," he hissed. Once again, his tongue was back in my ear. "Tell me," he growled.

I started getting a little light headed; I took a serious double take at the parking lot now, and those same three cars were still there. I didn't see anyone else but us. I unbuttoned my trousers, and he slid his hand in my panties. I threw my right leg over onto the passenger side. "Don't stop until I fucking cum," I breathed.

Jyme slid two fingers in me moving in and out repeatedly. "Three," I breathed.

He slid another one in, and I could barely stand it. I watched the parking lot tracing back and forth, back and forth. Jyme was back at my ear, and I was about to fucking scream.

"Tell me," he hissed.

"Jyme, I'm about cum," I told him.

"You better tell me what I want to hear, or I'm going to stop," he teased.

"No," I whined.

"Tell me!" He stopped abruptly and pulled his fingers out of me.

"JYME!"

He put all three, super wet fingers into his mouth and sucked them.

I was about to combust all over the place. "Put em back," I growled at him. He slid them back in; going faster than before.

He was back at my ear. "Tell me right fucking now!" I was now at the top of the roller coaster. "I love you," I breathed. Then, the roller coaster collapsed.

"I told you, we were meant to be," he said.

*****

At my last assignment for the day, I made my order at the drive thru. There was no possible way I could walk straight, and I was so terrified the ocean would emerge once I stood upright. I ordered a Naked Juice and parfait. My hands shook so badly when I handed the drive-thru attendant my credit card. He probably thought I was some druggy or something. I had very visible raccoon eyes, smeared lipstick, and just looked disheveled. I needed a hot shower and my bed.

When I pulled into the garage at the condo, I barely waived at the attendant. I got out of the rental and popped the trunk. I pulled my knee-length trench on and sprinted towards the elevator. I was the only occupant; thank God. I pressed the tenth floor button four times. The elevator doors finally shut. I relaxed against the wall, and then the elevator stopped on the first fucking floor. "SHIT."

The doors opened, and D'Artagnan stepped in; this was so not my fucking day.

"Cricket, hello" he gleamed.

I gave him a small smile, trying not to make too much eye contact.

"Cricket, are you alright?" he asked.

"Yes, I just got caught in a little rain," I giggled.

"Where? It has been sunny all day, not a cloud in the sky. Out of all the days for the PNW not to have rain, this was it."

"Oh, no, it rained."

We got to the eighth floor, and D'Artagnan got off. "Let's do lunch tomorrow and compare notes," he smiled.

"Alrighty," I smiled back at him. I felt so nasty and dirty, I needed a shower badly.

As soon as I walked through the door, I pressed the call button. Randy answered the call, and I went straight into him full blast, as I started peeling my clothes off me piece by piece. "Randy?"

"Yes, Cricket."

"Mr. Samson is probably going to show up asking for me or asking to come up."

"But Cricket," he rushed.

"LISTEN TO ME," I yelled. "He is not allowed to call me or to come up here. Is that understood?" I hissed. I stood there buck naked glaring at the box.

"But, Ms. Cricket…"

"RANDY, DID I MAKE MYSELF CLEAR?" I yelled in to the box.

"Yes, crystal clear. Ms. Hooper, do I need to call the police?"

"No. No, I just don't want to see him right now, that's all," I explained.

"Ms. Hooper, he's already in your apartment," Randy said. I looked up at the kitchen, and there was food on the table. I turned, and there stood Jyme, seeing me in nothing but my birthday suit.

CHAPTER 7

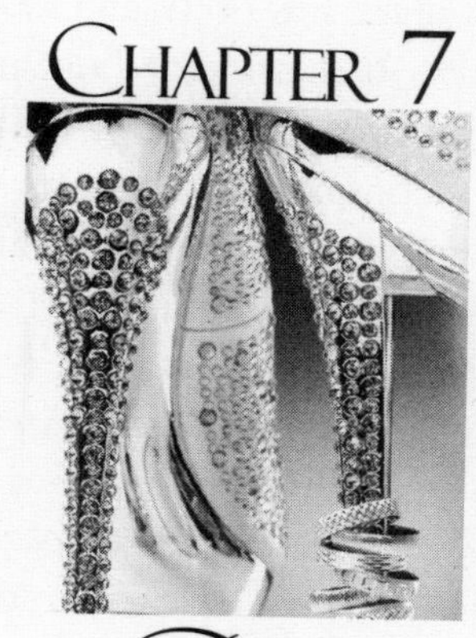

Ducati

"Ms. Hooper?" Randy called. I stood there looking at Jyme looking at me looking at him.

"Cricket?" Randy called.

"Randy, everything's okay. Thank you." I pressed the speaker box, and then I cringed inward. He didn't even have the audacity to turn away from me. I just slid down to the floor, pulled my knees up to my chest, and wrapped my arms around my legs hiding my face.

I heard his footsteps leave the room and then come right back. He wrapped his arms around me and pulled me up from the floor. I wrapped my arms around his neck and squeezed tight. Jyme carried me through the condo and stood me upright in front of the bathtub. He was just as naked as I was. He pushed the shower curtain around to the other side of the French tub. Jyme tested the water with his hands and then pulled the band out of his hair and twisted it into mine. He held his hand out for support, and I stepped into the tub. The water was a little too hot, but that was just fine for me. He kneeled down to the floor and rested his knees on a fluffy towel. I pulled my knees up to my chest and wrapped my arms around my legs. He dunked my luffa and squeezed the hot water on my back. He repeated this over a dozen times. I leaned back in the tub intertwining our fingers. He pulled one leg up at a time scrubbing them all the way down and repeated the action on my feet, arms, shoulders, back stomach, butt and even Ms. Juicy.

Jyme scrubbed every inch of my body. He pulled my bathrobe off the back of the door and held it out for me. I sat down on the bed, and he lathered me down with my Aveeno. He pulled his boxers back on, and we went to the kitchen.

At the table, he held my chair, and I sat down. He pulled two plates out from the warmer. He had reordered the same exact meals we had for lunch. I didn't even really get to taste mine earlier. Jyme got in the shower after our delicious meal. We still hadn't said a word to each other. I slid on a nightgown and then crawled into bed. I was almost asleep when Jyme slid in behind me; he pulled me up against him. He kissed my neck, and then I drifted off.

Sometime later, I woke and looked at the clock; I had another hour to sleep. I turned and slid on top of Jyme, waking him with neck and face kisses. He held both of his hands on my shoulders, paralyzing me for a moment.

"You hurt me bad last night," he stated.

"I know," I whispered.

"Don't do it again; I won't stay next time."

"I know," I breathed. He released my shoulders and I slid off him.

"Come back." He reached for me.

"No," I whispered. I slid down to the foot of the bed.

"What are you doing?" he asked.

"I'm making it up to you," I whispered. Then, I licked the tip of his anaconda and took as much as I could into my mouth.

"Cricket," he called through his moans and stretches. "Cricket," he called again.

"What, Babe?" I answered through sucks.

"Never mind."

"Never what Babe?"

Then, I stopped, and it hit me. "You've never been sucked off before?" I asked.

He shook his head from side to side, and I knew I had to put on a performance of a lifetime. I sucked him so hard that I could taste the blood from my wounded mouth. Jyme writhed and writhed and writhed some more. He yelled my name over a dozen times and beat the hell out of my mattress. He finally climaxed, and I couldn't swallow all of it. Jyme's climatic seizures looked violent.

Afterwards, I lay beside him, tracing his stomach ripples softly. He grabbed my hand and kissed my fingers. "I love you," he jerked.

I lay there. This was that moment that would make or break him. "I love you, too," I said.

*****

I arrived at my first assignment with a good fifteen minutes to spare. I called the office, and O answered. I asked her for the name of the best florist in town. She swore by Toppers European Floral. I ordered an arrangement called the Modina with a bottle of Veuve Clicquot Brut for Randy at the front desk. I also got the door attendant three months of free dance lessons for two at the Century Ballroom Dine and Dance. On Randy's card, it read, "I'm sorry for everything," and inside the door attendant's free passes, I wrote, "Until we dance again." O handled everything for me, and she sent a messenger to deliver the passes. I called Toppers European Floral again and ordered the most peculiar arrangement they could think of and had it delivered to O.

Beyoncé sang out to me, and I answered.

"I miss you," he said.

"I miss you too," I grinned.

"Lunch?"

"I can't, I have to meet with my boss today," I explained.

"The drunk?"

"I'm not sure he's a drunk. I think he just had way too much to drink that night."

"Where is he taking you?"

"Hold on just a sec. He sent me an email. Some restaurant called Slicks," I explained.

"Babe, that place is inside a mall."

"It is?"

"What does he think? You're some slut from the streets or something?" he accused.

"JYME?" I snapped.

"You deserve WAY better than that shit."

"Well, he picked the place; he must like it."

"Don't eat shit there; we'll go to a quick good lunch after that."

"Jyme."

"Cricket, I'm serious," he said sternly.

"Alright."

"I love you," he said.

"I love you too."

I walked into the shop and ordered a latte and a breakfast sandwich. The shop was busy, and no one greeted me when I walked in. The floors needed a good mopping, and the condiments needed refilling. The counters and a few of the tables were dirty.

I sat down in one of the accent chairs. I opened my laptop and noticed several of the customers had wandering eyes. I didn't want anyone to see the company's logo pop up on my screen. I decided to do some catching up on my personal life. I pulled up my personal Yahoo page to check some emails. I hadn't checked my Facebook or personal emails in almost three weeks, and I had three hundred new emails in my inbox. I spammed all the junk mail and then filtered the rest.

"Excuse Me," a voice said. I looked up and saw a very attractive African American man.

"Yes?"

"Is this your paper?"

I looked down and saw a newspaper on the floor.

"No." I picked the paper up and handed it to him.

"You don't want to read it?"

"No, it's all yours," I answered, looking back at my screen.

"Do you come here often?" he asked.

"Oh my God, that's your line?" I laughed.

"It needs work, doesn't it?" he chuckled.

"Um. Yeah." I laughed.

"Okay, how about this one? Hi. My name is Garrett."

"Hi Garrett. I'm Cricket,"

"I just opened an all organic restaurant," he beamed.

"Well, congratulations."

"See? I'm in the paper," There was a picture of Garrett standing in front of a waterfront restaurant. "Maybe you and some of girlfriends can come in sometime; beautiful women would bring more people in."

"Garrett, that was ten times worse than the first one."

"I'm sorry. I'm no good at this."

"I would actually have to bring my boyfriend," I explained.

"Damn, I knew you were too good to be true."

A motorcycle crew pulled into the parking lot, at least eight of them. Their bikes were loud, and they were showing off. Everyone in the shop looked towards the window trying to detect the source of the loud noise.

I looked at the clock and realized I was running about fifteen minutes behind. I closed my laptop and collected my things.

"Hey, they're all Ducati's," a man in line said to his friend.

"It's probably a gang," another man in line said.

"A gang of Ducatis? You're an idiot," another man said.

"Wait, don't go," Garrett said.

"I'm sorry. I'm running late. Have a good day." I walked past the bikes and headed for the rental. I placed my laptop bag on the hood of the car so I could fetch for my keys in my purse.

"Cricket?"

I turned around, and Garrett was jogging towards me. "I forgot to tell you the name of my restaurant," he shouted over the bikes.

"Oh," I shouted back. I pulled the keys out of my purse.

The bikes were loud now; they were seriously trying to get some attention. Garrett looked over at the bike crew and threw his hand up to his ears. Two of the guys on the bikes gave him the finger, and then they really started revving their bikes up. *This may be some sort of gang like the man said.*

"Here's one of my restaurants cards," Garrett shouted.

"Alright," I shouted back.

"Bring that card in, and your first meal is on the house."

"Thanks."

Garrett said something, but I couldn't hear him because of the bikes.

"What?" I shouted.

Garrett moved in closer and leaned into me. "I said, don't lose the card or the number," he shouted in my ear.

I laughed and nodded okay at him. When I looked up three of the bike guys were standing right in front of us. One of them stood closer to Garrett and I, and the other two flanked his sides. One of them was holding a chain. I screamed and threw my purse on the ground towards them. I backed up away from Garrett and the bike gang. The shop manager came out, and so did a few of the patrons. What the hell did this gang want? It was broad daylight for Christ's sake. The chainless man on the leaders' right tugged at his arm and the other bikers left fast. The man with the chain jogged back over to his bike and jumped on it. He revved and revved again. The leader bent over and picked up my purse off the ground. He held it out to me, but I cringed away. Garrett reached for the bag, and the leader of the bike gang swung back as if he was going to hit Garrett. Garrett screamed and drew back.

I moved to the back of the rental then. The leader shrugged my purse at me again. I walked over towards him and took it. I heard the police sirens, and all of the bikers jumped on their bikes and flew out of the parking lot. The police took statements from Garrett.

"Ma'am, how many bikers would you say were here?" Officer Carter asked.

"I think it was like eight or nine."

"Ma'am, what race were the bikers?" she asked.

"I couldn't tell. They were covered from head to toe in those race car jump suits.

"What about their hands?"

"They all had on gloves. None of their skin was exposed."

"Ma'am, about how tall would you say the man that gave you your purse back was?"

"Umm, six two; six three."

"Well, you're one of the lucky ones. Thank you for your cooperation. If you think of anything else, here's my card, and please don't hesitate to call."

I turned from the *almost* crime scene and got into my rental. I now had thirty minutes to meet up with D'Artagnan. I punched in the location, and my GPS came to life. My phone beeped and chirped, but I didn't have time to check it. Beyoncé sung to me and I pushed the radio screen to answer the Bluetooth.

"Babe, can I call you back? I'm running super late."

"Are you alright?" he asked.

"Yes, I just had a hell of a morning."

"Tell me what happened." Jyme made me go all the way back to when I got to the shop. He asked who I talked to and what we said. He mentioned I may have been a target of some sort, and then he demanded to know everything about Garrett. I told him everything I knew, and he repeated everything back to me. I told him everything the police said, and then I pulled up at the mall.

I disconnected with Jyme and rushed in. D'Artagnan was sitting at a table already; I sat down and had to explain the whole entire situation again. D'Artagnan required that I contact him or O after every assignment from now on. He rubbed my shaky hands with his with genuine concern.

We compared notes, and he gave me all of the shop managers'

excuses. I ordered a salad and picked at it. Jyme was not joking; this place was disgusting. D'Artagnan walked me out to my car, and I saw three motorcycles sitting in some spaces in the mall parking lot.

"D'Artagnan, do you know anything about motorcycles?" I asked.

"I own a Yamaha."

"What does Ducatta mean?"

"Ducati," he corrected.

"Oh."

"It's a type of bike; they are very expensive."

"Well, one of the guys in the shop said that all of the guys were driving Ducatis," I explained.

"Well, if they all had Ducatis, I bet you they are a part of some kind of organized crime. A gang of bike riders who all have a Ducati? That's unheard of."

D'Artagnan opened my car door and placed both of his hands on my shoulders. "You be careful out there, and call me any time... day or night."

"Thank you." I patted his arm.

As I pulled out of the parking lot, I noticed that one of the bikes in the parking lot was orange just like back at the coffee shop. I drove back through the parking lot again and pulled out a pen and piece of paper. I drove by the bikes slowly, writing down all of the tag numbers. Beyoncé sang to me, and I silenced her; I didn't feel like talking to Jyme right now. I had to make up two more shops this afternoon.

I pulled out of the mall parking lot and headed to the next assignment. Jyme called three more times, and I silenced the Beyoncé song every single time. I had two more assignments, I needed to cover them both and handle my paper work before I could end my day.

I pulled into my next assignment and took out my phone to text Jyme.

"I am seriously backed up at work. I cannot talk right now, and

I will be late this evening. I will call you when I get to the condo." Then, I put my phone on vibrate.

I checked out the clean parking lot, and then I walked into the shop and went straight to the ladies' restroom. I did this same routine for the next three shops. I tried to stay at least an hour at each location, and now I was fighting afternoon traffic with two more shops still left to visit.

I was in standstill traffic when I felt my phone vibrate. I pulled it out and I had twenty-seven missed calls. My last six calls were from Chelle, and the eight before that were from Ayashe. I clicked on Chelle's name. And the Bluetooth started dialing.

"Oh God, Cricket! You had us all worried," she yelled.

"What's wrong?" I asked frantically.

"You need to call Jyme as soon as you hang up with me," she said.

"What's going on?"

"Okay, all that motorcycle shit this morning has escalated to an attempted murder charge. Jyme called Sheen, who then called Ayashe, who then called me, and filled me in on what happened," she explained.

"What the hell?"

"I don't know all the details, but you should really talk to him."

"That's why he's stressing out about this."

"He's just trying to make sure you're okay."

I see that now; I should call him back, I feel terrible."

"Well, it's a good thing he is freaking out. That guy that was standing outside with you during the attack--"

"Almost attack," I corrected her.

"WHAT THE FUCK EVER, CRICKET!" she yelled. "Anyway, he got jumped and beat the hell up. Girl, he is in intensive care."

"What?!"

"Girl, it's all over the news, and they are saying this is some kind of organized crime mob shit."

"SHIT," I yelled.

The phone beeped; it was Jyme.

"Chelle, call Ayashe, and let her know I'm alright. This is Jyme calling me now."

"Okay, call me back," she demanded.

I clicked over.

"Hello?" I breathed.

"CRICKET, WHERE THE FUCK ARE YOU?" he yelled.

"On my way to Federal Way."

"COME TO THE CONDO NOW," he growled.

"Jyme, I just got off the phone with Chelle and she told me what—"

He interrupted me. "I CALLED YOU SO MANY FUCKING TIMES, CRICKET. WHERE WERE YOU?" he shouted.

"Please, stop yelling at me," I cried.

"WHERE WERE YOU?"

"Jyme, I was working."

"I'M GOING TO ASK YOU ONE MORE TIME WHERE YOU WERE AND IF YOU TRY TO SUGAR COAT YOU'RE WHEREABOUTS AGAIN, I'M COMING TO FIND YOU!"

"Jyme, I haven't been anywhere, but work; haven't done anything, but work today, I swear," I cried out.

"Then why didn't you answer your phone, Cricket? Are you cheating on me?"

"NO!" I felt another attack coming; I was getting way too upset. "Why would you say that to me?" I asked through sobs.

"You're cheating on me because my dick is too big, and you're scared it will hurt; you're cheating because I live on the reservation and I come from shit."

I felt the full-blown attack coming over me. I pulled the car over and put it in park; the doors unlocked automatically. Jyme was still accusing me of cheating and comparing me to Elle. I was trying to shut him out by covering my ears and rocking violently. Two young girls were beating the windows on both sides of the rental. Jyme screamed my name over a dozen times, and I couldn't speak back.

I heard someone scream off in the distant, "She's having an asthma attack."

I ripped my top three buttons off my shirt, trying everything I could to get some air down my throat.

One of the young girls yanked the driver's side door open. "Miss, the ambulance is on the way. Do you have an asthma pump?" I touched her throat twice and shook my head. Jyme started shouting something to the girl, and I blacked out.

When I woke, my throat was throbbing, I tried to touch it, but my arm wouldn't go that far. I opened my eyes, but they felt so heavy now. I heard a beeping sound and looked above my head. I had two machines on my left and one on the right, all connected to me. I tried to yell, but something covered my mouth, and I felt a tingle in my throat. I let all of the memories come to surface, and I realized something: every single time I've had one of my panic attacks Jyme has been the sole cause of it. If I didn't know any better, I'd have said he was toxic.

I growled out a couple of cries, and the door flew opened. Jyme's was the only face I saw, but I heard other voices in the room. Jyme held my hand and kissed my forehead. The doctor from the restaurant parking lot was there, too. He smiled at me, and I pointed at him.

He held my fingers in his hand and rubbed my neck with his old hands. "Cricket, you're in the hospital, love. You had another attack and lost consciousness," he explained. "Give me a thumbs up if you understand me." He held my hand out, and I gave him a thumb up. "Now we're going to pull that uncomfortable tube from down your throat. I need you to cough as hard as you can when I tell you to, okay?"

I gave the doctor a thumbs up without him even telling me to. He grinned and told me I was a good girl. Two more people entered the room and moved Jyme back away from me. I stretched and reached for his hand; I shook from side to side in protest. His hand reappeared in mine, and I calmed instantly. They shifted around Jyme, and then the good doctor counted to three. He told me to cough now, and I did as he said. They yanked the tube out, and I gasped for air. The air was cold and stung my throat in a good way.

"Cricket, I don't want you to try to speak until tomorrow morning," the good doctor advised. I gave him the thumbs up, and he smiled. Jyme still held one of my hands, and the good doctor had the other one. A woman was unhooking a mouthpiece from around my mouth and neck. Once I was free of the contraption, I smiled. Jyme kissed my cheek and then my forehead. The good doctor told me he would be right back; he was going to see if, and when, I was going to be discharged. I gave him the thumbs up again and he rubbed my hand.

Jyme pulled a chair up to the side of the bed. He had bags under his eyes. He turned the palm of my hand up, and he melted into me. He closed his eyes and rubbed his face into my palm and fingers. He laid his head down on my lap, and I felt the tears rolling down his face. I tried to pull away from him, but he wrapped his arms around me; not letting me budge. He held on to me so tightly, with his heaving, and I heard his whispered cries. I shifted my legs and tried to kick my leg out. He didn't turn to look at me, so I gave up. I wanted him off me; I couldn't trust myself with him anymore. I needed to think this out, but with him wrapped up around me, there was no use in a clear thought. Tears welled up in my eyes just as the good doctor came back in the room. Jyme stood up, walked away from the bed, and still didn't look at me.

As soon as the doctor saw my face, he turned to Jyme. "We talked about this. I told you she needed to stay calm," he scolded.

Jyme turned and our eyes locked; his face was red, and tears streamed down his cheeks. He looked beautiful when he cried; I've always thought men look so sexy when they cry.

I looked around the room, and there were so many arrangements of flowers and balloons. I pointed at the balloons, and the good doctor smiled. "Yes, you are well loved."

I shook my head and tapped on my wrist three times.

"Oh, the time?" The doctor pulled back his coat sleeve; I shook my head at him.

"Twenty-two hours," Jyme said.

The good doctor understood now and nodded. "You will be discharged first thing in the morning, and I want to see you at three o'clock tomorrow afternoon in my office."

I gave him a soldier's salute, and he called me a cheeky girl. The doctor left the room, and Jyme, now dry-eyed, walked back over to the bed. He held my hand and straightened his back like he was about to say something, but there was a knock at the door. Jyme told the visitor to come in, and at first, all I saw was nothing but balloons. Then, she stepped in.

Mrs. JJ held a potted plant, balloons, and a wicker basket. Jyme stood up and helped her with all of her belongings. There were a couch and two chairs across on the farthest wall in the private hospital suite. I lay back and wondered who in the hell I had killed in a previous life. I had been handed a hot bowl of shit these last few days. Now with her here, it looked like a shit buffet.

She kissed Jyme on his cheek and came to the doctor's side of the bed. She bent down and kissed my forehead and then turned away from me. I wiped her kiss right off my forehead like a first or second grader would do. I was pathetic. Jyme watched me with a smirk and started whispering to Mrs. JJ. I wanted to pull the covers over my head until she left. *Why was she even here? This woman couldn't stand me.*

There was a knock at the door. And Jyme called out for them to come in. It was a nurse with a tray of food; she asked me if I wanted the chicken or beef broth. I pointed towards the chicken; she gave me two containers of applesauce and two cartons of apple juice. I sucked half the broth down and drank both cartons of juice.

Jyme and Mrs. JJ were in some kind of major conversation on the couch. They were so close that their foreheads almost touched. They were whispering and they both looked strained. Jyme noticed me watching them; he walked back over to the bed and pulled my hand into his. I tugged away from him, but he held on and sat down next to me on the bed. "Babe, I have to leave for a few hours, and Mom is going to sit with you until I get back," he stated.

I shook my head frantically at him. I was pissed at him right now, but I didn't want to be left with her.

"Listen, if there was anybody else I trusted, they would be here. Chelle and Ayashe are both at work, and Mom is already here."

I looked around the room, then put my pinky and thumb up to my ear. He turned around and unplugged my phone from the socket by the windowsill. He handed it to me. When I touched the screen, the security swipe was gone. I frowned at the phone and looked at Jyme.

"I had to reset the security code on your phone. I needed to get in there. No one knew what had happened to you." I thought about that for a minute, but it didn't seem right. My phone would let anyone answer even with the security code in place. All he had needed to do was to wait for someone to call. No, Jyme wanted inside my phone for some other reason.

I laid the phone down and slid deeper into the bed.

"You need to get some rest," he said. He leaned down to kiss me, and I turned away from him. He rolled his eyes and sucked in a deep breath. "I'll be back in a few hours," he said. I kept my head turned from him as he walked out the room. Then, I closed my eyes, praying for sleep.

I woke up at a knock. Mrs. JJ went to open the door instead of shouting the ok to come in. There was a corner wall between me and the door, blocking my view of the visitor. Mrs. JJ backed up, and O walked in. I grinned and waived frantically at her. I was so happy to see O, and she ran over to me and hugged me.

"How are you?" she asked.

I pointed to my throat and mouthed, "Better."

"Are you in any pain?" she asked.

I mouthed "no" at her and shook my head.

"We miss you so much, and poor D'Artagnan has been going cray cray without you," she said.

I poked out my bottom lip, showing my sympathy for him. Then, there was another knock at the door.

"Oh, let him in. It's our boss," O called out to Mrs. JJ.

D'Artagnan walked in with a weary look and gave me a small smile. He sat in Jyme's chair next to the bed and pulled my hand into his. "Cricket, you looked fine at lunch yesterday. If I had known I could have…I should have…" he broke off.

I shook my head at him. There was no need for D'Artagnan to feel bad. They both filled me in on everything I had missed at work. O showed me the arrangements that were from the office, and then D'Artagnan showed me the flowers Randy and the dancing door attendant, whose name was Robert, sent me.

Just then, Jyme walked back into the room then and glared at D'Artagnan. I could see the tension in Jyme's eyes, and I could tell he was holding back some rage.

O turned to me and said, "Well, we should let you get some rest." I shook my head in protest, and Jyme interrupted by agreeing with O. She gave me another hug, and D'Artagnan squeezed my hand.

D'Artagnan walked straight up to Jyme and said, "I'm sorry. I've seen you a couple of times, but we've never been formally introduced. I'm D'Artagnan Crain. I'm a coworker of Cricket's."

"Yes, we always seem to meet when someone's shitfaced drunk." Jyme chuckled, D'Artagnan shifted, and then he cleared his throat.

My mouth dropped open, and the two men shook hands awkwardly. I couldn't believe Jyme had just said that to him. D'Artagnan bid us all a goodnight and quickly left the room.

Right away, Jyme started whispering to Mrs. JJ again. I just pulled the cover up to my chin and turned on my side. I only had one machine now, and it had a long cord. I heard the door open and shut.

I raised my head to see Jyme sitting in the chair next to the bed again. I turned my head back from him. "We need to talk about yesterday, but I think we should wait till you get your voice back," he stated. I didn't acknowledge his words or his presence. We sat there in silence for a long time. I watched the wall, refusing to turn back towards him.

The door opened again and Mrs. JJ stood there looking at the both of us. She stayed in the hospital room with us that night. She stretched out on the couch, and Jyme slept in the chair beside me. There was a knock at the door the following morning. Officer Carter and her partner walked in with an envelope. She asked Jyme and Mrs. JJ to excuse us. Jyme didn't budge. Mrs. JJ exited the room, and Officer Carter and her partner advised Jyme that either they could speak with me in private there or they could take me down to the station. He sat there for a moment and then he stood and stepped out of the room.

Officer Carter opened the envelope and slid some photos out. "Ms. Hooper, I really hate to do this to you right now, but we need to know all the information while it's still fresh on your mind."

"It's alright. I understand. I don't mind helping anyway I can."

"Ms. Hooper, Garrett Smith's restaurant was burned to the ground last night. We're starting to think the standoff yesterday was related to an upcoming attack on Mr. Smith."

Officer Carter took a deep breath and continued. "In saying that, we need to know if you've ever had a relationship of any kind with Garrett Smith."

"No," I answered.

"Ms. Hooper, if you're afraid that your boyfriend will find out and if you're not in a safe environment, we have people that can help you."

"Wait a minute. What are you implying?" I asked.

Officer Carter pulled the pictures out of the envelope, but she kept two of them in her hands. The pictures she laid out for me to view were photos of Ducati bikes. The pictures were taken at some street bike race. The majority of the photos were at night, but there were a few in the daylight. And in these photos were a burnt orange and a lime green Ducati. I remembered these two bikes because the guy with the chain rode the lime green one and the leader rode the burnt orange one. I didn't recognize any of the men on the bikes in the photos. I couldn't see much of them because of their helmets, but I didn't recognize what I could see of them.

Officer Carter looked over at her partner, and then she set the other two photos down in front me. "Do you recognize any of these guys in these photos?" she asked. I picked up the first photo, and I recognized both of the men. Sitting on the lime green Ducati was Loon and on a yellow and red Ducati was Kanoke. My hand started to shake, and then I looked at the last photo. It was the burnt orange Ducati, and its rider was Jyme.

CHAPTER 8

Bootylilcious

I felt sick and handed the photos back to Officer Carter.

"Ms. Hooper, were you aware that your boyfriend was part of a bike crew called 'The Whistlers?' They are known to be an organized group who has a lot of 'street cred,' so to speak. They race cars, bikes, boats, and ATVs illegally. Their crew's net worth is around five million dollars unofficially. That is not even including the other dozen of businesses they own. Do you know what your boyfriend's net worth is, Ms. Hooper?"

I shook my head, too afraid to speak.

"Ten million; and that's supposed to be from selling fish at a market on the weekends," she said.

"I don't know anything about any of this, I swear to you."

"Well, now you know, so what do you do? Turn a blind eye, or wake up?"

I sat there in shock. I could feel something had been off about him. I'd felt it ever since I met him. I knew he had skeletons in his closet. It always felt like he was trying too hard with me. He had told me repeatedly that he didn't think like the old reservation ways. But that was all a lie; he was still in that mentality. He was living a double life, and I didn't know why he sought me out. Everything we had was now tarnished.

"Look, Ms. Hooper, you seem like a real nice girl; you're still young, you have a good job, and you have excellent credit. Why don't you find another boyfriend and settle down with somewhere?"

I turned my head towards the window and stared at the buildings.

"We don't have enough to get them right now, but we will eventually. And everyone that's part of their crew, whether it's a girlfriend or the girlfriend's friends…they are all going down."

Officer Carter and her partner started walking towards the door.

"Officer Carter," I called out, still focusing on the buildings outside. She turned, and we made eye contact.

"Why do you think the person that did this, did it?"

"I think that person normally gets exactly what he wants, and he's not use to a challenge. I think the girl he has his eye on excites him. I think he got jealous because someone else was trying to holler at his girl."

They both left the room, and about a minute later, Mrs. JJ and Jyme returned. I sent a quick text to Chelle and Ayashe. Mrs. JJ watched me carefully; she was looking for something in my face. But this woman knew nothing about me and my ability to turn everything off. Jyme loaded up the gifts, flower arrangements, and the balloons. He didn't make eye contact with me on purpose. Mrs. JJ watched us both like hawks, but she wouldn't get a show from me. I pressed the nurse's button, and one of the nurse's came in. I asked if she could take all of the candy, flowers arrangements, and balloons to the children's ward.

"Are you sure?"

"Yes, hopefully they get a little joy out of them as well."

"That is such a sweet thing to do." she smiled. I grinned back at her.

Jyme and the nurse loaded the giveaway items onto the cart and the nurse pushed it away.

My phone buzzed; I looked at the screen, and it read, "We're on our way." I sat the phone back down on the bed.

"Mrs. JJ, could you give us a minute?" I asked, not looking at her; I kept my eyes on Jyme. Mrs. JJ looked a Jyme for a long moment, and then I saw her pain for him. Her face was crumbling right before me. She went from concerned to heartbroken. She had a sickly and pained look on her face. He eyes watered and I knew then, she knew what was coming, and she wanted to be strong for him. She walked out the room, shutting the door all the way.

Jyme stood up straight and turned towards me. Still not making eye contact with me. He walked over to the window and stared at the buildings with both his arms crossed.

"Why did you do it?" I asked.

"Cricket, don't do this," he begged.

"Jyme, look at me," I demanded. He turned around to face me and finally looked me in the eye.

"You'd be so much more scared of my truth than a lie," he sighed.

"This is why I don't let people in my heart," I breathed out.

Jyme walked over to me and kneeled down right in front of my face. "You didn't let me anyway near your fucking heart; don't kid yourself. I couldn't hurt your precious heart if I tried."

I turned my head away from him, and he nuzzled his face into the side of my neck. I closed my eyes and let the tears fall.

"Cricket, please don't do this," he begged.

"Stop it," I pushed him away from me.

"Cricket, let me love you," he begged through falling tears now.

"You don't know how to love me," I cried.

"You don't know how to let me love you."

There was a knock at the door, and Jyme turned and yelled, "NOT NOW!" I heard two sets of feet shuffling.

I crossed my arms around my chest and squeezed my eyes shut. "You need to go now," I told him.

"Cricket?" Chelle whispered from outside the door.

"Where am I supposed go without you?" Jyme weakly responded.

"Back to your life."

"I had no life before the 28th of October. You kick started me up."

Then, the 28th made sense now. Those flower arrangements had twenty-eight flowers in them.

"Lil Samson, we should go now," Mrs. JJ said nervously from a distance. Jyme kissed the side of my neck, and then he kissed my wet cheek.

"I'm cutting you off completely and don't try to contact me!" I said sternly.

Jyme grabbed my face in such a quick movement, I gasped. He was grabbing my cheeks so hard that my lips puckered up like a duck.

"Get the fuck off her," Chelle yelled.

I could not turn away from his hold on me. My cheeks started to burn, and Jyme was staring at me with a crazed look.

"Sorry, I don't have a cutoff switch," he growled. Jyme then pressed his lips down to my painful puckered lips and bit down hard.

I thrashed from the pain, and I felt hands tugging in all directions. There were so many voices shouting now, but my eyes focused on the black pair right in front of me. I could taste the blood on my tongue. Jyme sucked on my lips so hard, and then he took a loud swallow. He pushed me back onto the bed, and pushed every single person dangling from his arms, neck, and torso to the floor one by one.

Mrs. JJ followed Jyme right out the door.

Ayashe made it off the floor and to me first. "OH MY GOD!" she screamed.

Chelle jumped up off the floor and yelled, "He fucking bit her. She's bleeding!"

Two nurses started working on me immediately. A doctor in a white coat ran in with a syringe and injected something into my lip. I ended up having to get six stitches, and my lips stayed swollen for over a week.

*****

I cried myself to sleep for weeks, and the pounds started shedding off.

The front desks at the condo and at the office were notified by D'Artagnan not to let any packages, or anyone – who was not authorized on the now very short list – to come through. I am not sure how long the flower deliveries would have lasted if D'Artagnan hadn't stepped in. I was receiving arrangements at the condo and at the office. D'Artagnan insisted on me working only in the office for at least a month. He picked up all of my territories, and I did all of our paperwork.

We were a great team and started to become good friends. We began carpooling, and we would leave the condo every morning by nine and always retuned by a little after five. We ordered take out for dinner Monday thru Friday. D'Artagnan was now the big brother that I never had. Our relationship was professional and platonic. He never once asked me about Jyme, and I appreciated that. I had a new-found respect for my *new* friend, D'Artagnan.

My *old* friends, on the other hand, had been begging me to have a full girl's night out with them. When I told them I was not up for partying, they agreed to have drinks instead and catch up. It had been a few months since that dreadful day in the hospital. I met the girls that Friday night; we all met up at Pink Ultra Lounge. I went right after work and caught a cab downtown. The girls were already sitting at a table, and they both had drinks. They didn't see me walk up; they both turned around scoping out the bar. I sat down and took a swig of the drink in front of Chelle.

"So who are we scoping out?" I asked. They both turned to look at me, and then both of their faces showed horror. Chelle gasped, and Ayashe squeezed her eyes shut.

"What?"

Neither one of them said anything.

"Is something on my face?" I asked, touching my lips and then my jaws and chin. "So, I haven't seen you guys since Thanksgiving. What's been going on?"

They both just sat there staring at me, and then a waitress showed up and took my drink order.

"Uhm, so the kids are dying to have a grown-up dinner party, and they wanted me to invite my friends for dinner; they've been watching the food network and they want to cook," Ayashe said with a fake smile.

I looked over at Chelle; she was looking down at the table.

"Sure, that sounds great, just let me know when." I smiled.

Ayashe looked over at Chelle, and she kept her eyes on the table.

"So, I got a promotion and I'm thinking about putting the kids in private school; I can finally afford it." Ayashe stated.

Ayashe and I both looked over at Chelle, and she was still looking down at the table.

"So, how's everything at work?" Ayashe asked.

"Oh, I've been really busy, we have these two new products coming out for the spring and we—" I was interrupted.

"How much weight have you lost?" Chelle demanded.

Ayashe gawked at Chelle and then widened her eyes and started looking at the table.

Chelle was glaring at me as if she hated me.

"I don't really know," I answered. Now I was the one not making eye contact with her. I looked everywhere in that lounge except at her.

"What size are you now?" she demanded.

"Oh, I'm a 16, "I lied.

"Bull fucking shit!"

"I'm a 14/16."

"14 going on 12 soon," she whispered, shaking her head.

"I'm trying to be healthier," I lied.

"Cricket, you're an 18; you've been an 18 since high school; you're a fucking 18," Chelle said.

I looked down at my martini and cringed.

"Has he tried to contact you?" she asked.

I shook my head and took another swig of my martini.

"So, now the only way we hear from you is if we contact you?" she asked annoyed.

"No, it's not like that."

"You know, Cricket, I've known you since our freshman year in college, and I've seen you through over a dozen breakups and three engagements, and you have NEVER looked like this before. You look like something someone drug from the crypt."

I looked down and reached into my purse. I laid out the money for my drinks and a five-dollar tip. Then, I drank the last of my Martini and slid away from the table.

"Cricket, no, wait," Ayashe said.

I stood up and made eye contact with Chelle.

"No, let her go. This is what she does best: RUN," Chelle snapped.

"Cricket, please we're your friends, but it's so hard to see you like this. Let us in. We can help you," Ayashe pleaded.

"She doesn't know how," Chelle said.

"Honey, you will bounce back, and you'll be fine. We will stand strong with you." Ayashe smiled.

"'We will stand strong?' Is that what you said?" I asked through tears.

"Yes, honey, we will," Ayashe said.

"I can't stand anywhere if I'm barely crawling," I cried out.

I turned and headed towards the door. Outside, the heavens had apparently opened the floodgates. I hailed a cab and slid in out of the rain. As soon as I shut my door, the other back door opened. He slid into the seat right next to me. He gave the cab driver a hundred dollar bill and told him to drive. His mouth was on mine instantly, and I couldn't stop him if I tried. His tongue was so hot, and he was panting as if he had been running. He kissed the side of my neck, and then he went for my ear. "You don't look good, Babe," he whispered.

"I know," I breathed.

"Fix that."

I nodded with my eyes shut.

"Look at me."

I shook my head no at him.

"Why not?"

"I don't want this memory in my head."

"Cricket," he sighed.

I turned from him and curled into a ball facing the car door. He pulled away from me, and as soon as the cab stopped at a light, he got out.

I sobbed into the sleeve of my trench coat. The cab driver never said a word. We rode around for thirty minutes in pure silence. "Miss, you have fifteen dollars left on the hundred," he said.

I gave him my address, and when he pulled up at the condo, I owed him four dollars. I handed him a hundred dollar bill and opened the car door.

"Miss, this really isn't necessary."

"Yes, it is. Thank you."

Robert held the car door open for me and held my hand as I got out. The tears were starting again, and I needed to be in a cold, dark place.

"I got you, Ms. Hooper," Robert said as he pulled the front door open.

He whistled once, and Randy was to his feet running towards the elevator. Robert and I made it over to the elevator just as the elevator doors opened. Randy stepped in and pulled me into him. He pressed the tenth floor, and I began to sob. He walked me to my door and used his master key to unlock it. The door opened before he could turn the knob.

Ayashe and Chelle stood there, looking frantic, I stepped into the condo, and Chelle pulled me over to the sofa.

"Let it out, Cricket. Let it all out," she soothed.

I obeyed every word she said. Two full meltdowns, a box set of

Sex in the City, and six weeks of this passed.

By February I was almost 90% of my old self. I had been hanging out with the girls more and more. The insisted on taking me out, we ended up at a sketchy looking building called Cat's Nip for my birthday. I thought, well, they did ask me what I wanted to do, and I did tell them I didn't care. I guess Chelle took that to mean I wanted to see some stripers.

"Oh God, it looks like Cupid threw up in here," Chelle frowned.

"Who has a birthday on Valentine's Day? That is just so wrong on so many levels," Ayashe stated.

"I know, and I've hated this fucking day every year," I said.

"Well, Happy Birthday to the most bootylilcious size 18 I've ever seen," Chelle crooned. We clinked our glasses and slammed the shot down our throats. All three of us hissed from the strong drink.

"Okay…Okay. No more drinking. We have another destination for the evening." Chelle said.

It was true I was back in my size 18, and I'd never felt better. Some people are meant to be size 4s and 6s, but I am a bonafide bombshell 18 and extremely proud of it!

A man in velvet—and I do mean velvet—red suit got on the stage.

"What is the place?" I whispered into Ayashe's ear.

"Shhhh," she teased. The announcer introduced a band called Sensation, and the crowd went wild. When the lights hit the stage, there were four women dressed up like a bad eighties video, and then they started the concert with Pat Benatar's "Love Is A Battlefield."

My mouth dropped open, and Chelle burst out laughing. "I know how much you love eighties music, so here you go," she beamed. I hugged her around her neck, and then we all started shouting back at the stage.

I looked around, and everyone in the lounge was a woman, seated in a party of three or more. There was not a man in sight; well, except for the half-dressed waiters; they wore bow ties and things.

The band sang everything from Cyndi Lauper to Whitney Houston. It was amazing. An hour had passed when Chelle and Ayashe took me to our next destination. We made it to an underground bar in Tacoma.

Chelle knew I loved good music, and she told me this club was off the radar. She said the stuff was so underground here that the CD's don't arrive until twenty minutes before the set. The bar was called No Judgey, and there was no telling what went down in here.

We went down a flight of stairs and walked for a few steps, and then hit another flight of stairs. I would have taken my heels off and jogged down like everybody else passing us now, but I was sure I would need a tetanus shot if I did. Apparently, this was the spot where Ayashe and Sheen could be incognito. Ayashe knew almost everybody in here, and there was some kind of code. Sheen wasn't from around these parts but he felt safe here with her. They both seemed so at ease in the setting. Chelle said they played nothing but Underground music here.

We finally made it down to the concrete floor and entered a set of double doors. The space was huge and freezing. Good thing I wore my jacket over the little, sparkly, off-the-shoulder shirt I loved so much; well, the one the mud god adored so much. I wore a pair of black skinny jeans, sparkly heels, and silver hoop earrings. My hair was down, and I had on very little makeup.

I started noticing that each song they played in this club had a sort of grind beat to it and everyone was grinding up against each other.

"Do you like it?" Ayashe asked.

"Yes, it kind of reminds me of dirty dancing," I explained.

"But in a good way, right?"

"Yeah," I agreed.

The crowd was wild, and the club had a nice, flowing rhythm to it. I didn't know any of the songs they played, but I desperately wanted the CD. If the songs weren't filled with driving beats, they talked about sex and seducing somebody. On my third warm beer, I was standing up cheering Ayashe and Chelle on the dance floor.

The music was amazing, and we were all having fun. Ayashe was dancing with Sheen, and Chelle was grinding on a local. I shot my eyes over to the side and saw a huge pole entering the dance floor. I was not sure if something was about to pop off or not, but I was ready for whatever.

A guy walked out on the dance floor and pulled Chelle up to him, right at a song change. Chelle's previous partner didn't mind and he found another dance partner right away. She caught the beat to the new song and really laid it to this partner. I caught the side of his face, and it was Kanoke. I felt a ping in the pit of my stomach, and I was just about to turn and go back to my original watch spot when I felt someone press up against my back and then a hand moving my hair to the full shoulder side of my shirt. A pair of warm and familiar lips was at my ear on my shoulder that was now fully exposed. Those arms were wrapping around me like a vice. I breathed in, and I could smell fresh Irish Spring in the air. I felt the tingles rising inside of me. No matter how hard I tried to hate him, and no matter how much I tried to prepare myself for this encounter, it wasn't enough. He was my kryptonite, and our past problems didn't matter to me at all. They all melted away with just one touch.

Jyme sang in my ear, matching the same deep tone the singer was belting out.

"Can you lie next to her and give her your heart, your heart as well as your body. Can you lay next her and confess your love, your love as well as your folly." My skin rose in chill bumps, and my toes were tingling. He swayed me in his arms, and I couldn't think of any other place I would rather be.

Jyme sang, "Tell me now where my fault was in loving you with my whole heart."

I was a little scared of him, but I pushed every fear and every negative emotion down. My body and mind craved for this man, I was so lost in him now; he had completely hypnotized me, and I didn't want to ever wake. He grinded up against me, and I tried to turn around so I could see his face, but he yanked me back in place.

"Don't," he growled in my ear. Just hearing his thick deep voice, made chills run across my neck and back.

I was so caught up in him. I pressed back and bounced my ass slowly up and down on his anaconda. Jyme slid his tongue in my ear, and my insides went crazy. The singer's voice coming out the speakers all of a sudden got angry. The song still kept its slow grinding tempo, but the vocals now sounded like thick molasses and razor blades. The singer was mad and his words cut: "A white blank page and a swelling rage. You didn't think when you sent me to the brink; you desired my attention but denied my affections."

"Cricket, come with me," Jyme demanded. I nodded and gripped his arms around my stomach and torso tighter. He turned us around, still not letting me see him.

"Walk," he growled in my ear, and I started moving straight through the crowd. He guided me by pushing or tugging. Why won't he let me see him? Had he gotten beaten up or maybe he had a fishing accident? Surely, someone would have told me that; I mean if he was now deformed someone would have told Ayashe or Chelle.

My heart pounded as we rushed through the crowd. The song was at its climax, and everyone was rocking to it. A man I hadn't seen before stood at a door. He nodded and let us pass through. We were in a pitch-black room, and I could hear a train in the distance. If Jyme wanted to fuck me right here and now in this dark cramped room, I'd let him.

"We can do it here," I breathed.

"What?" he asked. I stopped, and he pushed me, but I didn't budge.

"Fuck me here," I whined. He pushed me ahead towards a hallway with a dim light. He pressed me up against the wall in the dimly lit hallway. He brushed my hair away from my neck, and then he was at my ear. I tried to reach for his face, but he yanked my hands back down.

"Why can't I see you?" I breathed.

"Wait," he demanded. He slid his hands under my shirt and pulled both of my breasts out of their cups. He kissed down the side of my neck and massaged each nipple repeatedly.

I felt tears coming to the surface. I had longed for his touch; I had ached for him.

"Jyme!" I cried out.

"Shhhh, I'm here," he explained.

"Where have you been?"

"Cricket," he sighed. He buried his face in the side of my neck.

"Jyme, I hate you so much."

"I know you do, Babe," he said, kissing the side of my face.

"You're a bad person, and a liar."

"I'm sorry, Babe."

"Just leave me alone."

"I can't."

"Stay the fuck away from me, Jyme. You disappeared once before; you can do it again."

"I've always been here, I never left, and you know that don't you?" Jyme slid both hands out of my shirt and unbuttoned my pants.

"PLEASE," was all I could call out to him. He unzipped the tight jeans, slid his hand in, and slipped two fingers into Juicy. Juicy was so hungry for this; she made a slurping sound every time his fingers would went in and out. It was as if she was talking to him. I spread my legs wider, and Jyme went in even deeper adding the third finger this time. I was already at the edge; I knew it was not going to take long. I'd gone without any release for so long that I felt like I was about to explode. I was so hot that sweat drenched me. I felt the lightness coming, and my knees started buckling.

"Jyme," I cried out to him.

"I got you," he said. He held a tighter grip around my stomach. Jyme slid his fingers in with two more good thrusts, and I exploded. The tingles crept up my legs and thighs, and then they entered into

Juicy. The lightness was now gone, and Jyme was pulling his fingers out.

"Don't stop!" I choked out.

"Again?"

"Don't stop," I yelled at him, slamming both hands against the wall.

Jyme pushed the three fingers back in, thrusting faster and harder. I felt both knees buckle under me, and then the climatic volcano erupted. I screamed out and then stomped my right foot and then my left. Jyme could barely keep a hold on me. This was the biggest orgasm I had ever encountered. I pulled my legs together tight, trying to calm the orgasm.

"Are you still cumming?"

"OH GOD, JYME. OH GOD!" I yanked my head back and squeezed my eyes shut. The tremors eased up and then settled. Jyme kissed the back of my wet neck.

"Turn around," he whispered in my ear.

I turned around and let the wall hold me up. When I looked up at the man standing before me, I barely recognized him. Jyme had a very low buzz cut, and he looked darker.

"Jyme." I smiled.

He smiled back and pulled my hand up to rub it over his head. I pulled him close and kissed him long and slow. I traced my acrylic nails up and down the back of his head.

"Babe, that feels so fucking good," he said between kisses.

My phone buzzed, and we ignored it. His phone buzzed, and we ignored it too. This reunion was too sweet to be interrupted. My phone buzzed again, and I yanked it out my pocket.

"What?" I snapped into the receiver. Jyme had moved from my lips to both sides of my neck.

"You got a ride, bitch?" Ayashe taunted.

"Am I riding with you?" I whispered in Jyme's ear.

"Mmm hmm," he mumbled.

"Yes," I breathed.

"BYE," Ayashe and Chelle yelled into the phone. I disconnected, sliding the phone back into my pocket.

"You fixed you," he breathed.

"You told me to," I explained.

"You look so good."

"You're not so bad yourself. I love the cut."

"Better than the hair?"

"I loved the hair, too."

"Which one do you love better?"

I pulled back so I could get a better look at him. I rubbed my hand over his scalp again, and he pulled me closer into him. "You."

"Can I have you this weekend?" he asked.

"Yes."

"Can I have all of you this weekend?"

"Yes."

Jyme guided me to a flight of stairs, we went up them and then we were outside in a back parking lot. We went to the spot where his SUV was parked and got in; his truck smelt the same as it always did. We pulled into some place called Suncadia Resort. Jyme and I walked hand in hand. The woman behind the counter nodded twice and smiled at him. Jyme had a look on his face that I didn't recognize. We stepped into the elevators, and he held me tight. At the room, he pulled a key out and slid it into the door.

He opened the door, and there was a warm glow coming from within the room, which was wide and filled with candles. This room was a kitchen and a living room. Jyme pulled my jacket off and then removed his. He wore a black fitted Henley with a white tank underneath. He was so fucking hot.

He guided me to a small circular stairwell, and there was a warm light coming from upstairs as well. At the top of the stairs, we entered a massive bedroom with a deck and a hot tub outside. A privacy fence kept me from seeing anything but the sky through the opening above. Jyme pulled me over to the middle of the room right in front of the bed, then reached over the back of his shoulder and pulled his shirts off with one hand. I felt a ping inside of my stomach. He stared at me, not saying a word and I knew then what he wanted from me. I sucked in a deep breath and blew it out slowly. He still stood there, and the look in eyes let me know he needed this much more than me.

I reached down to the end of my blouse and pulled it over my head. He still stood there, never letting his eyes leave mine. I reached behind my back and unhooked my bra; sliding both arms down and letting my bra fall. Jyme closed his eyes for one brief moment and then stepped into me.

He kissed me so softly; it reminded me of the old saying about butterfly kisses. Jyme unbuttoned his jeans, as did I. We both shrugged out of them and stepped out of our shoes. Jyme pulled his boxer shorts down, and there he was, the beast of many names: boner, cock, dick, ding dong, one-eyed snake, knob, meat, pecker, pee-pee, peter, pole, stick, wanker, woody, and my all-time favorite: anaconda. I knew he could grow bigger than the size I saw before me, and it made my mouth water. I took another deep breath and pulled my lacy numbers down.

Now Juicy was fully exposed. Jyme stood there and looked me over. I wanted to cringe and was just about to cover Juicy with my hands, but Jyme caught me in the act.

"Don't." He pulled me towards him and moved the left side of my hair to the right. "Cricket, you're perfect. Don't hide from me," he whispered in my ear.

"I love you," I breathed.

He smiled and guided me into the bathroom. There was a tub and a separate shower. Jyme walked towards the tub about to fill it, and I couldn't let him do that.

"Shower?"

"Babe, we got all-night," he smiled.

"Shower," I demanded.

He chuckled, went over to the shower, and started the water. We both walked into the dimly lit shower that was big enough for four people. I washed him, and he washed me; we were both sparkling clean when we exited. We towel dried together and reentered the bedroom.

Jyme pulled the bedding down; there were sheets and sheets and more sheets. Jyme stood in front of me and pressed down on my shoulders. I sat at the side of the bed, and he kneeled down. He spread my legs wide open and dug in. That tongue of his was amazing, and he knew just how to get me off. I came once on his tongue, and he was nowhere near a stopping point.

"Jyme, I already came," I panted.

"Not enough."

I fell back onto the bed, and Jyme pushed my legs up and slipped his tongue over my dirt box.

"OH MY GOD!" I screamed.

"Scream as loud as you want. There's no one above, below, or on either side of us."

Jyme licked me from my rooter to my tooter. I came again, and he still was not satisfied. He slid three fingers in me and talked filthy, nasty, dirty shit in my ear. He was driving me fucking crazy; I was climbing and kicking all over the place.

"Four!" I yelled.

Jyme slid the fourth finger in, and it didn't take long for me to cum at all. After the third climatic explosion, Jyme slid on top of me. He was not even sweating, and I was completely gone. I heard the ripping of foil in the distance.

"Look at me" he demanded. I obeyed, and his eyes were so bright. He looked so happy. "Happy Birthday," he whispered.

"Thank you," I whispered back, then Jyme slid inside me, and it hurt so good.

G STREET CHRONICLES
A LITERARY POWERHOUSE
WWW.GSTREETCHRONICLES.COM

Chapter 9

Happy Valen-Birthday

The pain was excruciating, and I had to fight back the tears. Jyme was so gentle and he went so slowly. It felt so good to finally have him inside, and it would have been so perfect if my insides were not screaming.

"Do you want me stop?" he whispered.

"NO!" I shouted.

"Babe, I can tell I'm hurting you."

"I'm okay."

"But I'm hurting you." He pulled out.

"Jyme, don't stop."

"I can't do this to you," he whispered.

"Jyme, we only tried for like five minutes. This will take time, and you said we had all-night." I smiled.

"I love you," he said.

"I love you too." He kissed me on the side of my neck, and I got an idea. "Can we try a couple of other positions? It may help."

"We can do whatever you want."

"Let's try it from the side," I suggested. Jyme rolled to his side, and I slid in front of him. We shifted and twisted and then he slid into me.

"Oh, that's so much better."

"Yeah, it is. Shit it is," he stated. Jyme slid in and out repeatedly, and the pain was almost gone. Jyme still took his time, never rushing inside of me and never going too far in.

"Oh God, Jyme. Right there, right there."

"Cricket, does that feel good? It doesn't hurt?"

"It feels so good, so fucking good!" I yelled.

"Babe?"

"More!" I yelled.

"Are you sure?"

"MORE!" I shouted, tugging at the sheets. Jyme slid some more in me, and I knew we were finally ready. "Get on top," I panted.

Jyme slid out of me and then got on top. He slid his anaconda into Juicy, and they were happy to finally meet. We both came violently, and Jyme had some serious after cum jerking going on. I rubbed my fingers over his scalp and traced the back of his drenched neck. He lay on top of me for a long time, and I thought he was crying, but I would never ask.

Four condoms, eight "I'm cumming's", and twenty-three "I love you's" later, we passed out a little after four a.m.

When I woke, Jyme was sound asleep on his back. I slid out of bed. I tiptoed into the bathroom, dreading the first pee after a night of what John Mayer would call, "Sexual Napalm." The pee was painful, and Juicy was out of commission. She was swollen and throbbing, but she is a strong cookie and held up all night.

I turned on the shower, and Jyme stepped in right behind me, turning it off. "We are taking a bath in that big ass tub together," he said sternly. I grinned and went and stepped into the tub. I turned on the water, and he threw in some bath salts. He laid three towels down and then he stepped in. He sat on the opposite side of the Jacuzzi tub.

"Come here," he demanded. I walked over to him and straddled him. "You like it when I take charge, don't you?" he grinned.

"Sometimes," I answered.

"You like it all the time."

I kissed him and then stood to turn the water off. I went back to straddle him again. But he shifted under me, and I slid down on him this time.

"Oh" I breathed.

"Babe we need a---"

I slid up and down slowly on his anaconda until his head fell back. "Just pull out when you need to."

"Okay."

Then I kicked it up a notch and rode him like a bucking horse. Jyme went ape shit, and we both had chill bumps afterwards. I tied the big fluffy robe around me, since I didn't have anything else to put on. Jyme watched me with a big grin on his face.

"What?" I asked.

"Do you think I'm slow?"

"Slow?"

"Retarded. My elevator doesn't go to the top floor. Stupid?" he chuckled.

"No. Why?"

"Because you're looking around like I haven't been planning this for months. I got you, Babe."

"I'm sorry," I apologized.

Jyme went over to the closet and opened it. He beckoned for me, and I walked to where he was. There were four garment bags hanging in the closet, two bags from my favorite clothing store, and three boxes of shoes.

Jyme pulled out one of the garment bags, and it held men's clothes and shoes. He pulled an outfit out with all the trimmings. He was about to get dressed when I slid into him.

"I want you," I breathed.

"Babe I want you to, but we really need to go," he said.

"Four minutes?"

"Um, I'm going to be longer than four minutes."

"I won't," I said and slid down on my knees and put him in my mouth.

Five minutes later, we were both dressed. As we started for the door, Jyme pulled something out of one of the nightstand drawers, but he didn't let me see what it was. I took my phone out of last night's jacket. I had four missed calls and a dozen text messages.

Jyme reached over me and set two small boxes on the counter. He brushed my hair to one side and wrapped his arms around me.

"Happy Birthday," he whispered in my ear, and I pressed back closer to him. "And Happy Valentine's Day," he said and gave me another kiss.

"I get two presents?" I beamed.

"It's two different occasions, isn't it?"

"Thank you."

"You haven't opened them yet."

"It doesn't matter. Last night and this morning were absolutely perfect."

"Open them," he demanded.

I picked up the box on the left, and Jyme sucked in a breath. I sat that one back down; that one was a deep gift, I could tell by his body language. I opened the one on the right and the sparkles almost blinded me.

"JYME!" I shouted.

"Put it on," he grinned. This box held a very gaudy, diamond cricket ring. The ring was as long as my pinky finger and the cricket had diamond eyes and diamond wings. "Please whatever you do, don't lose that ring."

Just those words alone made me swallow hard. "Is it insured?" I asked.

"YES," he growled.

"I am sorry. I am so sorry. I know you thought all of this out, and everything is covered."

"Thank you."

I slid the ring on. It was heavy as hell, but it looked fabulous on my hand.

"Now the other," Jyme insisted.

I picked up the other box, and Jyme shifted. I opened it slowly, and there was a sterling silver keychain with a four-leaf clover, a horseshoe, a rainbow with a pot of gold, a wishbone, and a star charm hanging from the key ring. Jyme reached around me and slid a key on the key ring. He turned me around, and I kept my eyes on the keychain.

"The charms represent you of course," he said.

Jyme had told me before that his people believe crickets are a symbol of good luck. So I understood the charms, but the key had me stumped.

"The key is for you to come and help me make a home."

I looked up at him, confused, and he gave me a small smile.

"I bought a house," he said.

"Oh," was all I could say.

"What are you thinking?" he asked with a worried face.

"That you're fucking amazing and that I don't know how I'm going to compete with you on your birthday," I rushed out.

"This isn't a competition," he grinned.

"Where is it?"

"Federal Way on Puget Sound Beach."

"Oh, it's a beach house." I smiled from ear to ear.

"Oh yeah, I forgot. You don't like the beach," he teased.

"If it was not for the beach, we would have never met."

"We would have met," he said sternly.

After the beautiful exchange of his two present, we left the room and headed for the elevator. We went down to the lobby and he held my hand. We stepped off the elevators, and he guided me to a side hallway. We walked in a set of double doors, and then they all yelled surprised. Chelle and Ayashe made it to me first. I was so not expecting this.

"You look so hot," Ayashe belted out. Jyme had gotten me four different outfits. One of the four was a Red Margaux dress with tonal red sequins all through the fabric. I wore the pair of black stilettos he got me with silver teardrop earrings, and I finished my outfit off with my brand-new diamond cricket ring. Chelle and Ayashe looked at my cricket ring and gasped. Then, the ring had an audience of its own. People were greeting the ring before they would even say Happy Birthday to me. Jyme was so proud, and everyone gave him the big ups for getting the ultimate gift.

There were about twenty or so people at the party. But I only knew about fourteen of them; the other six were mystery people. All of Jyme's friends and close family members were there. I saw O across the room and that made me smile. I looked for D'Artagnan, but I didn't see him anywhere. Then I thought about it, Jyme probably didn't invite him.

There were two big round tables with gold pillar candles lit in the middle of the table with huge flowers as the centerpieces. It was breathtaking, and Jyme made sure I saw every bit of it. He kept pulling me away from people trying to greet me to show me something. The room and decorations in it had a whimsical feel, almost as peculiar as a scene from Alice in Wonderland; but still very classy. There was a table full of gift bags and gift boxes.

D'Artagnan walked up, and I gave him a wide smile, but it ended fast. He forced a smile and kissed me on my cheek. He walked away, not saying a word. I tried to watch where he went, but the crowd blocked my view.

O approached next, and I pulled her into a quick hug and whispered in her ear. "What's wrong with D'Artagnan?

"He's not happy about the reunion." She pulled back, faking a wide smile for the wondering eyes.

"You look amazing," she chimed. I pulled her in for another hug. "I need to talk to him," I demanded. She nodded and was gone.

The next set of guests was approaching me, so I pulled out my phone to send D'Artagnan a quick text. Then I remembered I didn't have his number in my phone; it was in my Blackberry on the counter at the condo.

"What's wrong?" Chelle asked.

"I need to talk to D'Artagnan." I answered with a frown.

"Why?" Jyme asked from behind me. I froze, and Chelle's eyes got as wide as mine felt.

"You need to open your presents," Chelle said and tugged me away from Jyme as we headed towards the gift table.

I ended up with six IPods, the new Lady GaGa CD, the new Rihanna CD, the new Shakira CD, the new Adam Lambert CD, the new Michael Crichton novel, the *Gone with the Wind; 70th Anniversary Edition* Blu-ray, *The Wizard of Oz: 70th Anniversary Edition* Blu-ray, two Kindles, a bottle of Light Blue by Dolce & Gabbana, a pair of Ugg boots, a digital camera, a new Blu-ray, a one hundred dollar Visa gift card, and a two hundred dollar Visa gift card.

As I finished opening the pile of gifts, a waiter came out with a bell and announced that lunch would now be served. Everyone went to the tables and found their nametags. Jyme and Chelle were next to me. There was an empty seat next to Jyme until Mrs. JJ came in from a hidden sidewall and sat down.

I gripped Chelle's thigh under the table, and she followed my eyes before turning to me and pretending to unsnag something on my shoulder.

"Where did she come from?" Chelle asked.

"I don't know. Did she just get here?"

"No, but I haven't seen her for at least an hour." Chelle pulled back from me, and then we both felt the burning stare from Jyme.

He slid over and leaned into my ear. "What's wrong?" he whispered.

"Nothing."

"Do you not want my mother here?"

I looked at him and saw the hurt in his eyes. "I never said that," I whispered.

His phone buzzed and his attention shifted. I looked at all of the people at my table and I realized I didn't recognize four of them. I wondered who these mystery guests were at my birthday party. Jyme must have really been strict with the dress code for today. The women all wore black cocktail dresses and the men black suits and black ties. Jyme was the only man wearing a red tie. With the way this room was decorated, I wondered what the invitations looked like.

"Did he send out invitations?" I asked Chelle.

"He was not sure how this was going," she thumbed towards Jyme and me. "So he had the invitations made up and asked everyone to RSVP to me and Ayashe just in case it didn't work out."

"Oh," I said.

"And no one could bring a guest. It was single invite only, and he stressed that."

"Why?"

"I don't know. He never said. There's a guy back there at the side entrance for this room that has the list and the names of each guest." She jerked her head behind us.

I looked back there and saw nothing.

"There's a secret wall," she continued.

I nodded, and just then, the servers came out with trays. We first had a bowl of potato soup, then a dinner salad, then our main courses: steak, salmon, or lobster. Sitting in front of me was a lobster tail and a steak.

"Why does everyone have something different?" I whispered to Chelle.

"It was in the invitations."

"Oh, my God."

She nodded. "Oh, how did last night go?" she asked with a serious look now.

I was really shocked that Chelle of all people was okay with Jyme and me getting back together.

"Are you alright with all of this?" I tossed my hand to the side gesturing at the party. She took in a deep breath and then she stared at me.

"He swore to me that he would never hurt you, ever again. And I believe him because he loves you so much and you him."

I beamed at her, and she beamed right back at me. We both

started giggling.

Ayashe leaned over, practically sitting in Chelle's lap. "What are you two bitches over her snickering about?"

Chelle whispered to Ayashe, and her eyes shot up at me. She mouthed, "how was it?"

I gave her a wide smile, and we all started giggling. Jyme's hand suddenly was creeping up my inner thigh, and he was caressing the seat of my panties. I turned to look at him and he kneeled down under the table pretending to pick up his napkin. I opened my legs wide for him and he sneaked around the seat of my panties and slipped one quick finger into Juicy, and then just like that, it was gone. When I looked over, he was sucking on that same finger.

My mouth fell open, and I shifted in my chair. I looked at him, but he wouldn't meet my eyes. He sat there as if nothing had even happened. The sneaky devil. I realized then that he must want some attention, so I decided to give it to him.

"Where's the food from? It's so good." I asked.

He grinned and turned to me. "Palisade."

"You will definitely have to take me there."

"Anytime." He kissed my forehead.

The two main doors opened, and three servers wheeled in a giant form in the shape of a volcano. At the top, there were sparklers. Everyone stood to their feet and sang Happy Birthday to me. Jyme held his hand out and guided me to the volcano. I blew out the sparklers. Everyone clapped and cheered. I noticed the little round cupcake shapes that made the volcano looked familiar. "The CONFESSIONAL" I tugged at Jyme. Jyme had taken me to "The Confessional" on the dessert portion of our first date. It was fabulous, and now there was a mountain of cheesecake.

I hugged Jyme tight and looked up at him.

"Thank you so much this is the best Valen-Birthday ever."

After everyone ate their dessert, people started leaving. I didn't want the party to end, but it was still daylight outside, and it was Valentine's Day. I looked at my phone and it read, 4:00 p.m.

Everyone gave hugs and kisses when they left.

O walked up to me. I looked behind her and still no D'Artagnan. I pulled her into me.

"He left Cricket. He said he couldn't watch this train wreck." She pulled away and mouthed, "I'm sorry."

I gave her a small smile.

"He told me to tell you that he'll see you on Wednesday."

"Why Wednesday?" I asked. She cut her eye over at Jyme. He was watching our every movement. "He said to enjoy your birthday to the fullest," she chimed.

"Okay, I'll see you guys on Wednesday then."

She squeezed my hand, and then she was gone. A couple walked up to me next, and Jyme stepped over to us. He put one arm around my waist and gave them his full attention. He spoke to them in his native language, and I just stood there and smiled. I noticed Mrs. JJ, Loon, Kanoke, Sheen, and Ayashe all staring at us. The man shook my hand; then the woman gave me a hug. They nodded at Jyme and then left. Jyme never introduced them to me. He did this same thing with the next two couples. They walked up; I smiled; and he spoke to them in that language and then they left.

When the strangers were all gone, I looked up at him and frowned. He noticed my face and said, "Later." Then, he was gone. He went to talk to Mrs. JJ, and I wondered if I should leave and go back to the room.

Ayashe and Chelle said they were going out with Sheen and Kanoke to some lounge in the city. I yawned and told them to have a good time for me.

"Oh, you're going to have a blast tonight." Ayashe grinned.

"What?" I asked.

"You'll see."

Then they, too, were gone. I stood there at the entrance while Mrs. JJ and Jyme stood in the corner of the room talking. Neither one of them even noticed that I was the only one left in the room now. I would have gone back to the room, but I didn't have a key. I thought of something and walked out to the front desk.

There was a cute, blonde-haired woman behind it.

"Hello," I said.

"Yes, ma'am, how may I help you?" she asked.

I explained to her that I was the birthday girl, and she knew what party I was with. I told her that I left the key in the room, and she gave me another key then handed me a package. I knew it was Jyme's and not mine, but I took it anyway, planning to put it in the room.

I walked over to the elevators and was just about to get on when someone caught my arm and tugged a little too hard. I pulled back, and one of my slits on arm sleeve ripped all the way down. I looked up, and it was Loon.

"What the hell, Loon?" I snapped.

"Jyme's looking for you," he said, not giving my now ripped dress another glance.

"I'm going upstairs; if he's looking for me, he knows where to find me." Loon pressed a button on his phone and said, "She is at the elevator." Then, he turned back to me. "Don't move."

I stood there waiting, and Jyme came from around the corner. He held his hand out for me, and I stood there looking at it. I was not budging until he started talking. He mumbled something to Loon, who quickly disappeared.

Mrs. JJ came around the corner. She walked up to me squeezed my shoulders a little too tightly and gave me a kiss on my cheek before she walked out the front door. I rolled my eyes long and hard at her.

"This thing with you two has to stop." he scolded me

I stood there as if I was a statue; I was not talking or budging until I got some answers. Jyme ran his hand over his head as if looking for his hair.

"They were some very important people that I was trying to impress."

I stood there and crossed my arms with my eyebrows raised.

He pulled me closer to him and away from the elevator. I only budged a little because he gave me a little info.

"I'm trying to start up some businesses, and I need their support," he said.

I started tapping my foot on the marble floor.

"A casino," he whispered. I frowned at him, and he let his eyes wander around us. "Later, please." He looked down at his watch and said we needed to go. "Are you okay for two more hours in those shoes?"

"I'm a fucking lady; I can wear these shoes until my feet bleed."

"I believe you." He grinned wide, and then guided me out the front door. He helped me into the truck, and then I handed him the box that was at the front desk. "Where did you get this?" he asked in a panic.

"It was at the front desk. I went to get the key, and she told me we had a package." Jyme yanked his phone out, dialed a number, and then pressed it to his ear. He spoke quickly in that native language again. Then he hung the phone up and shut my door. He walked toward the front of the truck and Loon met him. Jyme handed Loon the box, and then Loon went back in the direction he came from.

Jyme got into the truck, and I didn't say a word. He sat there for a moment, and then he started the truck. I pulled the seat belt over me and locked it. Jyme pulled out his phone and made another call. He spoke in his language and glanced over at me.

When he hung up, I stared at him.

"I know I owe you a ton of explanations, but please just give me some time to get everything in order.

I nodded, and then he pulled out of the parking lot. We drove in silence for about two miles. Jyme's mind was working, his eyes were so crazy, and his hands were clenched around the steering wheel.

"I love you," he said.

If I ever had any doubts about whether he really loved me or not. That look in his eyes now confirmed everything.

After a few minutes' drive, we arrived at the port. Jyme led me toward a small speedboat and stepped inside.

"I can't swim," I told him nervously.

"I can."

"See the thing is, I don't like small spaces, and this boat is hella tiny."

"Cricket, get into the boat."

I stepped back from him, clutching my small purse to my chest. "I don't want to."

"Cricket," he soothed.

"I don't want to."

Jyme jumped out of the boat and pulled me to him. I cried into his chest. A couple of footsteps came up to us fast, and I gripped Jyme tighter.

"Lil Samson, is everything alright?" a man asked.

"Yes, it's just my girlfriend doesn't like boats."

The man laughed.

"Well, hell. How does someone live in the Pacific Northwest and not like boats?" another man stated.

I glared around at him, and when he saw my face, he stopped laughing.

"I think you better shut the hell up, Chuck. Oh, pardon my French, ma'am."

"I don't like small boats." I growled.

"Oh," Chuck said.

"Well, take my boat. It's slower than your speed racer, but it will get you where you need to go," the other man said.

"You don't mind?" Jyme asked.

"Shoot," the man laughed. "I think you're good for it." Both men laughed now.

"Listen Miss. Lil Samson's been driving since he was six," the man told me.

"Five," Jyme corrected.

They all looked at me, and I nodded. Jyme kissed my forehead and pulled away from me. He stepped back into the small boat and shut it down. He stepped back on the dock and pulled out his wallet. He handed the man a hundred dollars and then told him he was renting his boat for one hour. Before the man could even protest, Jyme slipped another hundred out and said, "Well, we better make that two hours." I saw the look in Jyme's eyes, and he was thinking nasty thoughts. My toes tingled.

"Your money's no good here," the man protested.

"Take your wife out to an expensive Valentine's Day dinner," Jyme suggested.

"I'm taking her out to Grady's already," the man answered.

"Grady's Fish Shack?" Jyme asked in disgust.

"And you know it," the man said proudly.

"Take her to Palisade for a nice lobster dinner," Jyme demanded, looking down at me and smiling. I smiled right back at him.

"The steak is really good, too," I beamed.

"Well, I won't be able to get reservations for tonight," the man announced.

Jyme pulled out his phone and shoved the money into the man's hand. Jyme spoke into the phone briefly.

"You have reservations for eight thirty," Jyme told him.

"Well, shoot. Thank you, Lil Samson," the man said.

He handed Jyme the keys and made plans for Jyme to return them. The men bid me farewell and were off. Jyme and I stepped into a boat that was obviously used for working, but it was clean and far bigger than Jyme's. I felt much safer in it.

We entered into the dark waters. I stood behind Jyme with my arms wrapped around him. He was operating the boat, and it was the sexiest thing I'd ever seen.

"That song last night," I shouted over the motor.

"What song?" he shouted back.

"At the bar, when you first came to me."

"Yeah, what about it?"

"What's it called?"

"They're an English band."

"What kind of music is it?"

"Folk rock."

"What's the name of the song?"

"White Blank Page."

Jyme parked the boat at a beach. We walked down the dock and up a flight of stairs. He unlocked a side gate, and we got into a golf cart. My heart was racing from the excitement. I had no idea where we were going, and I didn't care. We made it to a residential area, and he turned down a street with a huge gate. He punched a code in, and the gates opened. We rode down the street, and there was nothing but gates, more gates, and more gates.

At a dead end, Jyme pulled in front of the gate and punched another code in. The gates opened. In the driveway, we got out of the golf cart, and Jyme guided me to the door. He unlocked three locks. Inside, the house was pitch black. Jyme reached against the wall and flipped on the light. And what a light it was. I looked up, and there was nothing but ceiling.

Jyme pulled me further into the house. My shoes clacked against the hard wood floors. We walked past a stairwell, and Jyme looked at his phone and grinned wide. He was up to something, but I didn't know what. We walked through a living room with a stone fireplace. We entered a kitchen with a brick oven. The room was wide open, and the back wall was nothing but windows, but I couldn't see a thing because it was so dark. We walked over to a side room with French doors, obviously a dining room. We strolled into another hallway. There was a bathroom, a laundry room, and the door to the two-car garage.

We ended up right back at the entrance, and then we moved on to the second floor. He rushed me through three different bedrooms. I had a feeling there was a main event coming somewhere. He opened the only door we hadn't been into yet. He pulled his phone out and hurried me over to the huge window, not bothering to turn on the lights. I faced the window and he stood behind me; and then the explosions started.

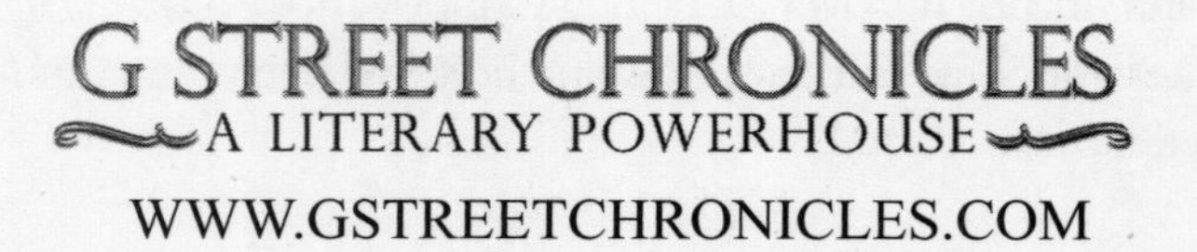
G STREET CHRONICLES
A LITERARY POWERHOUSE
WWW.GSTREETCHRONICLES.COM

CHAPTER 10

The Safe House

The sky filled with a million sparkles, and my eyes widened. A ton of little balls exploded into the sky. I heard whistles and crackling sounds. Jyme brushed my hair to the opposite side of my neck and nuzzled his face in.

"Look." I pointed out the window. "You're going to miss it, and it's amazing."

"I know it is," he answered, staring at me. I turned my face to his, and he kissed me. We watched the fireworks show for another five minutes or so.

Then, he walked from the window and went to turn on the lights. There was a mattress on the floor with full bedding. This was the only room in the house with a piece of furniture in it.

"Have you been staying here?" I asked.

"Yes, but I wouldn't ever ask you to, not like this."

"I've seen worse," I assured him.

He gave me a puzzled look, and I changed the subject. "So how are you going to decorate this room?"

"I don't know. I've never decorated a house before."

I walked into the bathroom, and there was a Jacuzzi tub just like the one in the bathroom this morning. There was a door and I figured it was the bathroom's closet. My attention went back over towards the tub and just the thought of this morning's tub session made my toes tingle.

"Why don't you do it for me?" he asked me. There was something else in his voice.

"I've never decorated a house before either," I advised.

"Please," he asked, pressing up against me.

I leaned back on him.

"You didn't answer my question earlier."

I knew exactly what question he was talking about, but I was in no shape to answer it now.

"How long have you been staying here? I asked, stepping away from him.

He held on to my hand as I walked all over the master bedroom. I opened a door in the bedroom and stepped into a closet heaven. There were shelves, hanging rods and even an island dresser in the middle of the closet. Towards the back of the closet, there was another door. I opened it and walked into the master bathroom. The door I assumed was the bathroom's closet door was not. It was a door that entered into a closet heaven. We stepped out of the bathroom and I saw another door next to the main closet door in the bedroom. We walked over to it and he let my hand go, I opened it and there was only small rods going up and down, from the ceiling to the floor of the small room.

"What is this?"

"You don't know, Ms. Pink Bottoms?" He teased me by calling me my favorite brand of shoes. And I knew then, it was a shoe closet, and my heart jumped. He really bought this house for him and me. I mean the closet alone would make anyone sign on the dotted line. That shoe closet really got me. My mind starting wandering; I could imagine every single rod in that closet full of nothing but pink bottom shoes. I had to wake up from the trance he had forced on me with these amazing closets. I couldn't think clearly, everything was happening too fast. I walked over to the wall where the light was and I shut it off.

"Cricket, wait."

I turned and wrapped my arms around his neck. I kissed him softly and pressed myself against him.

"Last night, this morning, my party and the fireworks, I've never had—I…I've just never had anything like that before," I choked out. "I will never forget this for as long as I live."

"I beg to differ, just wait till next year," he assured.

My mouth fell open and I felt a ping in the pit of my stomach. I couldn't take much more of this; my heart was already on the verge of stopping.

I slid from his arms and turned, heading back down the stairs. He didn't follow me right away. I had made it down to the entrance before he even started coming after me. He shut the last of the lights off and faced me.

"You don't like the house?"

"God, yes," I laughed. "What's not to like? It's perfect."

"Stay here with me then."

"I can't."

"Why not, Babe?"

"We don't know each other well enough for all that yet."

"What are you afraid of?"

"Nothing. I just don't think we're ready to move in together yet."

"Cricket, we've known each other long enough."

"And we've actually only been together maybe four full weeks. We were broken up longer than we were together."

"You know everything about me," he stated.

"No, I don't. That's what happened to us last time. I thought I knew you, but I was wrong, and now with that shit at the party and that fucking box…" I threw my arms up at him.

"You don't tell me anything," he growled.

"Well, my lifestyle won't get you locked up or have the police asking you questions." I took a step towards the door and twisted the knob.

"I want you here with me."

"Alright then, what was in the fucking box?"

He stood there looking torn, and I just stared at him because I didn't have anything else to say.

"It's not important right now?" he exhaled.

"Really?" I yelled.

"You're the only one I want, and I can't be here without you," he said.

"Where in the fuck have you been then?"

"What?"

"You gave up. You were supposed to fight for me. That's what they do in the movies," I told him.

"Cricket, you never responded to anything I did, but I never gave up on us. Ayashe and Chelle said I had to do something big. They said you wouldn't take me back unless I really meant it. And I did! But I had to do something big for you to listen to me. You couldn't hear me or accept me any other way. I knew it had to be something to astound you.

Cricket, when I saw those tears stream down on your face in the cab that night and you told me you didn't want the memories, Babe that broke me. It reduced me to my core. And I knew when I came back, I had to come correct. But I never gave up on us. Never."

He pulled his face down and rested his forehead against mine. "I need to tell you everything, right now."

He locked the top two locks, flicked on the lights, and guided me back to the kitchen. He helped me up on the granite counter where I sat as he paced the floor. He cracked his fingers and dug in.

"I started fishing with my dad and uncles when I was three. My dad was never a good fisherman; he was never good at anything but drinking. My mom worked cleaning houses and babysitting to pay the little bills we had on the reservation. Living on the reservation, a lot of your housing and utilities are covered or they help you with other bills. It is the way of life there; they look out after their own.

Well, with my mom and dad both there, we had our share of

bills we had to pay, but we didn't have a car, and my dad was always drunk. When I was five, I was a better fisherman than most grown men. My uncles used to let Loon, Kanoke, and I drive the boats and fish with them. We would go to the fish markets because we were short and cute, and the women would buy the fish from us just to be nice. I made out good, and we got by in the house.

After a few years of that, I decided I wanted to do my own fishing and work for myself. Loon, Kanoke, and I worked like fucking dogs for a year; scraping any and everything we could find. Patty was three, and my mom was working odd and end jobs to get us by. We had enough to buy a truck, but none of us were old enough to drive. We needed the truck so we could fish in the deep waters for salmon until we could afford to get a boat. My mom helped us buy the truck, and she put it in her name. Kanoke's mom worked at a school cafeteria, so we had a place to store the fish, and now we had a truck.

Our first weekend out at the markets, we made five hundred dollars. And after six months, we bought our first boat. It was not much, but it got us the fish we needed. About a year after that, we had two boats and then the business just skyrocketed. When I was twelve, I had more money in my bank account than any man on the reservation. I've worked hard all my life because I've had to. My dad fucking sucks and he has never really provided anything for us. I was, and have always been, the man in my house.

We started racing boats for fun back when I was fifteen, and then we got serious about it. We knew how to handle them all because we worked on all types of boats. Kanoke liked working on vehicles, and Loon knew boats inside and out. We started racing a lot of stuff: three-wheelers, four wheelers, dirt bikes, and bikes. I had plenty of money, but it was never enough. Something was missing, and I was trying to find out how to fill the void; I still don't know how. I was a man in my mom's eyes when I started paying the house bills. No one could tell me anything, and I would beat the shit out of anyone if they tried.

Then, puberty hit me big time and Elle couldn't hang; that drove me fucking crazy. I couldn't fuck her, and I needed to fuck. Jacking off did it for a while, but then that was not working anymore. I needed more. She tried to oblige me; I'll give her that. And my mom and grandma tried to help her deal with my size because they both knew how it was for them dealing with the men in my family, but Elle has a very small frame, and she couldn't ever handle it no matter how slow or how deep I went.

Her folks wanted her with me so I would take care of them and her. So their affection towards me was bias. My grandmother said my dad and grandfather went through the same thing, but my mom and grandmother went to this reservation back when they were young, and they saw a medicine man that helped them with ways to stretch themselves…down there. But that medicine man has since died; and no one knew his secrets; so we could not get Elle any help.

No matter what we tried, she couldn't handle me, so she went elsewhere. After Elle, girls on the reservation wouldn't come near me because everyone knew I was the boy with the monster dick."

Jyme walked over to me and slid between my legs.

"My grandmother told me the girl I'm supposed to be with would be from far lands and she wouldn't know of our people. She said that my dream woman would have a wide frame and that I would fit her. She said, my woman would stretch well and that we would have three children; two boys and a girl."

"Jyme," I sighed.

"Okay, okay. So my mom came to me back in September and she said she knew of this land that was for sale and that I should buy it up and start up a casino. I have the mind for it, and it would be easy money. Well, ever since then, some of the other reservations found out I had a bid on the land and that I actually have the money to buy it. Let's just say, it's been shit ever since."

I crossed my arms over my chest, not saying a word. He sucked in a deep breath and pulled away from me.

"There have been threats, theft, vandalism, harassment, carjacking, and now two people have come up missing," he explained.

"JYME!" I shouted, jumping down from the counter.

He followed me as I walked towards the foyer and then I started pacing back and forth. He stopped me and held both sides of my face.

"You must tell me now. Are you afraid of me?"

"No." I yelled.

"Are you afraid to be with me?"

"NO," I shouted.

"Why are you mad?"

"BECAUSE YOU DIDN'T FUCKING TELL ME."

"CRICKET, YOU HAVENT BEEN AROUND!"

He had a point, but I didn't want to hear his point right now. I jerked from him and started pacing again.

"Why did you freak out about that box?" I asked.

He walked over to me and I pulled away from him again.

"Come here."

I stepped further away.

"Come here, Cricket!" he demanded. I went to him, and he placed both hands on my shoulders. You must not tell anyone what I just told you, not Chelle and especially not Ayashe. "Okay? Listen to me. You can't ever let anyone know about this place. No one knows I bought this. No one," he said sternly.

"Not even your mother?"

"She doesn't have a clue, and I want to keep it that way."

"Why?" I stared into his eyes.

"This is ours," he assured me.

He pulled me into his arms, and I let myself melt into him.

"Cricket, this is why shit got so crazy with Garrett. We thought he was targeting you for someone else to get back at me. Sheen let things get out of hand and that is what happened."

"Why didn't you tell me all of this months ago? It's been hell living without you, and I thought—" I cut off.

"You thought what, Babe?"

"I thought you were some crazy jealous guy that couldn't control his temper."

"OH, BUT I AM."

I squeezed him tighter.

"But in Garrett's case that was only fifty percent of the problem."

"Oh," I said.

We stood there holding each other. "Jyme, why did you get so mad at me that day?"

"After the shit went down in the parking lot, we had to get out of there. Everyone that I had on backup watch was on a bike, and the bikes weren't good to have anymore that day. I risked a lot going to that mall where you met D'Artagnan, and when you wrote the bike's tag numbers down, I about fucking lost it. I couldn't let you see us, so I couldn't follow you right away. Then, you wouldn't answer your phone. Sheen kept talking shit in my ear about Garrett being a snitch or some kind of spy for some of the other reservations. I just let him handle it. Sheen means well, but he has a hot head and went way too far."

"Wait you said you watched, and then you said you couldn't follow me?"

He took a deep breath and pulled me from him. We made eye contact, and then he started.

"At first, it just started out as me wanting to see you. Then, I did get a little obsessed with it, but then, shit started happening and I couldn't risk you getting caught up in the mix of it."

"But Jyme, I'm right slap in the middle now."

"Not really, no one knows who you are. You're not from here; you drive a rental under your company's name, and you live in corporate housing," he explained.

"Oh." He had a point.

He pulled me back into him again, and I held on.

"But Jyme, all that's going to be changing in the next month. I have to get a car, and I have to find an apartment."

"Hence the house. Follow me."

We walked to one of the closed doors, when Jyme opened this door before he hadn't turned the lights on; all he had said was, "here is the two car garage." Now the door was open and the light was on. I saw the monster tank sitting there.

"What the hell is that?" I frowned.

"Take your shoes off."

"I'm fine."

"No, there's a lot of cracks in there and I don't want you to ruin your shoes."

"Oh," I sighed.

I slipped out of my shoes and he sat next to the stairwell. We stepped down into the garage and walked over to the tank.

"It's a Cadillac Escalade."

"Why is it so fucking big?"

"You need the room."

"Ex-fucking-cuse-me!" I yelled.

"NO. NO. NO. Not that kind of room. I mean so we can ALL go somewhere if we need to."

"Who is all? It's just me and you."

"And Kanoke, Chelle, Ayashe, Sheen, Loon, and his flavor of the month."

He unlocked the car doors, and I stomped away from the beast.

"I think you're obsessed with big things, hence the girl standing in front of you."

Jyme licked his lips and tugged at his anaconda. My toes started tingling at once; I stepped back into the house, trying to hide my face. I put my shoes back on, and he beckoned for me. We made it back to the front door. And he shut off the lights once again. He closed the door and locked the three locks. We got back into the golf cart and headed back to the docks. When we made it back to Jyme's truck, he was all lovely dovey once again. He kissed me about a dozen times, and our fingers had been locked since we got in the truck.

"So, let me get this straight. You're not a part of some organized crime, nor are you the leader of one?"

"No," he laughed.

"So you don't kill people or blow up buildings?"

"No Cricket."

"And you love me, unconditionally?"

"Yes." He offered nothing more than those simple answers; and for my heart, those were enough.

When we made it back to the room, I was exhausted. We ordered a ton of room service and watched T.V. We both realized we loved *The First 48 Hours*, *Crime 360*, and *CSI;* the original version.

I lay in his arms, and I had never have felt safer.

Jyme let me shower alone and I was grateful; I needed to think. I took a super long shower to melt all my worries away. I thought about something Jyme never answered in my questions.

What was in the box?

I had a strong feeling I didn't want to know. I would have to bring it back up to him again, for my own curiosity; but not tonight. Tonight I had too much else to absorb.

I got out of the shower and slid on one of the nightgowns.

Jyme stepped in the room as soon as my nightgown touched the floor.

"OH, SHIT. Babe. Please don't go to bed yet."

I turned and stomped my foot at him. When I did, I noticed the mountains jiggled like Jell-O. I knew why Jyme had picked this gown out. He walked past me buck naked now heading for the bathroom.

"If you fall asleep, I'm fucking waking you up! You can best believe that!"

I wondered if he noticed his own double meaning, and then again I don't think he cared. After our very tiresome session, we laid in the bed wrapped up in each other. Jyme was tracing his fingers up and down my arm in a soothing motion. I was right on the edge of passing out. Jyme sat up and then laid back down.

"Happy Birthday," he whispered.

"My birthday is over."

"You officially have five more minutes."

I smiled and pulled him a little closer.

"Cricket?"

"Yeah?"

"Please?"

I lay there not saying a word while he caressed my arm.

"Have you ever heard that song by Foreigner called, 'I Want to Know What Love Is?"

"I don't think so."

"Mariah Carey did a version of it a few years back."

"I've never heard it."

"Well, the lyrics are, 'I'm going to take a little time to look around me. I've got nowhere left to hide; it looks like love has finally found me. I want to know what love is. I want you to show me. I want to feel what love is. I know you can show me.'

He turned me onto my back and sat up on one elbow. "Will you open up completely to me?"

"I'll try," I told him.

"Then I'll show you."

*****

We got back to the condo Tuesday evening after dinner. Jyme helped me out of the truck, and we headed towards the door. Robert wished me a belated birthday, and he shook and patted Jyme's hand.

Randy came from behind the counter and greeted us both. He handed me an envelope and wished me a belated birthday.

"I still have your spare key, and Sergio will be right around to pull it into the garage for you." He shook Jyme's hand and told him he was glad to see him.

We got on the elevator, and D'Artagnan stood inside with some pretty young thing (PYT) in the famous words of MJ.

We spoke to each other awkwardly, and then the silence around us killed me.

"I looked for you Sunday evening, but you had already left," I told him.

"I was not feeling well."

"Baby, you were fine Sunday night," the PYT slurred.

"Well, I'm glad you're feeling better now, D'Artagnan." I said.

"D'Artagnan, you told me your name was Jyme," the PYT slurred.

My mouth dropped wide open, and Jyme burst out laughing, I elbowed him to shut up. The elevator dinged at the eighth floor. D'Artagnan snatched the PYT off the elevator, and she yelled at him. Her shoe came off, and D'Artagnan still pulled her even in her protest about her shoe. I picked up her shoe and chucked it down the hall. When the elevator door shut, I heard, "Ouch, bitch."

At the tenth floor, I stormed off the elevator and bustled through the door. I slammed my bag and purse on the counter and went straight to the bathroom, not saying a word. I cut the shower on and stepped out of my clothes. I got in and let the tears fall silently. D'Artagnan used to be my friend; he was my best friend for a few months. Now, he had turned back into that thing. He is not Mr. Crain, and he is not D'Artagnan. I fixed my face and got out the shower. I slid the robe around me and yanked my clothes off the floor, chucking them in the hamper. I walked back into the front room a little more cool now.

I went straight to the counter to retrieve my clothes. Jyme had set my garment bags over the couch, but he was not in sight. I looked out on the patio, but he was not there either. I checked the spare bedroom and bath, but still couldn't find him. I called out to him, but he didn't answer. I went back to the front door, and it was locked. I opened it and poked my head out, but he was not there.

I pulled my phone out of my purse, and I had no missed calls or text messages. I shoved the chain lock on the door and shut off all the lights. I sat my phone down on the nightstand in its cradle. I hung all my clothes up in the closet and found something to wear to work for the next day. I put on a nightgown and got into bed. I tossed and turn until I finally settled. Beyoncé belted from my phone, and I turned away from her singing. Then the doorbell rang, and I shot straight up. I walked over to it and peeped out the peephole. I opened the door, and I just stood there in his way so he couldn't get it. Jyme stood there holding a bag from Best Buy. "You went to the store?" I asked.

"You didn't see my note on the counter," he asked. I looked over on the counter, and there was not anything on it. Jyme slid his jacket and shoes off. I looked around on the floor, and there was a note in the kitchen doorway.

"Oh."

He walked past me and went into the bedroom. He sat down on the bed and pulled something out the bag. I sat on the bed looking at him; he was hiding what he had…I stood up on my knees, peeking over his shoulders.

"Dang, nosey," he teased.

"What's in the damn bag?"

He handed me a CD.

"Um, thanks," I said, frowning. The CD had four men standing in a shop window on a deserted street.

"Put it in the CD player." I went over to the CD player and slid it in.

"Number five." he said.

The song started with someone playing a guitar. I turned to face him in protest, and he snatched me back around towards the CD player. Then he was at my ear.

"Listen" he whispered. "Remember?"

I nodded at him, and Then I picked up the case; the group was called Mumford and Sons.

"It came out today, and I wanted to get it for you but we never left the room. So I couldn't."

"Thank you."

He kissed the side of my neck, stepping out of his clothes.

"What other songs are good on here?" I yelled over the shower.

"I haven't heard anything but like three songs on there, but what I've heard is good."

I listened to the whole CD, and my absolute favorite was the one Jyme sang in my ear that night, but I loved a song called, "The Cave" and "Little Lion Man." They said *fuck* in that song a lot, and I loved it.

I woke up the next morning to Jyme's kisses. I smiled at him.

"There she is," he crooned.

"You need to stop spoiling me like this. I can get greedy and start demanding these morning kisses daily."

"You don't have to demand," he breathed.

I looked at him. There was heaviness in his eyes.

"What is it?"

"It can be a reality if you want."

I watched him. He was so serious now.

"I know what you're thinking, but if we're a mistake, I want you to be my best mistake."

I didn't say anything. I didn't want to upset him anymore than he already was. "Hey, what are you doing today?"

"Nothing really."

"I think your fedora hat is here."

He said nothing; just let the wheels runaround in my head. I told Jyme my game plan, and he was all for it. If we were meant to be, we would see.

I had to follow up on my favorite shop this morning. I walked in and, of course, everything was perfect. I was greeted within first thirty seconds of me walking into the shop. Everything was white glove clean, and all of the condiments were full to the rim. The smiley faced girl was there again; I caught her name now: Raven.

"Hi there, and welcome back," she smiled. It had been about three months since I had last been here, and she still remembered me. She was great.

"We still have some of our Valentine red velvet cookies with the cream cheese frosting," she teased, bouncing her eyebrows up and down while she nodded her head.

I took the bait again; this girl was good. I ordered a latte and two of the specialty cookies. I heard the door chime twice while I was making my order, but when the third chime hit the door, the look on Raven's and the other female employees faces behind the counter was priceless. I knew it was show time.

I thanked her, went, and found a two-seater in the crowded shop. I pulled out my computer and began writing on my new laptop with the privacy screen up so wandering eyes couldn't see what I was doing. I laid my Blackberry on the table next to my laptop. About a minute after that, I heard someone clearing his throat, and I looked up from my laptop.

"Excuse me, is this seat taken?" the mud god asked. Jyme had these certain looks that would transform me back to the very first day we met. It was a smile here or there or even a clearing of his throat. I'm sure he was unaware of these small little things, but I always noticed. And just thinking about that day so long ago now, made my insides warm up.

"No," I assured him. I looked back down at the laptop and began typing again. I heard a couple of women two tables over say, "Is she blind?" I coughed back a laugh, and I grinned at my screen.

"Something over there must be pretty amusing," he said. I looked up at him.

"Yes, it is."

"Well, I bet I can tell you something that's way more interesting than what you're reading."

"Alright." I agreed. I closed my laptop and gave him my full attention. He rolled up both of his shirtsleeves all the way up to his elbows. Then, he went into a show of all the scars he had collected throughout the years. Some were funny, and some were sad. By the end of his journey, I noticed we had an audience sitting at the tables surrounding us and standing in line. A few employees were even captured by him. Before I knew it, an hour had gone by and it felt like five minutes.

He walked me to my car, and I told him, "I would have given you my number this time, but we have more light in the day, so we will see."

"Girl, I'm going to get your number every single time." he grinned. And that he did.

We met up at two more of my assignments that morning, and then had lunch at Pike Place. We then went to three more of my assignments that afternoon, and played out the same scene; he won my attention, and I would have given him my number every single time. I had so much fun with Jyme that day; I saw another side of him. He showed me his more vulnerable side and I melted like chocolate when he gave me those killer grins. He seemed so light and animated; his dark and bruiting side had slipped away somehow. I saw how people flocked to him no matter what; he was sharing his soul, and people like to be around that.

Jyme told me he needed to make a few runs before we went to dinner. We decided to meet up at the condo at 7:30. I desperately needed to go to the store for household products. I made it to the front of the condo at 7:15. I had six bags to haul in, so I went through the front. Robert held the door, and Randy met me at the counter with a floral arrangement that was obviously from Jyme. There was also two other packages for me. Randy helped me upstairs with the packages and he set them on the counter.

"He sure does know how to pick an arrangement that grabs your attention," Randy admired.

"He sure does."

This particular arrangement was remarkable; it had a wild forest feel to it. There was so much going on, that you could barely keep up. There was a knock at the door, and Randy opened it. Jyme greeted us both and walked in. He saw what we were gawking at and grinned.

"You need to write this stuff down for the rest of us poor

smucks, Mr. Samson."

"I'll get right on that, Randy."

Randy left, and we showered and dressed for dinner. While Jyme was finishing his shower in the guest bedroom, I decided to organize the mail, which was now piling up into a mountain. Most of it was junk mail, and then I remembered I had two packages from downstairs. I brought the packages and my letter opener over to the couch. There was no return address on the first letter-sized manila envelope. I slid the contents out, and there were two hand drawn pictures from Ayashe's twins and two birthday cards from Chelle's boys. They were so fucking sweet, I loved those kids dearly. Jyme passed through in a towel and came to see why I was gushing. He grinned at the pictures and read the birthday cards.

I opened the other package with the letter opener and slid the contents onto my lap. Three bloody human fingers and a gold ring fell out, and I screamed at the top of my lungs.

G STREET CHRONICLES
A LITERARY POWERHOUSE
WWW.GSTREETCHRONICLES.COM

Chapter 11

Cricket

Jyme had his arms hooked around me like a backpack. My arms and legs were free from him, but he still secured me like a turtle shell.

"Shh. I know, Babe, I know," he soothed in my ear.

I cried and cried, but I didn't feel trapped by him. I still felt free enough to breathe, and I didn't feel an attack rising. Dr. Barnes, the good doctor, had me practicing some breathing techniques, and I took a little white pill every day. I hadn't had an attack in months, but I hadn't been around Jyme for months either.

I calmed down, and Jyme released his grip on me. He turned me to face him. "I want you go into the bedroom and play that new CD until I come and get you, okay?" he said sternly. I nodded and went into the bedroom. He shut the French doors.

I looked at the clock. It was 7:50. Jyme came into the room at 8:58. The CD had started over all by itself. He came over to the bed and laid behind me. I snuggled up to him, and he held me.

"We're going to dinner, and we're not staying here tonight."

I nodded, and he kissed my forehead. Jyme asked me to get only the bare necessities. He had the clothes, underwear, and shoes under control. I got a big purse and put everything I needed in it. I grabbed my laptop bag, and we were off.

We said nothing to each other in the truck, just held hands. We pulled up at a restaurant called, Buenos Aires. Jyme ordered me a glass of wine right off the bat. Then, he ordered a porterhouse, and I ordered a Caesar salad. Jyme stopped that order immediately. He ordered me filet mignon with mashed potatoes and sweet potato fries.

"Jyme? Two starches? Really?"

He and the waiter chuckled. Then he scratched the sweet potatoes and ordered grilled vegetables. I had two more glasses of wine during dinner.

We got back to the docks and boarded the loaner boat from before. I held onto Jyme the entire ride. We made it back to the dark safe house, and Jyme lit up every room with the soft lights. We went upstairs, and he pulled four garment bags from one of the spare bedrooms. He took them into the master bedroom and hung them in the big closet.

"You have sleepwear in there," were the first words he had spoken directly to me since the condo.

I nodded and waited for him to exit the closet. I unzipped one of the bags, and it was filled with dresses. I unzipped the next one, and it was filled with blouses. I unzipped the next one, and it was filled with jeans and pants. I guess the fourth one would be the charm. I unzipped it, and there were nightgowns and sleep separates.

Jyme came back with two bags and three boxes of shoes. He set the bags on the floor and left the closet again. I changed into a sleep separate set and dug into the bags filled with underwear, leggings, tights, stockings, and bras. He had thought of absolutely everything. I unpacked everything and put it up into the closet drawers and cabinets. I put the three pairs of shoes in the shoe closet, and Jyme watched me from the bed.

"I picked those out for you a while ago," he said.

I said nothing; I just put the shoes away. I walked back to the bedroom, searching for something to do.

"I need to stay busy."

"Okay." He watched me and started to get up off the bed.

"We could have sex all-night long, or I could clean all-night long. How many condoms do we have?"

Jyme's faced dropped and then his head fell back.

"FUCK," he yelled.

I knew then that I would be cleaning all fucking night.

"I need socks."

"Babe, I could pull out like in the tub that morning."

"SOCKS," I shouted.

I had to hurry up and get away from him. He was my kryptonite, and if he got anywhere near my ear, I would be pregnant by the morning. He jumped up and got some socks out of his closet. Jyme stood awkwardly while I slid on the two long and too big socks.

"Shit my overnight bag."

I knew exactly what he was thinking. He had condoms in his overnight bag in his truck at the docks, and there were also some at the condo. Jyme couldn't just go to the quickest corner store to get a box. He had to order his special from Durex online. He twitched and then stopped, I glared at him.

"YOU ARE NOT LEAVING ME HERE BY MYSELF TO GO AND GET SOME FUCKING CONDOMS!"

"BABE," he growled, tugging at his anaconda.

"NO," I growled back.

I headed for downstairs to start my night of excessive cleaning. Jyme didn't follow me, and I seriously didn't want to know what he was up there doing to himself. He showed up after I placed everything back into the now pristine fridge. This was one of those big refrigerators with the freezer at the bottom.

I looked at him, and his face was all flushed.

"You are so disgusting."

"So," he snapped back.

"You could have at least let me watch."

"Oh, there will be a round two, I promise you."

I started laughing hysterically, and then he slid behind me and went straight for my ear. I didn't have a chance in hell. I woke the next morning sore and sticky. Jyme had nutted everywhere but inside of me; we fucked until we couldn't fuck anymore.

The view outside was breathtaking – the water and the boats and then more water and then more boats. I untwisted out from under Jyme and pulled one of the sheets with me. I went towards the window and stood there. The sun was peeking over the water, and it was so beautiful.

"Come back to bed," he called out sleepily.

"No, you nympho." I laughed.

He rubbed his eyes and stretched.

"This is beautiful." I pointed outside.

"I knew you'd like it," he said. "I'm starving."

"I'll make us some breakfast."

"REALLY BABE?"

"My God, I can hear your heart beating all the way over here," I told him.

"I just have this *MAJOR* fantasy of you cooking me breakfast in nothing but a white, long-sleeve, collar shirt."

"Well, I can do breakfast, but I can't get the twins in any of your shirts.

"I GOT ONE ALREADY. I ORDERED IT A LONG TIME AGO," he said a little too loud and too fast.

"Okay, okay...calm down. Let me get a shower, and we will live out your breakfast fantasy."

"I'll go and get the shirt and leave it in the bathroom for you."

I sent D'Artagnan and O a quick text that I would be working from home today. I went to get into the shower, and I heard Jyme when he came in.

"Babe?"

"Yeah?"

"No socks, okay?"

"Okay." I laughed.

I fried a couple of pork chops, eggs, and potatoes with onions. I toasted some bread and cut up some fruit. Jyme walked in wearing nothing but a bare chest and very well stretched out boxers. He had really gotten himself excited with this breakfast fantasy.

I soon found out that Jyme's so-called fantasy was not a fantasy at all. Jyme wanted a wife to wake up to and cook him breakfast every morning. He wanted to set up house and have babies to fill the rooms upstairs. Jyme wanted a son to take fishing, and he wanted his business of Samson and Son to be for him and his son. The one thing Jyme longed, dreamed, and ached for was something I didn't have a clue about giving him.

Jyme sat on the kitchen island and ate everything I put on his plate. "I thought you said you couldn't cook."

"Babe, if you call this cooking, then I am a fucking gourmet chef."

"Well, hello, chef."

I went and collected his plate and poured him some orange juice. Jyme wrapped his arms around my waist and rested his head on my stomach.

"Please cook me breakfast every morning," he begged.

"I didn't know you liked breakfast so much. I hardly ever see you eat it."

"That's my favorite meal of the day. We just don't ever make it or have time to eat it."

"Okay it's a deal."

"I know you need to work today, but can you please order us some furniture and have it delivered TODAY?"

I stood there in utter shock. I didn't know anything about the shit he was asking me to do.

"Jyme, I'm not that kind of girl. I don't know the first thing about ordering furniture and stuff like that."

"Cricket, you're the best-dressed woman I know. Order whatever you like."

"What pieces of furniture do you want me to order," I frowned.

"Are you serious?"

I turned from him, trying to fight back the tears; he thought I was a freak because I didn't know how to do this shit. I pulled away from him and went back to the sink. I started washing all the dishes. Once I was done with that, I cleaned the pots and skillets.

Jyme walked over to the sink and started rinsing the dishes.

"Why don't you ever talk about your life before you moved here?"

I didn't answer; I was so not ready for this conversation. It was too soon for all of this shit. I went up behind him and slid my wet hands in his boxers.

"Cricket." He pulled away from me.

"Come on. You know you want it." I slid in front of him and kissed him. He kissed me back.

"Cricket, we need to talk," he said through kisses.

"I'll make you feel real good, Daddy," I said while kneeling to the floor.

"What?" he asked breathlessly.

"You can shove it down my throat till I choke."

"Cricket what the fuck?" he asked in a high-pitched whisper.

"I might even let you try another hole if you're a good boy." I slid his anaconda out, and Jyme jumped back from me.

"What's wrong?"

"Why the fuck are you talking to me like that?"

"Like what? Did I say something wrong?"

"You're talking to me like a whore, and I don't like that."

"Oh, I'm sorry." I put his anaconda back in his shorts for him.

He started right back rinsing, and I kept wiping everything down I could find. He put the dishes in the dish racks, and there was nothing else to do. I had wiped down the island and all the counters, and I was on my third wipe of the fridge.

Jyme pulled the dishrag out of my hand and turned me to face him. He pulled me close to him and rubbed both of my shoulders.

"Listen to me. I know you're not ready to talk about your past, and I don't want to pressure you, but we're going to have to have this conversation eventually. Cricket, I want to wake up next to you every single day for the rest of my life. You promised you'd open up to me."

I stood there looking down at the floor. Jyme released me, and I headed upstairs. I slipped back on what I wore at dinner last night. Jyme walked in, and I was pulling my purse on my shoulder. I bent over to pick up my laptop bag.

"I thought you were working from here," he asked.

"I need to go home."

"Cricket, are you coming back?"

"No."

"Babe, why?" He walked over to me. "Cricket, please don't leave me."

I stood there looking at the floor.

"I won't ask you anything else about your past, I swear," he whispered.

"Don't ever, or I'm out of here. I'm real good at disappearing," I warned him.

"Cricket, please don't disappear. If I were to ever lose you, I don't know what I'd do. I'd go fucking crazy. Promise you won't do that to me."

"I promise," I lied.

Jyme had to go and handle some business. He left the car keys, a stack of cash, and two credit cards. He reminded me to fill the house up with furniture and have it delivered today. He said he would be back around six. I promised a hot meal on the new table when he got back. He almost peed himself with excitement. He reminded me that no one was to know where we lived. The credit cards had Jamerson and Jamerson construction on them. He told me to sign everything Jamerson Jamerson. I answered emails, and then I called the one person I knew who would know what I needed.

O answered on the second ring, I told her I was helping a friend who just got a new house and that I needed a place that could do it all and deliver it today. She asked what kind of money they wanted to spend. I told her the sky was the limit. She told me that the only place I could get everything today would be IKEA. I could order everything online, and I would have to pay a hefty price if it needed same day delivery.

I went to the website and got started right away. O was right. They had absolutely everything. I ordered for each room in the house, and I bought what I thought was pretty. I called the store in Renton, and after I begged, pleaded, and paid an additional four thousand dollars, they agreed to have the furniture here by 3:00. I was checking a few more emails when my phone rang.

"We need to talk," Chelle said in a dry voice.

"Okay, can you meet up for lunch?"

"Yes, where?"

"How about Maxwell's in Tacoma?"

"That's fine. See you then." I wasn't sure what that was all about, but I was sure I would find out soon.

I worked a little more on the laptop, and then Beyoncé was singing to me from my phone. I answered, and he just sat there. We both sat on the phone in silence. I refused to say anything before he did. He called me; I didn't call him. I didn't say anything. His fight he was having with himself would have to work itself out.

"I'm sorry about this morning."

"Already forgotten" I assured him.

"How do you do that?"

"Do what?"

"Turn it on and off. You can be mad one minute, and then the next you don't even care."

"Some call it bipolar, but I think I've got a magic switch that I can control," I answered.

"Cricket?"

"Yeah?"

"I'm in love with you, and if you ever leave me, I would go fucking crazy," he said.

"I shouldn't have threatened you like that this morning, and I'm sorry. But I felt like you were attacking me, and that's the only coping mechanism I know."

"Don't apologize to me for anything that happened this morning. It was all my fault and I shouldn't have said what I said."

"Jyme, I love you."

"Say it again," he asked.

"I love you."

"I love you, too, Cricket."

"I'll see you when you get home," I told him.

"Um, that sounds so good."

I got into the tank and sweated bullets every time I had to turn a corner. It took me almost ten minutes to park in a parking space in the parking lot of the restaurant. I met Chelle at Maxwell's for lunch and I had a strong feeling this was not going to be a good visit. She was waiting on me at a table in the corner. I took in a deep breath and sat down across from her. There was lemon water waiting for me at the table already, and she said she ordered us an appetizer.

"So, what the fuck did you do to him?"

I looked up from my water to meet her eyes.

"We met for coffee this morning, and he was torn up; he went on and on and on about how you flipped out on him this morning. He said you talked to him like some whore, and then you threatened to leave him. He was a complete and utter mess.

"What did you tell him?"

"All I said was you had a real fucked-up childhood, and you don't like to talk about it."

"What did he say?"

"Nothing, he just listened to every word that came out of my mouth," she explained. "Look Cricket, I know you're scared, and I know it's hard for you to trust anyone, but I think he's really in love with you. You should just come clean with him. I don't think he'll care about that stuff,"

"You know, I thought I at least had till March before all this stuff started to happen. I didn't even make it six months."

"Cricket, please don't do this to him. It will kill him."

"What do you expect me to do then, huh? Tell him the truth so he can look at me in *that* way? Tell him all about my family roots?" I asked.

"It's not just you that will hurt. Ayashe and I will be the ones sitting back watching him fall apart, and then we have to hear the voices of his best friends. Did you think about that?"

"I never asked for you to--"

"OH, I KNOW YOU DIDN'T. You never ask for anything. Not one damn thing."

The tears started, and I knew I had no control over them now.

"Honey, I know you love him. I can see it in your eyes when you look at him. That night in the bar on your birthday, when he had you all hemmed up in his arms. I could tell you were at peace, and he is your peace."

I wiped at my face, and the waiter brought me more cloth napkins without saying a word. "I don't know how to do this with him, he has so much baggage and his life is . . ."

She interrupted. "Cricket, you carry all of your baggage in your heart and mind; you have to let some of that baggage go. He's got strong arms. Let him carry some of that for you."

We sat there for another hour or so, and Chelle tried her best to convince me to come clean with Jyme, but I just couldn't see how. There were major things in my past that he should never know about.

I made it back to the safe house a little after 2:00. The one good thing about this monster tank of a car was that it held fifty-seven household item bags like a champion. I felt so small driving it, and that does not happen often. I unpacked everything from the bacon and eggs for the fridge to the Irish Spring body wash for Jyme to feminine products for me. I went to work for another thirty minutes, and then there was a massive ding-dong sound vibrating through the house. I yanked all the bedding off the bed and headed for the door. The washer and dryer came in first just as I had requested. As soon as the washer and dryer were set, I went to work on it. I set all of the furniture and kitchen appliances the same way I saw it online. I went to IKEA's website on my phone and had the workers put everything exactly like the pictures on the site.

Two hours later, this house looked like it belonged in *Better Homes and Gardens*. Jyme said he would be here by six, and I needed to start dinner. I ran upstairs and hopped in the shower. I put my morning fantasy outfit back on as he had requested through a text message earlier. But I wore a pair of his socks; I would peel them off when he got there.

I made spaghetti with fried catfish; I am not a baker, so I got a Mrs. Smith's cobbler. I was mixing the salad when I heard the front door open. I pulled my socks off and threw them in one of the laundry baskets.

"Cricket?" Jyme called from the foyer. I walked to the stairwell, and there he stood with a massive flower arrangement.

"Do we have a dining room table?"

"Yes, we do."

He walked towards me and gave me a quick peck on the cheek. Then, he went down into the dining room. He set the flowers on the table, and they looked great there. He turned around and pulled me up against him.

"You smell good. What you cooking?" He smiled wide.

"Dinner will be ready in about twenty minutes," I kissed both sides of his neck and tugged at his ear with my teeth.

"I'm going to take a shower," he croaked out.

"Alright," I said and turned to walk back to the kitchen. He grabbed my arm.

"Come with me?"

"I just got out, and I need to finish dinner."

"What are you cooking?"

"Spaghetti, fried catfish, and cobbler."

"Is the spaghetti done?" he asked in my ear now.

"Yes."

"The catfish?" he asked licking my ear.

"No, I haven't put them in the grease yet."

"And the cobbler?" His tongue was in my ear now.

"Yes," I growled.

"Shower."

I took off for the stairs. I looked behind me, and Jyme was hopping on one leg, pulling his shoes off. I laughed at him and then stopped abruptly.

Jyme gave me this look, and I knew he was about to fuck the shit out of me. I was undressed and in the shower when he got there. "Don't get my hair wet," I warned while pulling it all up in a ponytail.

He nodded, pressed me against the back wall, and put the water on blast. I came twice, and he came hard once; we were exhausted. This wild kingdom sex was really tiring me out.

We were both starving, and Jyme had me give him a piece of fried catfish straight out the grease onto his plate. He ate absolutely everything again and wanted second helpings.

"I've never had sweet tea before," he told me.

"It's a southern thing."

"And catfish with spaghetti. I've never had that, but it's so damn good."

"Another southern thing. Next time, I'll make you collards with fried catfish and corn bread."

"Tomorrow?"

"I guess so, if you want catfish again," I laughed.

"Yes, please."

"Alright."

We sat there in silence, and Jyme examined the kitchen from his seat.

"Do you like it?" I asked.

"Do you like it?"

"Yes," I whispered.

"Then I love it."

I smiled at him as his cell phone rang. He silenced it at once and set it back down on the table.

"Aren't you going to get that?"

"We're having dinner."

"I met Michelle for lunch today at Maxwell's."

Jyme wiped his mouth with the brand-new cloth napkins. I held my hand up to stop him.

"It's alright; I know why you did it. I just had a horrible childhood. I want to talk to you about it, but I am not ready right now. And I know that's not fair to you, but I can't give you more than that right now. I am letting you in more than you will ever know. All of this is terrifying me, and I am hanging on the edge, trying hard not to fall off. I need you to not push me and be patient with me on this."

Jyme placed his hand over mine, and I gave him a smile.

"I'm a patient man; I just needed something to go off of. I'm sorry I went to her, but you were all ready to leave me this morning, and I was not sure if you were going to be here when I got home."

"I'm here."

"And I see that."

"I spent $27,000 today. All of the receipts are in the top drawer in your office," I told him.

"Did you get everything we need?"

"Do you want a TV, desk computer, stereo, or Blu-ray player?" I asked.

"We might need that stuff at some point."

"Well, I can call Best Buy tomorrow and see if they can deliver and install."

"Can you be here tomorrow during the day? I've somewhere I have to be," he asked.

"Sure, I can work from home."

"Home," he crooned.

"Yes. Our home."

"You made this house a home."

"And in less than twenty four hours."

"Spend however much you need to make us comfortable here."

"Is there anything you want?" I asked.

He smiled at me with a raised eyebrow.

"Besides me lying flat on my back?"

"I don't know, I'm kind of partial to the shower now."

I raised my eyebrows then; the shower was very good, and we got clean right away.

"I'm planning on having sex with you in every single room in this house," he said.

"Well, alright then."

I woke the next morning to Jyme's kisses all over my bare back. "Oh, that's nice." I stirred.

"Cricket, what's this?"

"What?" I asked sleepily.

"It's a scar; it kind of looks like a bullet wound."

I rolled over on my back at once, and I pulled him into me and kissed the side of his neck. Jyme laid his head on the two soft mountains. Then, he sat up slowly, staring at my bare stomach. "Here's the entry wound and back there's the exit."

I lay there not moving and hardly breathing.

"Cricket, please."

"It's just a cigar scar," I assured him.

"Cricket, in the front and the back?"

"I had a mean grandfather," I told him. I got up and went straight to the shower. He joined me a few minutes later. "Jyme I'm really not in the mood right now."

He pulled me into him and took a couple of deep breaths. "I can't do this," he whispered.

"You want me to leave?"

"God dammit, Cricket. NO!" He found the almost invisible scar on my back with his fingers. "I will protect you," he assured me while rubbing his wet fingers over the bullet wound. I cried in his arms, and he just let me without saying a word. I made waffles in the waffle maker with eggs and bacon for breakfast that morning. Jyme had two waffles and was now working on his fourth piece of bacon. His phone rung, but he ignored it again. I watched him, and he looked frustrated.

"What about my stuff at the condo?" I asked him.

"What about it?"

"I need my things."

"What do you need there that you don't have here?"

"Jyme, it's my stuff."

"Is there anything there that isn't replaceable?"

Why was he acting like this with me? I needed my shit. It was mine. I worked long and hard for everything I had. I stood and started clearing the table; I dumped all the extra food down the garbage disposal.

Jyme stood beside me, handing me his empty plate.

"Look I'll get everything of yours moved out today, but I don't want you going back there by yourself."

What did he think I was going to live here forever? And I still had to get a car.

"I still need to find a place of my own and a car. I don't mind spending ninety percent of my time here, but I really need my own place, Jyme."

"Why?"

"Just because, and I am not going to get in some big dropkick fight about it."

"Where do you want to live?"

"I was thinking about trying to get a condo in the same building."

"WHAT?"

"Jyme that place is the safest. No one can get in. Yes, granted, someone sent me an unwanted package, but no one can get in. It's well secured, and you know it."

"I don't get a say in any of this?"

"A say in what?"

"Cricket, I bought this house for us—me and you and you and me."

"Jyme, I've no security. If we breakup, I'm stuck."

"Who's breaking up?"

"You know what I mean."

"If anything happens, you can just keep the house, and I'll move back to the reservation" he assured me.

"JYME!"

"That's it. Problem solved," he said, walking out of the kitchen.

"Jyme, we are not done talking about this." I screamed at him, following him to the front door. Jyme unlocked and opened it with me right on his heels.

The four figures at the door scared the shit out of both of us. Four women were standing there. One had a basket, another had a cake, another had some kind of casserole, and then the other had a bottle of wine with four goblets.

"Hi," they said in unison.

"Good morning, ladies," Jyme greeted them and turned around to give me a quick peck on the lips. He stepped around them and looked as though he was about to burst with laughter.

"Mrs. Jamerson, it's so nice to finally meet you. Mr. Jamerson said he was not sure when you would be back from your sick grandmother's house," the woman with the cake said.

"Down in Tennessee right?" the woman with the casserole dish asked.

"I'm sorry, ladies. I'm not dressed for visitors," I told them. I was wearing nothing but Jyme's white fantasy shirt and panties too skimpy to even be called panties.

"Oh, we can wait," the woman with the wine said.

"Oh well, please come in," I told all four of them. I guided them to the kitchen, apologized for the mess, and excused myself.

I ran up the stairs and yanked my phone off the cradle; I pressed my speed dial number one.

"What's our story?" I asked him.

"Tell the truth just add a couple of years to it."

"Alright."

"I love you," he teased.

"Fuck you."

"I should have before I left," he said and my toes started tingling.

"I gotta go."

"I love you," he said again.

"I love you, too."

"I'll see you at five."

"Four!" I stressed.

"Okay four."

I dressed quickly and went back downstairs. The women were all still sitting at the table.

"Mrs. Jamerson, I love the rich bold colors you used in the kitchen. Do you guys plan on leaving the walls bare?" Casserole asked.

"Oh no, the rest of our stuff is at our old condo," I told them.

"Oh my goodness, where are my manners. I'm Lori Shaffer, the casserole lady said.

"I'm Darlene Walters," said the cake lady.

The wine lady introduced herself as Jillian Rogers.

"And I'm Athena Jacobs, said the basket lady.

"Oh, it's so nice to meet you ladies, and thank you so much for the warm welcome.

"Well, Mrs. Jamerson, I see you have some fresh biscuits over there on that innovative oven. I make jams, jellies, and preserves." Athena pulled the small cloth napkin off the top of the basket, and there were at least eight jars of jellies and what not. I went and got five plates, knives, and soft some butter.

"Oh, what lovely saucers you have," Jillian admired.

"I just love the texture and depth. It's so urban," Lori said.

"So Darlene, what kind of cake is that?" I asked, trying to change the soon to be racial conversation.

"Hummingbird," she answered.

"Oh, I've never heard of that."

"It's an old family recipe," she answered.

"And Lori what kind of casserole is that," I asked. "It's a cobbler and it's Rhubarb," she answered. Neither one of those desserts sounded appetizing to me. "Ladies, I sure do hate to rush you off, but it is already ten and I need to start getting to work. Let me find something to put those wonderful desserts in."

"No, No, we will stop back by in a week and retrieve them," Athena said.

"Well, alright. Thank you so much." I walked them back to the door.

"Mrs. Jamerson, does Mr. Jamerson take his speed boat to work with him every day?" Darlene asked.

"Just about," I answered with a smile. "You ladies have a good day and see you soon," I beamed. They all nodded, and then the door was shut. I shook trying to get the freaky Wisteria Lane bunch out of my head. I locked the door and headed upstairs.

I was on my tenth email when Beyoncé started singing on my phone—Jyme's ringtone.

"Are they gone?" he whispered.

"Yes, finally. They left about twenty minutes ago."

"There will be two delivery men coming to the house to bring the rest of your belongings from the condo."

"JYME," I snapped.

"We're not having this conversation, Cricket."

I said nothing. What was the point?

"Have you had a chance to check out Best Buy's website?"

"No, but I will."

"Try to get them to deliver and install today."

"Yes, Sir!" I teased him.

"You still cooking dinner?"

"Yep."

"Okay, good. I love you."

"I love you, too."

Two loads in the washer, the cleaning of three bathrooms, the changing of sheets on our bed, and four hours later, the deliverymen and the Best Buy geeks arrived at the house within ten minutes of each other. Everything I owned fit in my new closet, and that made me sad. I unpacked all ten boxes, and I pushed all five of the portable closets inside of the big closet. We had three TVs mounted, two Blu-rays set up, two stereo systems connected, and a desktop hooked up. While the Best Buy geeks were mounting the TV in the bedroom, my phone rang. I didn't recognize the number.

"Hello."

"Who am I speaking with?" the male voice asked.

"The person you called."

"May I speak with Lil Samson?"

I clicked into my phone quickly and found the recorder. "I'm sorry, who?" I asked.

"Jyme" the male's voice said.

"I'm sorry, you have the wrong number."

"Oh, so are you not coming home tonight?" the voice asked.

"I'm sorry. What?"

"Did you get the little gift I sent you?"

"I'm sorry, sir. You have the wrong number."

"You can't hide forever, and when I do find you, I'm going to split you wide open."

I hung up the phone, and went downstairs. I stepped out the kitchen door onto the deck and dialed his number. I paced back and forth until Jyme answered.

"Someone just called my phone," I rushed out.

"I'm listening," I knew instantly Jyme was not alone. He never talked to me so formally. I filled him on what had happened and what was said.

"I will meet with you in a half an hour."

"K."

"I, umm," he stammered.

"I love you too."

We both hung up.

I was frantic, so I started cleaning like a mad woman. I swept and mopped the bathroom and kitchen. I was just about to start in on the dining room when I heard the garage door open. I went to the door and opened it.

Jyme got out of a black Dodge Charger. He went to the trunk of the car and pulled out two boxes. He walked up the three steps to the hallway, and I stood in front of him.

"The Best Buy guys are still here," I warned him before he started talking. He nodded and kissed me on my lips hard. I kissed him right back just as hard.

"Here's all your jewelry." He held the two boxes up. "I'll put them in your closet."

I nodded and went back to start on the dining room. I was on my knees scrubbing the hardwood when Jyme walked in.

"Babe, your clothes."

"I know, but I didn't have time to change into something else, and I have to stay busy."

"I know, Babe,"

"Mrs. Jamerson, we're all done," one of the geeks called from the foyer.

"I'll be right there."

I went to rinse off my hands, and then I signed the paper on his clipboard. He handed me the receipt and I let them out. I shut the door and locked all three locks and went straight to Jyme's office. I put the receipt in the top drawer of the desk.

Jyme walked in and looked all over the room and then smiled.

"This room is nice."

"It's all yours."

He walked over. "Do you still feel safe in the house?"

"Yes."

He sat at his desk and turned on his new computer.

"We have internet, so I guess we need to order some cable."

"You get whatever you want."

"Why aren't you taking any participation in this?"

"You need this stuff to survive. I don't," he explained.

"Jyme, you like stuff just as much as I do, if not more."

"I don't need it though; you can't function without it."

I said nothing and started to exit the room slowly.

"Cricket, I will do any and everything to make sure you feel safe, and being in control makes you feel safe. This is our house, and it's safe."

"I feel safe here," I assured him.

"You wouldn't be here if you didn't."

I went into the kitchen to start dinner. My mind was still on Jyme's words, and I wondered how he knew that about me. I didn't even know that about myself.

My cell phone rang while I was adding some ham chunks to the collards. It was another number I didn't recognize. I screamed for Jyme. He came running right to me. He nodded, and I answered it on speaker.

"Cricket?" the woman said into the phone.

"Yes?"

"Hi Honey. This is JJ." Jyme smiled wide and walked out the kitchen. If he only really knew how his mother terrified me, he would have stood right there.

"Yes, Ma'am."

"I was wondering if you had time for a little shopping tomorrow. I know it's short notice, but I have a dinner tomorrow night, and Lil Samson is always praising your style. Can you help me?"

"Sure," I said reluctantly.

"Oh, good. How about I pick you up at noon tomorrow?"

"I will meet you at Pac Place food court at noon."

"That sounds great. See you then."

I rolled my eyes hard and hung up.

Jyme ate his entire plate again, and then he had a slice of the hummingbird cake and a slice of that nasty looking rhubarb cobbler. Jyme told me about some of his fishing adventures and all the fishing mistakes he used to make. I laughed at the majority of his stories, and then he told me they were not supposed to be that funny; but they were. We made love all night and for the majority of the early morning. I hope he never gets enough of me.

I woke the next morning to an empty bed. I listened for the shower, but he was not there. I walked towards the stairs and heard murmuring. He was down there on the phone. I striped the bed and put on fresh sheets. With all of our lovemaking, I will be washing sheets every day. Thank God I ordered a dozen sets from IKEA.

I found an outfit for the day and hopped in shower. I was in there maybe two minutes when Jyme joined me. I turned to kiss him, but his face was distorted.

"Babe what's wrong?" I pressed up against him.

"I need you to do me a favor."

"Anything."

"I need you to stay at the reservation tonight."

"Where are you going?"

"I have to go to California today."

I swallowed and nodded. I turned back around and finished my shower. He rubbed soap in the palm his of hands and washed my back. He touched my bullet wound all the time now; it was like he was fascinated by its presence. I had many more scars he would never see.

"What makes you feel safe?" I asked him.

"Knowing you, my family and friends are safe."

"When you're scared, what makes you feel safe?"

"I guess I've never been that scared."

"You've never been bullied before?"

"No, I've gotten into fights before, but I was not scared of them. I knew I was going to beat the shit out of them, so it didn't matter."

Those words about him beating the shit out someone made my toes tingle and the feeling was rising, but I knew he was not in the mood for that. Oh wait, yes he was.

*****

I met Mrs. JJ on the fourth level at the food court. She wore a black tank top tucked into tapered jeans with a red blazer and suede boots. She looked a mess; we had to stop this train before it wrecked. Two growling stomachs and four hours later, Mrs. JJ ended up with a sequined blazer, three pairs of skinny jeans, a studded sweater dress, two sleeveless paillette dresses, two wrapped jersey dresses, a crepe dress, and four pairs of pumps. We decided to grab a bite to eat in the food court.

The day hadn't been extremely unpleasant. Mrs. JJ acted civilly, but every now and then, I caught her staring at me as if she was still dissecting me. When we sat down at the restaurant, we both ordered a glass of wine. I knew not to drink too much more because I had to drive us all the way back to the reservation. Jyme had arranged for Mrs. JJ to be dropped off at the mall so we would only have one car. I was not thrilled at all about having to stay on that reservation, but if this made Jyme feel comfortable, then so be it.

"I can't seem to figure you out," she told me.

"Well, how about we just stop trying to figure each other out and just enjoy each other's company?"

"No."

I rolled my eyes and hunched my shoulders.

"I know you're hiding something, and I can tell it's something big."

I sat there staring at her.

"Do you deny it?"

"No."

She nodded and grinned at me. "You have him fooled, but not me."

"The secrets that I keep have nothing to do with Jyme and me. I would never do anything to hurt him. I'd leave him before I let that happen," I explained.

"See that's what you don't understand. If you ever left him, that would kill him. You're in too deep, and the longer you keep this from him the more it's going to hurt him."

We both sipped our wine, and then our food arrived. "I won't pretend like he hasn't come back to life since he's met you, but I can't help but fear the storm that you're brewing," she said.

I ate my salmon in silence.

"Where are you from?"

"Tennessee."

"Where are your family and friends?"

"Tennessee."

"Why are you here?"

"My friend Chelle asked me to come to the Pacific Northwest, and I've never lived here before, so I came,"

"Where all have you lived?"

"All over."

"Where?" she demanded.

I wiped my mouth with my cloth napkin and took a gulp of my wine. "Um, let's see. New York, Pennsylvania, Virginia, Florida, Michigan, Georgia, Texas, Louisiana, Illinois, California, Ohio, New Hampshire, and Washington State."

"Why so many states?"

"Work."

"Have you always traveled?"

"Yes, I've always been in auditing and sales."

"So, I take it you make a pretty good living?"

"Yes, Ma'am."

"You must have had a lot of education?"

"The best money could buy."

"So why are you with a boy from a reservation instead of some white-collar millionaire?"

"White collar men aren't my type," I told her.

"So, what is your type?"

"Jyme."

"Why?"

"Because he understands me better than I understand myself."

Those words seemed to have had magic powers in them. Mrs. JJ melted right before my eyes. She smiled at me and told me; she understood what I meant. She talked and talked and talked for the rest of the day. She told me exactly how she met Big Samson and about giving birth to his children. She told me the way he used to be with her, and then the kids came and that everything changed. She told me about her childhood. And how things used to be on the reservation. She told me about Jyme when he started fishing and how he loved it. She repeated almost everything Jyme had already told me about how he started his business, but I didn't stop her. She seemed so laidback talking about her family and all of their adventures.

We talked about sex with the Samson men, and I gave her an inch of information. I had to share something in our bonding stage; this was crucial and Jyme wanted this.

"I know this is difficult for you to talk about, but you have to understand I encourage my children to be sexual and free. They can talk to me about any and everything. I don't want my children to be embarrassed about sex."

"Oh, he's not, believe me," I said.

"Oh, I know he's not, but he's reserved when it comes to you, and I don't like that," she told me.

And at that moment, I understood Mrs. JJ a little bit more. Jyme always went to her with all of his issues and thoughts, and now that had changed and she felt like she didn't know him anymore. Jyme protected me, and she did not know me so that annoyed her. I had to let Mrs. JJ in some kind of way, but she was a mother and I don't do mothers.

"He's so gentle and patient with me. Just looking at him, you'd think he was hard and rough, and he can be at times. But the majority of what I see, he's a tamed tiger," I told her.

She sat there in silence, and then I went on. "Our first time was beautiful. It felt like my first time ever in more ways than one." We both giggled. "He didn't think we could do it at first, but we had to rearrange, and then things were perfect. I don't know we just fit; I can't explain it, and I don't want to get too deep into this. Pun not intended," I said laughing, and she joined me. "Seriously it's just like our bodies know each other; they know each other better than our minds do," I explained.

"Kindred spirits" she whispered. She looked over at me in the driver seat, and then she laid her hand on top of mine. "I like you now," she said with a smile.

"I'm glad." I checked my phone three times, and I had absolutely no messages from Jyme.

Mrs. JJ wanted to know everything current about me, and I appreciated her for not trying to pry into my past. She wanted to know how Jyme's relationship and mine was and what we do together. After her tenth time of asking, "Is that all you guys do?" I had to tell her we were still in the honeymoon stage. She said she understood, and she backed away from that subject.

We made it to the reservation at 9:45. Mrs. JJ walked into Jyme's house with me and turned on all the lights. She told me if I was too scared to stay there by myself that she would stay the night, and I assured her I was fine. She put her number on a piece of paper by the house phone.

I showered and dressed for bed. The house phone rang, and I answered it.

"I miss you," he growled in my ear.

"Jyme," I breathed. I just sat with the phone for a minute; I think he was listening to my breathing because I know I was listening to his.

"I love your mom."

"I'm glad, Babe." I could hear the smile in his voice.

"When are you coming back?" I asked.

"The crack of dawn. I'll be there before you wake up in the morning."

"Well, you make sure you wake me as soon as you get here."

"Oh, I will."

"I can't wait to taste your tongue on mine."

"Cricket," he breathed into a growl.

"I miss us, and I miss our safe house."

"Me too."

"I love you, Mr. Jamerson."

"And I love you, Ms. Hooper." I slid into his soft comfortable bed and drifted off.

When I woke that morning, I could hear Jyme in the kitchen. I jumped out the bed and went into the kitchen. "Why didn't you wake me when you got here?" I scolded.

But I was scolding the wrong person. Jyme's sister Patty sat at the kitchen table, and Mrs. JJ was cooking something on the stove. I turned around and looked in the front room. Jyme's grandmother was sitting in her wheelchair staring out the window.

"Where's Jyme?" I asked.

No one said anything. I went to the house phone and dialed his number. It went straight to voicemail.

"He said he was going to be here when I woke up," I told them.

No one looked at me; they just acted like they couldn't hear me. I sat at the table and put my hands on top of Patty's. "What's wrong? He called last night and said he'd be here by eight o'clock, but he's not." I looked over at the kitchen clock, and it was nine thirty.

Patty and I sat there holding hands in silence and Mrs. JJ set food in front of Patty and me.

"The flight?" I yelled out.

Patty shook her head. "They missed it. I called this morning, and none of them were on it."

"Who all went with him?"

"Loon, Kanoke, and Sheen."

I jumped up at once and ran to get my phone. Patty followed slowly behind me. I dialed Ayashe's number on the house phone; it rang twice.

"Sheen?" she said frantically; my heart fell then. I knew she was waiting to hear from him if she saw this number thinking I was him calling her.

"Ayashe."

"Cricket, have you—"

"No."

"I told him not to go down there. I told him."

"Ayashe, what are they doing?"

"They are so obsessed with this fucking casino; they think this is going to be the ultimate pay off for all of them. They are going to get killed trying to make this happen. No one wants them in the casino business. Jyme has paid every fucking body off from the deserts of Nevada and now the palm trees of California. Loon is their only voice of reason, and they wouldn't even listen to him. Jyme is so determined not to have a paper trail that he delivers the cash himself. He doesn't send anyone else to do it; he does it himself. You cannot go around paying off all these Natives like this. It pisses them off that he has so much money. I don't know where they are, and I don't know what to do."

"Call Chelle, and I'll be at your house in three hours. Get baby sitters, and look up flights," I told her. I walked from the hallway and went to get dressed.

"Momma," Patty called frantically from the hallway. She watched me, and then Mrs. JJ joined her.

"Cricket, what are doing?" Mrs. JJ asked.

"I'm going to find him."

"No, the hell, you're not," she shouted at me.

"Mrs. JJ, I can find him, and I promise I'll get him home." I walked to the front door, and Jyme's grandmother wheeled over to me. She reached for me, and I kneeled down to her. She touched both sides of my face, and then her face went slack. She let her arms drop, and she started weeping and reached her hand out for me again. I walked out the front door. Patty and Mrs. JJ ran after me. I jumped in the Lac and sped down the hill.

I made it to Ayashe's in two hours; I drove ninety the whole way there. I walked in and both of them were packed and ready to go. Ayashe had tears in her eyes, and I knew Chelle had filled Ayashe in on my past. Ayashe watched every move I made. She was starting to piss me off.

"Listen, don't fucking look at me like that. If you can't handle this, you need to go." I snapped.

"I can handle this, and I can do this. I'm sorry," she whispered.

"So what are the flights looking like?"

"We have two hours, but they're expensive," Ayashe said. Then she closed her eyes in disgust with herself. I handed Chelle my credit card and walked towards the door.

"I need to run a quick errand, and then I'll meet you guys at Sea Tac." I left Ayashe's, heading for the safe house. On my way, I stopped at the bank right before they were closing and withdrew six thousand dollars.

I pulled in, and I sat in the garage for a minute. I looked over at Jyme's brand new Charger, and then I slid down out of the Lac, leaving the keys in the ignition. I thought about it, and then I realized I'd never felt safe enough to leave keys in an ignition. But Jyme did it all the time at the reservation and here. He knew what it truly was to feel safe, and now I did. I went into our beautiful home and sat at the kitchen table with a pen and pad. I wrote down the thoughts that were in my head. I finished the letter and headed upstairs. I packed my essentials in three bags. The only piece of jewelry I took was my Cricket ring.

I was heading back downstairs when I remembered something. I ran back into the bedroom and went to the back of the closet. There was my red birthday dress. I folded it in a piece of plastic and shoved it into one of the bags. I heard a horn outside and ran down the stairs. I opened the door and turned to take one last look at our house. It was absolutely perfect for us. I fought back tears, locked all three locks, and got into the cab.

When we landed, Chelle had everything under control, as I

knew she would. She had a rental and a hotel room already booked and paid for. We loaded up in a Chevrolet Suburban, and Chelle apologized immediately for the obvious distraction, which I didn't need right now.

"This was the biggest vehicle they had, and I was not sure how much room we'd need," she said. I nodded at her and kept driving.

Ayashe had a few numbers she had collected from across a few reservations, and we now had names of the Natives Jyme was meeting with, but we didn't have a clue how to find them. That is where my expertise came in handy. I knew the hottest streets to check, and I knew where to avoid. I changed clothes in the truck, and Chelle helped me by handing me this and that. I piled the makeup on and then jumped out of the truck.

"Stay as far back as possible, I whispered to Chelle. She nodded, and I shut the door.

I walked a half a block before I stopped, and then the games began.

"Baby girl, you look new and fresh," the man in the Infiniti SUV said.

"I am, I just got off of a plane," I said in a slow twang voice. Country Bumpkin was on for the evening. I walked over to the Suburban, and then all hell broke loose. That is exactly what I was looking for.

"Wait a minute BITCH. Who the fuck is you'? A high-pitched voice asked.

"I'm Cricket; it's nice to meet ya."

"I don't know a fucking Cricket, but you better get yo ass out of here before C.J. finds you."

She was a skinny, tiny thing, but I could tell she could hold her own. She wore a black spaghetti strap fitted dress with black boots tall as the sky and a long jet-black wig; it reminded me of the old wig Cher used to wear when she was with Sunny.

"I thought Ralphie ran this side," I lied.

"Hell, no girl. Where the fuck you been?"

"On the Southside."

"Shit, no wonder why you're confused. Come with me."

"Hey, baby girl," the Infiniti called out.

"Jeff, ain't nobody touching that little pencil dick of yours."

"Fuck you, Cinnamon," he said as he drove off.

"That's the problem. You can't," she yelled back at him, laughing. We walked into a pizza joint, and Cinnamon ordered us two slices and two sodas. I ate as if I was starving, and Cinnamon watched me.

"Shit girl, when was the last time you ate? You don't look like you have missed any meals, and girl, the white men are going to love your fat ass. They all come over looking for a video vixen. Girl, they see one Lil Wayne video, and they lose their God damn minds."

"I'm trying to make some money, so I can get me a place."

"Oh, you need a place to stay. Girl, C.J. will handle all that."

"How much does it cost?"

"Well, C.J. will protect you from the police and jerks. We have to bring him five, and we can keep one."

"So, where does the really rich men drive thru at?" I asked her.

"Well, alright then, somebody got they big girl draws on. I'm gone call C.J., and then I'm gone' take you to Rachel. She won't like you, but she knows money when she sees it."

We walked four blocks, and then we were on a busy street. Cinnamon hung up the phone and said, "Okay, he said to take you to Rachel and if Rachel says no, you got to go."

I shook my head with wide eyes.

"Don't worry. She just thinks she's the queen bitch."

We walked up to a bar, and there were a few tables outside. A couple of women were sitting out there talking. Cinnamon walked up and cleared her throat. Both of the women looked up at us.

"C.J. wants you to check her out," Cinnamon told her.

The woman sitting across from the tall blonde got up and went into the bar. The blonde pulled a seat out and gestured for me to sit down.

I did, and Cinnamon sat next to me.

"Let me see your arms," the blonde demanded. I slid out of my jacket, and she looked at both of my arms thoroughly. "Let me see your teeth." I opened my mouth wide, and she looked in. "Do you have any scars?"

"No," I told her.

"Go make three and come back," she told me. I opened my purse and gave her the seven hundred dollars I had stashed in my zipper.

"I made this tonight already," I told her.

"Shit girl, I bought a slice of pizza. You was holding out on me," Cinnamon said.

"Where you from?" the blonde asked.

I am originally from Tennessee, but I just moved here from Vegas," I lied.

"Why you leave Vegas?"

"Well, see my sister got in a little trouble and got me in some too, and she ended up getting herself killed, and I got out of there." I told her the truth.

"What's your name?"

"Cricket."

"What's your poison?"

"Rich men, clubs, casinos."

Since our four block walk, I would have to say we were now six blocks from The Three Strike Casino. I was not sure where Jyme and them were held up, but I was almost positive someone in that casino would know.

"Okay, Cinnamon take her over to the Three Strikes and see how she does," the blonde said. Cinnamon grinned wide, and she jumped up and yanked me up with her.

"What's a three strike?" I whispered loud enough for the blonde to hear me. I heard her chuckling, and Cinnamon laughed and told me to come on. We walked for about a block, and then I pulled out my phone. There were no messages.

I cringed and called Chelle.

"I need a ride," I spoke into the phone. I told Chelle where we were, and she came around the corner. I told Cinnamon those were my friends, and she got in with me. Once we got into the back of the truck, I turned to Cinnamon.

"Shit, you're a cop," she yelled and turned, trying to get out of the truck, but the child safety was on.

"I'm not a cop. I'm looking for someone. I will pay you a thousand dollars to help me out."

She thought about it for a minute and agreed. I gave her five hundred cash and told her I would give her the rest after we got out at the casino. I gave Cinnamon a brief and much edited version of what was going on and who we needed to find. So Jyme turned into Ayashe's boyfriend. and I was her best friend who was trying to help. Chelle was a friend and driver plus she spoke Spanish. I just threw that in there for a twist.

Cinnamon's eyes were wide. She thought this was so exciting. I thought for a moment and realized that I lucked out with her.

"You need to talk to Joey," she told me.

"Who is Joey?"

"He's a bodyguard over at Three Strikes, but he's cool."

"Do you know how to get in touch with him?"

"Yeah, he's a regular."

"Okay, can you call him and see if he has any friends that would like some company tonight because we're trying to make some serious money? Make sure you tell him you got a brand-new girl that can suck the chrome off a bumper."

I saw Ayashe's head whip over towards Chelle, but neither one of them said a word. Cinnamon called Joey. I used two makeup remover wipes and reapplied my makeup but with a little more class this time. I reached over Chelle and pulled my purse from under the seat and dug in for the little box. I pulled it out and slipped the cricket on my ring finger. I knew I needed something to distract me for what I was about to do, and this was it.

"Okay, he down. They're having a party, and he said the more the better," Cinnamon said looking at Chelle and Ayashe.

"No, just me," I told her.

"Cricket," Chelle said.

I rolled down my window and opened the door, and Cinnamon slid right out behind me.

"Hey listen, they gone want to *really* play once we get up here."

"Just remember what I told you, and if this works, there may even be a bonus in it for you."

After clearance with security, we made it to the penthouse. Cinnamon walked in, and I followed. There was a serious coke fest going on. This could be a very good thing or a very bad one. You never can tell with cokeheads. I saw six bodyguards, and they were all sober. The room was massive; there were at least five bedrooms as far as I could tell. One of the bodyguards looked at me and started over. Someone stopped him, and I went in the other direction.

Cinnamon came back and told me the man in charge was not there yet, but he was coming. She then pulled in a little closer to me.

"He's at his house dealing with some out of town issues."

"Do you know where he lives?"

"Slow down GI JOE. Let's get in the house first."

There were already some girls here, but the pickings were slim. This was better for me because the less skinny made the fat beauty look ten times better. I pulled out my phone and texted Chelle that everything was ok.

The elevator dinged, and three men got off. I knew the man who ran things was in this bunch somewhere. They all just had this aura about them; one was native, one was some kind of mixed race, and the other was black; and fucking shit of all fucking shit—I knew him. Our eyes met instantly, and I turned from him.

Cinnamon watched me and followed.

"What ya doin?" I kept moving

"Is that them?" she whispered.

"We gotta go," I rushed out.

Cinnamon turned and started going back up the steps towards the elevator and I followed. We almost made it to the top when an arm gripped mine.

"Where you going, Cricket?" the voice asked.

Then the bodyguard who was approaching earlier was now standing beside me. I now knew why he was coming towards me; he knew me too, and this was not good.

Troy and Trey knew me and my sister very well. We all used to strip together in Fresno. Troy and Trey were twins from Palo Alto; they were alright guys until they started drinking. And with the looks of this crowd, they've come a long way up from Fresno. They took us to one of the empty bedrooms, and Cinnamon looked like she was about to bolt.

"What ya doing here, Cricket?" Troy asked.

"I'm working."

"Nawh, you look too good to be working. You looking damn good, girl," Troy said.

"She still got that baby fat, but it's working for her," Trey said looking at my butt.

"Where's your sister?" Troy asked.

"Dead."

"Shit, what happened?" Troy asked.

"I don't remember," I lied.

"Bullshit," Trey said.

"They call it some kind of blockage that can happen when you're in a trauma," I told them.

"Well, you look too classy to be working. Now her, she's working," Troy said looking over at Cinnamon. She gave him the finger and told him to eat her.

"Hell fuck no!" he answered.

"So, what you guys doing now?" I asked.

"I'm Mr. Paul's right hand man, and Trey's one of his bodyguards," Troy told me.

"Who's Mr. Paul?"

"He owns this Casino and two in Washington State."

I swallowed hard and bit back the cry that was trying to get out.

"Cricket, can you still do that thing with your tongue?" Troy asked.

"Troy, that was child's play. I've so many more tricks in my bag now."

"I bet you do too, woo!" he said, reminiscing about the old days.

Troy looked over at Cinnamon and asked her who she worked for. She told him C.J.

"Cricket, what the hell you over there nickel and diming it for? Girl, you got way too many skills for the streets. You need to be inside a casino working on the floor with the high rollers."

"So, do you have a job for me?" I asked.

"You know what, as a matter a fact I do," Troy answered.

"Wait, what about me," Cinnamon asked.

"You can't do this job," Trey chuckled.

"I can teach her," I assured them both.

"Okay, she's your responsibility," Troy told me. I stared at him and licked my lips slowly. He laughed.

"Girl, you're good," Trey said shifting in the seat of his pants.

"Four hundred a head, and any tips are ours," I told him.

"Three hundred a head, you keep your tips, and free room and board," Troy negotiated.

I looked over at Cinnamon and then back at Trey and Troy. "You need to take care of C.J."

"Well, what about you?" they asked.

"I don't work for anyone but myself, you know that."

I stood, and Trey pulled me against him.

"Cricket, we're having a private party tonight, why don't you and your friend come out to the ranch?"

"Sure."

"Where you staying?" Troy asked.

"Nowhere actually. I just moved here, and I haven't had time to find anything yet."

Troy picked up his phone and dialed a number. "This is Troy. Mr. Paul has two new employees who will need a two-bedroom suite for, well, until otherwise." He hung up the phone. "It's taken care of. Just check in at the front desk, and give them this card," Troy said. He handed me a business card. I gave it to Cinnamon, and she slid it in her purse.

"Cricket, fix her tonight, and then tomorrow we can have you an account set up with one of the stores," Trey said frowning at Cinnamon.

"Blow me," Cinnamon told him.

"Hell no," Trey told her, shaking his head. "There will be a limo downstairs in two hours to bring you out to the ranch."

Cinnamon and I walked towards the door.

"Ladies, your employment starts as soon as you leave this room. Everything you see or hear from here on out is confidential," Troy told us both. We nodded and left.

As soon as we got back on the elevator, I texted Chelle, "On our way."

We got into the car, and Cinnamon started yelling at the top of her lungs. "YOU ARE FUCKING AMAZING. I LOVE YOU."

"What happened?" Chelle and Ayashe both asked. I filled them in on the very well-edited version, and I told them that Cinnamon was so stoked about us going to this A-list party. Ayashe seemed pleased, but Chelle stared me down through the review mirror. I asked Cinnamon if she needed anything from her old stuff and she said, "HELL NO."

We stopped at Macys in the Beverly Center so Cinnamon could get another dress and shoes. Ayashe went to the bathroom, and Cinnamon was in the dressing room. Chelle and I sat in the waiting area.

"You love him. You really do love him, and I can see that now," Chelle told herself this.

"Chelle if—"

She interrupted me. "You are going to find them, and you will get them back home. I know that. But I also know, you're not coming back with us," she said, not making eye contact with me.

"Chelle, I need you to get him out of here, and make him forget me and make him let this casino go," I told her through tears.

"What are you going to do?"

I looked at her and smiled, "A trade."

We made it to the ranch, and Chelle was about a mile back behind the limo. I told her to wait until she heard from me to do anything. We walked into the house, and everything was clean. There was music coming from all over the house. A server walked up to us with a tray full of champagne flutes. We both got one, and Cinnamon was about to chug hers down. I stopped her at once. We found the nearest plant and poured them out. We walked on into the house and saw Troy coming from a door. That door had steps going down, and I knew that had to have been the basement. He smiled at us and waved us in. He gawked at Cinnamon and said, "My brother has to see this."

We made our way to the main room, and there was nothing but rich cokeheads here. Trey walked up to us and hiccupped when he saw Cinnamon. I pushed her towards him, and he slid her over to Troy, and Troy wrapped his arms around her. Trey pulled me to the side, "I'd rather have the original," he told me.

I smiled at him, and then I got to work. "Damn, this is a nice house," I told him looking around up and down all over the house.

"Do you want a tour?" he asked.

"Sure, if it's okay,"

"Oh yeah, it's fine."

We walked upstairs, and he showed me his room and the other three bodyguards' room. There was a study, game room, and theatre. We went back downstairs, and he showed me the kitchen, two more bedrooms, a library, and a formal dining room. We passed the door Troy came out of twice, and Trey never said anything about it. We moved out to the backgrounds: there were horse stables, a walking path, a pool, the pool house, and another house a good ways off from the grounds.

"That's where Mr. Paul lives, back there."

"Why?" I asked.

"He doesn't like being around a lot of people, and he likes his privacy," Trey said.

We walked over towards the pool, and I asked if we could go into the pool house.

"Sure. Come on."

We went in, and it was so nicely decorated in cool colors.

"You know Cricket, we looked for you and your sister for a long time." Trey told me.

"I know, but we had to go."

"I know things got too hot and your sister…well, I know."

We walked back towards the house. I was just about to become frantic, and then I breathed through it. "I can't believe a house like this doesn't have a wine cellar or a basement."

Trey looked over at me and shook his head. "I forgot you were a serious wine drinker back in the day. It was your thing. I remember that."

"Yes, it is, and I would damn near kill for a decent wine right now." I pulled Trey closer to me and shivered.

"You cold?"

"It's a little chilly." He pulled me closer, and we walked back to the house.

We went in through a side door, and then Trey pulled me to the corner.

"We do have wine cellar, but no one's allowed down there right now," Trey whispered.

"Why?" I whispered back.

"Because Mr. Paul has some guys down there he's teaching a lesson to."

"Oooh, what did they do?" I leaned into him.

"This big shot Indian over in Seattle has been buying his way in, and Mr. Paul don't play that shit. He doesn't care how much fucking money you got. He runs the casinos in Cali and Washington State."

"Damn, Mr. Paul don't play," I giggled.

"Are there any dead bodies?" I asked with fake wide eyes.

"Nawh, Mr. Paul just had us beat the shit out of them for a few hours; he's letting them go tomorrow."

"Can I see? I won't say anything, and I swear I won't touch anything"

"Shhhh." Trey said, and then we walked over to the cellar door and started stepping down. We entered an almost empty room with a wall-to-wall refrigerated wine chiller. Trey tugged at my arm, and we walked towards the other side of the room.

We walked up to a steel door, and I looked through the small glass window. There were four Natives sitting in chairs that were all tied up to each other. None of them was facing each other; they were all blindfolded. There was food all around them, and then I realized they were in the refrigerator.

I looked around for something to hit Trey in the head with, but found nothing. I saw a small table to the side, and it had their cell phones and wallets on it. My mind was racing, and I was running out of ideas.

"You know they haven't said a word in English since they been here. They've been communicating in some old Indian language, and Mr. Paul is Indian himself and he doesn't even know the language," Trey told me.

"We need wine glasses." I told him.

"Shit, I forgot. I'll be right back." Trey headed for the stairs, and I pulled my phone out. As soon as I heard the door shut, I dialed Chelle.

"Let all the seats down in the back and don't come any closer to the house until I call or text you. Don't let him know I am here. Make him think I am on the reservation and cannot come to the phone. Call Mrs. JJ, and fill her in. From what I can see their all okay. I gotta go."

I hung up the phone and ran to the other side of cellar, looking for another door or a window, but there was nothing there. I still looked for something to hit Trey in the head with, but there was only the small table and that wouldn't do anything.

I heard the door open, and then Trey was heading back down. But the person on the steps was not Trey; it was Troy.

"What are you doing down here, Cricket?" he asked.

"Trey brought me down to get some wine."

"What are you up to?" he demanded.

"I want to make a deal with you."

"I'm listening."

"Me for them."

"What do you mean?" he asked.

"I give you myself completely for them."

"Why?" he asked.

"Because the only man who's ever loved me for me is in that room. And I'd die for him if I have to."

"My brother loved you, Cricket, and I think he still does. You've had many men who loved you," Troy said.

I stood there, and then Troy laughed. "Oh, but you love this one back. I get it. So if we were to let them go, what can you promise me?"

"You'll never hear from them or this stupid casino again, and I'll do anything you want."

"Love my brother even when he's been drinking, and I want to feel the tongue trick my brother has been raving about for eight years straight."

"I can do that."

"Which one is he?" Troy asked.

"Does it matter?"

"Which one?" We both looked in, and I said, "The one in the white shirt." Loon was wearing a white shirt; Jyme was wearing a black sweater.

Troy looked at me and shook his head. "Liar, that one in the white shirt is not your type. I can see you with…I see you with the one in the black sweater." I stiffened, and Troy opened the refrigerator door.

He untied them from the chairs but still left them tied up as if they were in a chain gang. He pulled Jyme out last just to fuck with me. I pulled Kanoke's hat off his head, and he shifted, messing up the coordination for the rest of them. I ran right dead smack into Jyme. As soon as our bodies touched, he started sniffing and sniffing like a dog looking for food. I knew he knew something, but I was not sure what. I pulled all of their phones and wallets off the table and put them in Kanoke's ball cap.

My heels were loud, and Jyme was listening. He kept stopping, and then he would start back up, walking backwards again. I pulled my phone out and texted for Chelle to pull the car up and wait for me to come out. I told her to have the back already opened because they were all tied up and blindfolded.

She texted me back, "I'm here."

We finally made it to the top of the stairs, and Troy opened the door. We all walked into the hallway. I wondered where Trey was. He told me he would be right back, but that felt like hours ago. My heels across the floor were so loud, and Jyme's face twisted and turned from side to side. He absolutely knew something, but hadn't put the puzzle together yet.

Chelle and Ayashe were waiting by the main gate. My heart was racing, and I knew I was about to lose it. The tears started first, and then I breathed and breathed slowly. The gasping of air caught everyone's attention, and I could tell Sheen and Loon were scared. Jyme and Kanoke acted as though everything was okay.

I wanted to touch him, feel him, kiss him, and tell him I loved him so much, but I couldn't . He would find the letter when he got home, and that is all that mattered. I knew all along he was too good for me, but I wanted to live in the bubble so badly that I pretended he was not. I knew we would never have a happily ever after, and I cursed myself for the months we had been apart. I would give anything to go back and fix it. He looked so strong and so confident. I loved him so much and I wished. I just wished.

Troy and I got them loaded up in the back, and I never once

touched Jyme. Once they were all in, we shut and locked the hatch. I opened the door and got my three bags out, and Chelle handed me my purse. I handed her the hat with their belongings. I reached into my purse and handed her the stack of money for the plane tickets, my rental car keys, and my Blackberry. She got out and hugged me tight. Ayashe did the same. We were all crying and sniffling and looked a mess now. I mouthed, "I love you: to Ayashe, and she did the same. Chelle stood there, and then she smiled at me.

"I know I won't ever see you again, and I will miss you. You're my best friend and I love you," she cried into my shoulder.

"Take care of him, and tell him I have this," I pointed down at the ring, and she nodded.

"Don't take those blindfolds off until you get to the airport; you have to convince him I'm not here," I told her as I pulled away from her. They both blew me kisses and waved as they pulled off.

I turned around and set all the bags onto the concrete. I pulled my phone out and slammed it to the ground twice. Then, I dug into it with my Stiletto heel. I left the crumbled up pieces of my phone on the ground and walked away from my current life, stepping back into my old one.

G STREET CHRONICLES
A LITERARY POWERHOUSE
WWW.GSTREETCHRONICLES.COM

Epilogue

I couldn't get her smell out of my head; I smelled Cricket everywhere, and I could have sworn I heard her heels earlier. She felt like she was right there with me. She was my true lucky charm, and I was missing her like crazy. She asked me what I was afraid of the other day, and I couldn't answer that, but now I know to smell her here, where we were, that scared me. To have Cricket around those monsters and for them to do to her what they just did to me—that scared me.

We were still riding, and I could tell Loon was about to lose it; his breathing was too sharp. I could tell we were in the back of an SUV. There was carpeting under us; there was a door on my side, and we entered through the back hatch. The person driving was not a good driver; we were slung all over the place. I was not sure if anyone was watching us or not. Kanoke kept asking if we could try to untie ourselves, but I told him no because we didn't know for sure. I had told them when all this shit started to not speak in English anymore. And so far it had worked; they didn't know what we were saying. We stopped all of a sudden, and then I heard two car doors open, but they didn't shut. There was running and then the hatch opened.

I heard Chelle call out to Kanoke, and then Ayashe cried out to Sheen. They took our blindfolds off first, and then I looked for her.

"How in the fuck did ya'll find us?" Kanoke asked.

"I got the numbers Sheen left, and then here we are," Ayashe told us.

"Cricket?"

"She's still at the reservation," Chelle said, not looking at me. She used a box cutter and then Kanoke was loose and in her arms now. We were at the end of a terminal. Kanoke let Sheen lose, then Loon, then me. We all rubbed our wrists. Sheen was in Ayashe's arms now, and I wanted Cricket badly.

"Give me a phone," I demanded.

"They're all dead, ours, yours. They're all dead, and we have to go now," Chelle said, still not looking at me. She had never not made eye contact with me before, but she was worried about Kanoke now.

We went through the terminal, and Chelle ran to buy the tickets. We all went to the bathroom. When we got back, Chelle had returned the rental and had our tickets waiting for us. We went to get something to eat, and Ayashe and Chelle kept away from me. I guess they're mad at me for getting everyone in this shit. Well, I was done fucking with these casinos and all their fucking rules.

I sat next to Loon, and we were both staring at our phones. A man and women were eating behind us.

"Excuse me. My phone just died. Do you mind if I use yours for just a second to call my mom?" I asked the man.

"Sure, man, here you go." I kept my body turned towards him so he wouldn't think I was trying to jack him. I called moms, and Big Samson answered.

"Son, they're next door, everybody is."

I hung up on him and dialed the other house. Patty answered on the first ring. When she heard my voice, she started screaming and crying to mom. Mom got on the phone, and I told her we were safe, but I was borrowing someone else's phone. "Let me talk to

Cricket."

"She's not here," Mom said.

"Where the fuck is she?" I stood up and looked down the hall we just entered from; something didn't feel right. I had been feeling this feeling ever since we got out of that fucking cooler. Something was off, and they were acting different.

"She went over to Gail's," Mom assured me.

"What? Why?" I demanded.

"She was going crazy just sitting here, and Gail went to the store and asked Cricket to come to her house for a while," Mom said.

"What's Gail's number?" I demanded.

"It's storming really bad here, and her phone lines are down. I've been calling them for thirty minutes," Mom said.

"Go and fucking get her. I'll call you back in ten minutes. GO AND GET HER!"

"Okay, I will." she said.

"Thanks, man." I gave the man back his phone. He and the woman got up from the table, and now I could see everyone sitting close to us was staring at me, and security was walking around watching me.

"Chill," Loon whispered.

We got to the other terminal, and I borrowed another phone from a college student. I called the house, and there was no answer. I called the other house and still no answer. I gave the kid back his phone. I sat there with my mind wondering. I guessed the lines are down all over the reservation.

We boarded the plane, but something kept tugging at me. I felt sick and something was missing. It felt like the air was too thin, and I was about to choke on it. I fell down into my seat; every breath was getting harder and harder.

"Chill man," Loon said. I closed my eyes and tried to calm my breathing. I ended up drifting off and woke when we were landing at Sea Tac.

It was going to take me three hours to get to the reservation, but

I had to go now. It was almost six thirty, and the sun was peeking out. When we got off the plane, I sprinted to the exit, Loon right on my heels. Kanoke and Sheen tagged along with Chelle and Ayashe. I knew they would be in with them for the rest of the day. I had to get to the reservation, and I knew I would be speeding the whole way.

We ran to the parking garage where I left the truck. I paid the toll, and we drove off. I plugged my phone into the charger and buckled my seat belt. After thirty minutes of charging my phone, I had a little battery life. I tried calling everybody, but no one answered their phones. The phones must still be down. I called over a dozen people over a dozen times.

After an hour of silence, Loon went back to sleep. We made it to the reservation in two and half hours. I pulled up at the house and ran to the door; I slid the key in and busted the door wide open. I went to my room, and she was not there. I called out to her and there was nothing. I ran next door, and Loon was walking behind me.

I opened the door, and everyone was at the table. I looked at each face and I didn't see Cricket's.

"CRICKET," I yelled. They all watched me, and then JJ put her hands on my shoulders.

"She's gone, and I don't think she's coming back," she said.

"WHAT THE FUCK, JJ!" I yelled.

I ran out the house and went back to the truck. I yanked my cell phone out of its cradle, and I ran into the house and dialed Cricket's number from the wall phone. It went straight to voicemail. I dialed it three more times, and it went straight to voicemail.

"Babe, call me as soon as you get this fucking message. As soon as you get this, call me!"

Everyone was standing in the living room watching me, and that was pissing me off.

"Why did you let her go? I asked you to do one thing, and you fucked that all up like you do every fucking thing else," I yelled at JJ.

I called Chelle, and she didn't answer; I called Ayashe and she didn't answer. The wall phone rang, and I answered it on the first ring. "Cricket?" I breathed into the phone.

"She's gone Jyme," Chelle said. We hung up the phone twenty minutes later with me knowing Cricket's whole life story. After hearing about Cricket's mysterious life, I now know that I've been defeated, and that I will never see her again. I walked out the door saying nothing to anyone. I got back into the truck and drove away. Four hours later, I pulled up at the docks and got into the speedboat Cricket hated so much. I was heading back to the safe house, hoping and now wishing, that somehow she would be there waiting for me.

G
STREET Romance

From Love to Loathe Series
Part Two

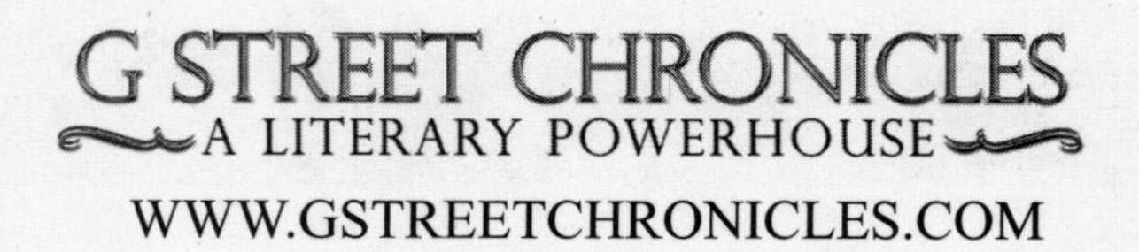
G STREET CHRONICLES
A LITERARY POWERHOUSE
WWW.GSTREETCHRONICLES.COM

Chapter 1
The New Cricket

The smell of cigarettes, cigars, vomit, and brown liquor lingered in the air. Today was my first day back from a ninety-day vacation. Cinnamon and Sugar had done a great job; so good we decided to keep Sugar on fulltime. We were some bunch of rejects though; Cinnamon was a mixed breed of some sort. She told me last October she wasn't sure what she was mixed with. Sugar knew her parents, but she tried to drink the memory of them away nightly. And I was the crème de la crème of fucked. I did not know my birth parents, my real name, or my real birth date. When I was little, my big sister Chyna asked me what my favorite day of the year was, and I picked Valentine's Day. I told her that women always got sparkly things on that day. So, she decided my birthday would be on Valentine's Day.

I thought of the very first day I met Troy and Trey as I walked to the cash box. Chyna had just broken up with one of her councilmen, and we were moving out of one of his condos that his wife didn't know about. Chyna and Chelle were loading up the car and I was a block away picking up our lunch. The first time I saw Troy and Trey they were on the corner I had just turned. Trey approached me first, trying his best to be suave.

"Hey beautiful girl, do you want to come to my show tonight?" A guy said as he jogged up to me. He had light brown skin, with curly hair. He wore jeans, a t-shirt, and a leather jacket.

"No."

"I put on a real good show, girl." He told me as he handed me a flyer. I held the flyer with my empty hand.

"Hey, let me get them bags for you, beautiful girl," he said, reaching for the bags in my hand. I moved them all to the arm farthest from him.

"That's alright, I'm good."

"Dang, you cold as hell."

"No, actually hell is hot and it's cold out here."

"You're mean too!"

"Trey, leave that girl alone; she's not interested."

"Thank you, he doesn't seem to catch a hint." I called back to the other guy.

"Can't you see she's too classy for us and she's out of our league?" Troy asked Trey.

It was obvious Troy had schooled Trey on what to say. All of his words seemed rehearsed. He stopped following me and I turned the last corner. When I reached Chyna, she was still loading the car. She turned to face me and I handed her one of the bags.

"Cric-kat, what did I tell you about bringing strays home." Chyna had been calling me Cric-kat for as long as I could remember. She told me that's how I used to say my name when I was little, and it just kind of stuck. I turned around and there were two, almost identical boys, standing right behind me; starring at the both of us. Chyna liked Troy instantly; we went to their show that night, and we started working at the club the next day.

I walked to the cash cage and Misty gave me my nightly dosage. "Good luck, honey," she said with a smile.

I walked over to the roulette tables and noticed Troy staring at the black tables. As I glanced around the room, I saw my mark. He was a short, paunchy something, wearing a white suit with bright red shoes. I could tell instantly he was a tit man The waitress couldn't get away from him fast enough. I smiled at her, and she shook her head as she walked past.

"Good luck with that one," she breathed.

When Troy made eye contact with me, he seemed to have relaxed a little. I winked at him, and he nodded as I walked over to the table and stood across from pudgy. I looked to my left and then made a show of looking towards the right.

"DAMN." he said, gawking at me. I giggled and started walking away from the table slowly.

"Wait, wait, where you going?" he called out. I stopped and turned back at him. He waved for me to come sit next to him.

"You sit right here, sweet thang, and give Uncle Ben some good luck." I sat down, and the twins came all the way to the stage. He stared, licked his lips, and cleared his throat. I crossed my legs and let the slit in my dress rise under the table. Then I pressed my inner thigh on his package and I felt a very small lump. He lost it then; he pulled out a hundred dollar bill and slid it between the twins. I giggled and pressed up against him even more. My leg slid up and down the inseam of his pants, and he grunted. I quickly pulled my leg back; I did not want any of that on me. I quickly stood, smoothed out my dress, and walked away. As I walked past Troy, he nodded and I smiled at him.

I made three more rounds through the casino and then took a break I went to Lecrux, one of the three restaurants in the casino. They had the best wine selection. I sat down, and Dax brought me a glass and filled it with a Pinot. I took one sip, and Cinnamon sat down across from me.

"Hey there, you looking for some company tonight?" she said with a smirk.

"I got a warm place you can put them cold hands," I replied with a grin.

"Mondays suck."

I nodded and took another sip. "Especially if it's your birthday."

Cinnamon smiled wide and started singing to me an octave way too high for her The entire wait staff at Lecrux was now at my table singing "Happy Birthday" to me. Chef Seal set down a perfectly round, saucer-sized slice of red velvet cake with crème cheese frosting. I thanked them all and gave Chef Seal a kiss on his cheek. I ate my slice in peace while Cinnamon played with her smart phone.

When I looked up, Trey stood next to me and asked if he could have a seat. I scooted over and ignored Cinnamon; that was our code for her to stay right where she was. Trey leaned in and kissed me on my mouth. I could taste the liquor on his tongue and knew it was going to be one of those nights.

"I missed you, Baby." He said.

"I missed you too," I lied.

"You couldn't call me once?"

"I told you Nantucket has horrible service and my poor aunt was really bad off."

"Baby, you've been gone for three months."

"It's actually been eighty-nine days. It was supposed to have been ninety, but your brother insisted."

Trey reached into his pocket and pulled out a small box. He set it in front of me and I stared at it.

"Open it, will ya?"

I picked up the small box and cracked it open; it held a ring with a round stone flanked by two smaller stones.

"Will you make an honest man out of me?" he asked.

"Dear God," Cinnamon moaned as she rose from her seat. "Happy Birthday Cricket," she said as she walked away.

I sat there looking at the ring.

Dax walked back over to fill my glass again. "Whoa. Let me get you something a little stronger," he said.

I nodded, and he bustled away. Dax came right back and poured some brown liquid in a glass. As he set it down, he widened his eyes and took a deep breath before he walked away.

"I mean, hell, Cricket, I know it's just you and me, so we should do this."

"I'm not ready to get married, Trey."

"You're not ready to get married, or are you just not ready to get married to me?"

"Does it matter?"

Trey slapped the drink out of my hand and yanked the hair at the back of my head so that I was looking at him. "See, that fucking smart mouth of yours is what makes me do things to you that I don't want to do."

Dax walked over and set a drink down in front of Trey.

"Trey, did you want the chef to make you something?" Dax asked, trying to help me out, and I loved him dearly for it. Trey released me and righted himself.

I looked down at my watch. "I need to get back work."

He waved his hand for me to go. I walked to the bar and handed Dax forty dollars. He smiled at me and squeezed my hand; I didn't react.

As I left the bar, I heard Trey call Dax back over to the table. Trey always got shit faced when he was stressed or upset about something. Since I hadn't said or acted the way he had outlined in that fucked up head of his, I knew I could hang it up on getting any sleep tonight. I knew he would be shit faced tonight and would more than likely take it out on me.

I made it back to the floor and did two more rounds, which were both successful. It was time for Sugar's shift, so I went back to the cash cage and turned my chips in.

"Have a good one, honey," Misty said.

As I boarded the elevator, Troy stepped around the corner and got on with me.

"I need a favor, Cricket," he said.

"What's up?"

"I need you to work the club room tonight."

"Alright. What time?"

"In an hour," he said, looking at his watch.

I nodded at him and faced the elevator door. He slid over to me and placed one of his hands on my butt and licked the side of my face. "You think you can sneak off from my brother tonight?"

"I'll see what I can do."

He laughed and shook his head. "Do you ever say no to anything?" The elevator door opened on my floor.

"Do I have a choice?" I stepped off and didn't look back.

In my room, I showered and put on a white shinny tank tee with tight leather pants and a matching jacket and stiletto heels. I put my hair up in a ponytail and carefully applied red lipstick. Then, I went back down to the bar and ordered a shot.

"What we got?" I shouted over the music to the bartender.

"High rollers are in VIP, and some computer guys sitting over in Spain." He yelled back at me over the music.

Three Strikes Casino and Hotel had two clubs in it; one was an upbeat hip-hop style club, and the other was a more laid back, reggae pop feeling spot. Tonight, I was working in the reggae club. My job was to make sure the rich guys were having fun with the planted call girls. I had to make sure their tables were full of women and drinks. The bartenders would let me know where the hot tables were, and I would send over what they needed. Everyone knew me and trusted me, and that was the way I liked it.

I'd been there an hour, and I'd over stuffed the computer guys section with pretty blonds and made sure they had plenty of champagne. Two guys in VIP were fucking four call girls, and the other three watched them with their dicks in their hands. I looked at the girls, and they gave me the thumbs up—they were oka. I told the bouncer to check on them in twenty minutes. I went back downstairs and sat at the bar with a rum and coke. On my second sip, the D.J. called me out and told me to get up and shake that sexy ass of mine.

"Your work never ends," the bartender said with a smile.

The D.J started playing my favorite reggae song, "Hold You" by Gypita. I stood up, and the strobe lights started. I handed the bartender my leather jacket. Then I pulled the twisty out of my hair and shook it around to hide my face. No matter how many times I heard this song it always made me tear up, and tonight was no exception.

As I walked to the dance floor, I thought about where I was a year ago and how perfect my life was. Now my whole entire world was a complete clusterfuck. I was fucking one brother, sucking the other off, and letting the old me do terrible things to me.

I stepped onto the floor and raised both of my arms and joined the crowded floor. Everyone was grinding and humping. I closed my eyes and let the tears fall. Someone pulled me to him, and I didn't even care. I danced with him and then another man pulled me and then another. I danced like that for the next two songs, totally uncaring.

When I made it back to the suite, Trey had three guys there. Cinnamon and Sugar were both drunk, and the guys were coked up. I spoke to them and sat for about ten minutes before I left and went to get in the shower. I locked my bathroom door and slid the vanity chair under the doorknob. I heard Trey try the door while I was in the shower. He started banging on the door, and I stayed in the shower until he settled down. I put a nightgown on and opened the door slowly.

When I walked out Trey slapped me in the face and I fell back on the wall. I had stopped screaming a long time ago, and I just stood there waiting for the next blw. He broke one of my gown straps and then yanked it up and slammed me against the wall. I fought with him until I was turned backwards. I had never let Trey inside Juicy; he always got it from the back. Juicy had only ever had one visitor, and I planned to keep it that way as long as I lived.

"Let me get it from the front," he slurred.

"I'm on my period," I lied.

"You said that last time."

"You know this is your special place. I don't let anybody else in there but you." I lied again.

"You don't let them old men in there, Baby?"

"No, never. This is your secret place. It's special."

Trey slid into me from behind and asked me if I loved hm. I

lied to Trey almost every single night; I always told him yes.

Trey was normally done quickly, but he must have been really drunk, or maybe he had done some coke, too. I'd have to turn my performance up a notch if I wanted to get some sleep tonight. I rode him reversed cowgirl style, this was Trey's favorite position. He loved watching my ass bounce up and don. This position was more painful for me because he squeezed my ass cheeks so hard that I had major bruising the next day.

After a long, gruesome, eight minutes, Trey finally came. He pulled out, kissed my back, and told me he was sorry. He walked away and fell on the bed.

I returned to the bathroom, slid the vanity chair back under the door, and got back in the shower. When I got out, I slid on another one of the nightgowns hanging on the back of door and threw the now torn one into the trash. When I walked back into the room, Trey was passed out and would be until the morning.

My phone beeped, and I read the text message. "I need you," Troy typed.

"Come on up." I shut the door and went into the living room. Sugar was letting one of those guys go down on her, and Cinnamon and the other two guys were gone. But with the moans and screeches I heard coming from the bedroom they shared down the hall; I knew they were in there. I saw stacks of money on the table. Cinnamon and Sugar had hit the jackpot with these guys.

I cracked the door and waited for him to get there. He walked in, locking the door behind him. He watched Sugar and the guy on the couch for a while and then he came over to me on the other side of the suite. We went into the spare bedroom like we always did.

I locked the door behind us and kneeled down. I took him into my mouth and went to work. He lasted maybe two minutes; Troy always punched the wall when he came. He had never asked me for sex, and I was glad for that.

"Girl, that mouth and tongue of yours."

I stood up and unlocked the door.

"Wait, did he do that to your face?" he askd.

I walked out the door and headed for the guest bathroom to wash Troy's juices off my neck and breasts. When I came out, I did not see anyone. Sugar was gone, and so was her guest.

I went to the hallway closet and pulled out my bedding. I stepped out on the patio, shut the door, and laid down on the cushioned lounge chair. I slept here almost every night.

G
STREET CHRONICLES

We'd like to thank you for supporting G Street Chronicles and invite you to join our social networks.
Please be sure to post a review when you're finished reading.

Like us on Facebook
G Street Chronicles
G Street Chronicles CEO Exclusive Readers Group

Follow us on Twitter
@GStreetChronicl

Email us and we'll add you to our mailing list
fans@gstreetchronicles.com

George Sherman Hudson, CEO
Shawna A., COO